EAST INDIAMAN

Book 1 in the East Indiaman Saga

By

Griff Hosker

East Indiaman

Published by Griff Hosker 2024
Copyright ©Griff Hosker

About the Author

Griff Hosker was born in St Helens, Lancashire in 1950. A former teacher, an avid historian and a passionate writer, Griff has penned around 200 novels, which span over 2000 years of history and almost 20 million words, all meticulously researched. Walk with legendary kings, queens and generals across battlefields; picture kingdoms as they rise and fall and experience history as it comes alive. Welcome to an adventure through time with Griff.

For more information, please head over to Griff's website and sign up for his mailing list. Griff loves to engage with his readers and welcomes you to get in touch.

www.griffhosker.com
X: @HoskerGriff
Facebook: Griff Hosker at Sword Books

Thank you for reading, we hope you enjoy the journey.

Contents

Real people in the book

Lord Mornington - Richard Wellesley. Governor of India
James Kirkpatrick - Resident of the Madras Presidency
Arthur Wellesley - Colonel of the 33rd Foot and future Duke of
Wellington, brother of Richard
Captain William Barclay - Sir Arthur's Adjutant General
Captain Colin Campbell - Sir Arthur's ADC
Captain John Blakiston - Sir Arthur's Engineering officer
Lieutenant General George Harris - titular head of the Army in
India
The Tiger of Mysore - Tipu Sultan, the ruler of Mysore and an
ally of the French
Mir Sadiq - 1st Minister of Mysore
Nizam of Hyderabad

East Indiaman

Prologue

I was a good thief when I lived alone in London. I still am a good thief. I know because I didn't get caught. Although that is not entirely true, I do not want to spoil the tale too early. Let us just say that I could steal and I made a good living from it. There is little point in false modesty for if I had not been so good at what I did then I would have died and none would know my story. One thing I will say, I never hurt anyone. That is not to say I did not defend myself. I did, for after my family left I had to defend myself.

I lived in an unforgiving part of England. I was what they called a wharf rat. We were the orphans who swarmed around the docks at Blackwall which was on the eastern side of London. How there came to be so many of us I do not know. The other orphans were the nearest friends that I had. They were not real friends; they were more like acquaintances in the same business of stealing to stay alive. There were many inns used by sailors and as most of them had sailed from lands many months to the east then the women who served in the inns and alehouses were readily sought. The children of such liaisons could easily find themselves alone. The whores and sailors often died young. There were others, I suppose, who were sailors and they simply did not return.

My story was a little different to most. Before he was taken from us my father had been a sailor on an East Indiaman. Those ships plied the seas, mainly to Asia, bringing spices and treasure home. It was a well-paid job and certainly safer and more profitable than serving the king in his navy. It was why we lived where we did. We had a small house with a bedroom, kitchen and a room where we ate and sat. Looking back it was almost luxurious. We ate reasonably well; we ate meat, sometimes five times in a month, especially when my father was home. I can barely remember him for he came home so briefly. He would land, reeking of salt and the sea with a skin that was burnished

7

brown and his hair tied in a pigtail. He would hug us all, even me
and he showered gifts on my mother and gave her hugs and
cuddles. I believe they loved each other. He gave my mother
money and normally fathered another child before he was off
again. The longest time I remember him being home was five
weeks. My mother accepted her life for we had clothes and a
roof and we were able to live better than many around us. Then
he died and our income dried up. His ship was sunk and my
mother had to bring up five children of which I was the eldest.
My mother was still pretty, despite having borne six children.
One had died three months before we heard the news of the loss
of my father and the doctor who attended that birth told her she
could have no more. It was bad news made all the worse by the
fact that he charged for his services and, with my father dead, we
could ill afford the expenditure. I was told that I would have to
earn money.

I found a job at the docks, fetching and carrying. It paid
pennies. I was a big lad, thanks to my mother's cooking, and I
was able to carry more than some of the others thus employed.
We were paid on a daily basis and I thought it unfair that I was
paid the same as they were and yet I carried more. I started to
pilfer goods when we entered the ships and the buildings. I found
I was able to take valuable items and secrete them in my
breeches. I learned to take better and better items and that was
when I began my thieving. I found that I could steal more if I
was not carrying boxes and sacks. I did not tell my mother but I
no longer went to work with the others. I went to work to steal. It
was simple stuff at first. I stole food from the market: a turnip or
a cabbage could provide a meal. Then I learned that if I hung
around the ships that docked and unloaded their cargoes I could
take bigger things like a sack of tea that could be sold. When I
began to bring silver into the house then my mother discovered
the truth. My mother was a good woman and she did not approve
but she was torn. The money she earned from cleaning the inn
did not pay enough to keep us fed. My thieving did.

When the Dutchman van de Meers chose her to be his
consort, he was quite happy to take on my four sisters but I was,
by then, too big and boisterous. They had met at the inn when he
stayed there. I took comfort from the fact that he appeared to

love her and she was just happy to have a man to look after her. She had been alone for more than a year and she had the girls to think about. As I said, she was still a pretty woman, at least I thought so. She knew that I could look after myself. She gave me a chest with my father's clothes and a tearful farewell. I was abandoned and the family left for the Dutch colonies in Java. My story was not unusual. I was thirteen years old and my mother, who had struggled to care for us all, saw that she had a chance to save her girls. To be fair to my mother I was already not only a thief but also able to handle myself. I knew how to use my fists and anything else to defend myself. I think that was another reason that the Dutchman chose to leave me behind. I think he was a little afraid of me. I still chuckle when I think of their departure as they sailed in the Dutch East Indiaman down the Thames for a new life in the Dutch East Indies. My tearful mother waved and my sisters called to me. The Dutchman was solemn not yet knowing that I had lifted his purse. By the time he knew he had been rooked, it would be too late. I waved and I smiled. When they departed that was the start of my life alone. The coins in the purse gave me some security. I did not spend them. Why spend when you could steal? The docks were like a market to me. I knew how to break into places and leave no sign that I had been there. I worked alone. There were other gangs of urchins but they had learned to avoid my fists. I did not bother them and so they avoided me. That fitted the way I lived.

I stayed in the room my mother had rented after my father had died but only for a week. The rent had been paid for that week and when I discovered how much I would have to pay then I left and found my own nest. I found a haven for myself. The docks and the buildings were old. They had been begun more than a hundred years earlier. Buildings had been added and older, smaller, places forgotten. I found one that must have been used to store ropes. It was at the back of a warehouse that was still used but the room I found was locked and I broke in through a window, leaving the lock intact. There were still a few old ropes left within. After ensuring that I would not be disturbed I made it my home. Over the next weeks, I added what I needed to and made myself comfortable.

It was then that I began to improve my skills as a thief. I needed more than the odd turnip or sack of tea. I needed coins. I deliberately chose not to be a footpad. I did not harm my victims and I never robbed those who could not afford it. There was no Christian mercy in my decision. I needed money and stealing from the rich made me more profit. I took purses. I broke into rich men's houses and stole belongings which I sold. I crept aboard the Indiamen when their crews went ashore, leaving a small watch on board. I learned where the officers' cabins were and took items from them. I stole swords and 'bring 'em nears' and I took well-made books and Bibles. I knew where I could sell them. I found my way around the ships even in the dark. I also plied the inns. Many men arrived at Blackwall and, having business in London, found it cheaper to stay in the inns and take a wherry into London. That was where I honed my skills. I had a quick mind and even quicker hands. I learned to study routines and take advantage of them. I knew when the rooms in the inns were cleaned and when the innkeepers would be busy in their cellars. It was then that I struck.

If my life sounds lonely then it was not. I lived alone and I stole alone but I met others and spoke with all. I had learned that a smile often opened doors and open doors meant information for me. It was how I gathered what I needed to make a profit. I made as few enemies as I could. I feigned friendship when necessary and people seemed to like me. Most were poor like me and so they were safe from my thievery. I determined that by the time I was a man I would have enough coins to be able to set up a business. I had no idea what that business would be but my time in the docks had shown me that it was easy to make money. The ships that arrived from India, Java and the Far East were laden with such riches that I could not see how a man could fail to make a fortune.

I learned to steal from people and houses. People were harder for you might be seen. I preferred breaking into houses. I was silent and agile. I could climb and find windows that were ajar. I could pick some locks and if the lock was too difficult I moved to another property. There were many of them and I was able to make enough coins to feed myself. I still stole from people but only when the rewards were worth the risk.

My life was a good one and, as I approached what I guessed was my sixteenth birthday, I almost had enough money gathered to think about a business. That was where I made the mistake I alluded to earlier. It could have been a fatal one but, in the event, it was not. I was a good thief but I made the mistake of stealing from a killer. I did not know the man was a killer. To me, he was just a well-dressed man with the tanned skin of one who has been abroad. The name, Ralph Every, was unknown to me. He arrived on an Indiaman and I saw how well-dressed he was. He wore rings on his fingers, and I recognised the silk shirt he wore. When he went to the best inn on the river, I knew that he had money to spare. He looked like a merchant and they were easy prey for me. I confess that it was my greed that was my undoing. I saw him and did not spend as long as I normally did watching him and seeing to whom he spoke. Within a day of his arrival, I had decided that his purse would be the one that would give me my passport out of Blackwall. It was simplicity itself to find which room he used and when I saw him leave the inn to find, I assumed food, then I slipped into the back of the place where he was staying. I had stolen from there before. I could sneak in through the back and up the back stairs. I knew the inn's routine and that I could do so unnoticed. The locks were rudimentary and I was a skilled picker of locks. Once inside the room and I opened his chest, it was as though I had found the treasure of the Mogul Emperor. There were jewels and sacks of coins. I saw fine weapons and I suddenly became fearful. I dared not take the jewels for I had no means of getting rid of them. That meant taking the coins but there were so many that I would not be able to carry them. My natural cunning took over. I chose one small bag but picked the one with the biggest and best coins. I could always come back for more. I slipped out and locked the door. I escaped the inn without being noticed and headed for my den. I put the coins with the ones I had already accumulated, and I counted them. I was becoming rich. I decided to celebrate. I headed west towards Limehouse. I had some better-quality clothes and I wore them. I went to the inn called '***The Grapes***'. They served good food and it was not too expensive; more importantly, I was not well-known there and I enjoyed, for once, a fine meal. I was no fool and I did not drink to excess. I ignored the advances of the doxies and enjoyed the steak and ale pie washed down with porter. I set off for home but, as was my wont, took a circuitous route.

It was as I neared the docks that Alfred rose like a wraith from his hiding place. Alfred was a younger version of me. He was ten and was the nearest thing I had to a friend. I had passed on some of my skills to him and when I had too much of anything perishable I shared it with him. It had cost me nothing for what I gave him would have been wasted. Now it stood me in good stead.

"William!"

My hand had gone to the dagger I kept in my belt but seeing it was Alfred I relaxed a little, "That is a dangerous thing to do, Alfred. Never sneak up on a man. What is it?"

"There are men looking for you, William. Many men who wish to hurt you."

A chill spread through my body, "Men?"

"A man was robbed at the Royal Garden. A newly arrived man from the east." It was clearly the man I had robbed. I said nothing. "The man is a pirate captain. He is called Ralph Every. He and his men are seeking you. Even the toughest of men are afraid of him and he has asked them to find you. He has put a price on your head. There is a reward of a guinea for information and five guineas if you are brought to him."

"Why me?"

"The innkeeper gave your name to the man. Everyone knows of your skill as a lock pick. He has men looking for you." He looked terrified. "He has said he will cut out your heart."

"How will he know me?"

Alfred shook his head, sadly, "You have enemies, William. They have described you and your haunts. Those who have no love for you will happily give your name and the places you might hide for a few coppers."

I had to think fast. I could not leave my treasure trove in the rope shed. "Alfred, come with me and, if you help me to escape, there is a silver shilling for you." I slipped my hand into my purse and drew out a coin.

"The dead cannot spend coins."

"And you will not die. Just come with me and if you see danger then whistle." I held the coin in my fingers, and he nodded.

I knew the backways and narrow places. We used those to get to my shed. I felt a certain satisfaction when even Alfred did not know this was my home. I slipped inside and gathered my treasures and my clothes. I had a linen belt with pockets and inside was my money. I took it from its hiding place and fastened it around my waist. I tucked in the shirt and then donned my jacket. I would keep my treasure about my person. If I had to discard clothes, food and weapons then the treasure would ensure that I could buy more.

Even as I took what was valuable to me, I was formulating a plan. I packed my clothes, food, and an ale skin into a sack which I slung over my shoulder and secreted my weapons about my person. I had four daggers. Two were concealed in my boots. A third was secreted beneath my leather jacket and the fourth was prominently displayed on my belt. Once outside I gave the silver shilling to Alfred. "Now, go and tell these men who hunt me that you can lead them to my home. That way you will be given a guinea." He looked confused. "I have left enough there so that they will know you speak the truth. They may give you coins but, at the very least, it will allay suspicion and prevent harm coming to you." I did not know until that moment that I had a conscience, but it pricked me. Alfred was too young to have his life snuffed out.

"And what will you do?"

"If you do not know then you cannot tell, can you?" He nodded. "I have left some odds and ends in my den. They are yours as is the den. I shall need it no longer."

"Thank you, William. Godspeed."

I waited until he had gone and headed back through the alleys to the quayside. I had, in my head, the names of all the ships that were moored. I knew that the ship, *HCS Campbelltown*, a relatively newly built ship, was due to head east although I knew not where but I had heard it was to be soon. I thought I could stow away and use my wits to avoid being caught. Once at sea, even if I was caught, it would be unlikely that I would be returned to London. The last thing I needed was to stay in

London where a bloodthirsty pirate captain hunted me. I was pragmatic. I could start a new life at whatever port she docked. Who knew? If I did not know where I was going to land then how would those who wished me harm? This might be the chance I had been seeking. It had been forced upon me but I was beholden to no one. Lurking at the back of my mind was the thought that, perhaps, I might see my mother and my sisters. I dismissed the thought. I needed no one.

I did not head for the quay at first. Instead, I went through my world; the world of alleys and back passages. I should have known that a man like Ralph Every would have involved anyone and everyone in his search for his treasure and my head. It was Jacob the son of the Cooper who found me. He was a hulking brute with hams for fists and he worked as a bully boy for anyone who would pay him.

He stepped suddenly from the shadows. He had chosen his hiding place well. It was close to a cesspit and that disguised his smell. "You are worth a pretty penny to me, my friend. You shall make me five guineas and I can sell your clothes when Captain Every has slit your throat."

He was confident and with good reason. He was at least a stone heavier than me and at least six inches taller. Working with his father hefting barrels had made him strong. If I was going to survive, I needed to use my wits. He had a cudgel in his hand and clearly intended to batter me with it. The pirate wanted to slit my throat and that gave me hope. Jacob would try to take me alive and earn his blood money. He was more than strong enough to carry me to collect his reward. The passage where he had me looked to be a perfect trap. I could not get past him easily and if I ran back then I would end up on a main thoroughfare. I needed to use cunning.

I dropped my bag and, opening my palms to show that I had no weapons, I moved towards him. I put fear in my voice. I was a thief who had learned how to act. I made my voice sound tearful and my eyes were wide, "Jacob, I beg you, let me go. I will make it worth your while."

He laughed, "When I strike you about the head then I will take from you whatever I please. I do not like you, thief. This is a pleasure. You have no words that will save you."

I kept walking for I saw that there were some timbers next to his right. They leaned against the wall and knew I could use them. "I have no treasure with me. It is hidden."

He shook his head, "Captain Every has men searching your home already. If that is the case how can you pay me?"

"I have another secret place. No one knows about it."

He frowned. I had a reputation for being sneaky and cunning. It was something that was believable. I was within two paces of him and I saw that the hand holding the cudgel had relaxed. His hand had dropped a little.

"Where is it?"

I stepped forward and pointed to his left although my eyes never left him, "On the other side of that yard."

His eye moved in that direction and I ran at him. My shoulder hit his chest and although he was a big man he overbalanced. He fell against the timbers and his head struck them. As he went down, I drove my right knee hard between his legs. No matter how strong you are having your manhood mashed by a knee brings tears. He screamed. I punched him hard in the face twice with my right fist, and when the hand holding the cudgel relaxed, I grabbed it and swung it at the side of his head. He was out cold. I dropped the cudgel and, after picking up my sack, I ran.

When I reached the end of the passage I stopped and peered around. I was looking for any of his cronies. I saw none. I crossed the road and took the next passage that I knew headed to the river. I had now put myself beyond the Pale. Jacob would seek vengeance. He had friends and with Captain Ralph Every and his men seeking me I had to leave London now or I would be a dead man…twice over.

Part 1

The Reluctant Sailor

Chapter 1

The hour was late when I reached the ship that I had chosen. I knew that she was due to leave soon for that day had seen the constant loading of supplies. That meant the crew would be enjoying their last night in port. They would be in the inns and whorehouses. The crew who were left aboard, on watch, would be fewer in number. I knew the layout of the ships for I had often stolen from them. I usually chose the day before they were leaving so that any theft would only be discovered when they were out at sea. There were two gangplanks in use but only one was watched. The deck watch gathered at one of them to smoke and talk. No doubt they would be grumbling at the injustice of having to keep watch while their shipmates were enjoying themselves. I saw that there were two marines with the four other men and they had laid their muskets against the gunwale.

The quay was busy, as it always was, both night and day. Other ships were being loaded. A carriage drew up close to the gangplank of the ship. I watched a knot of officers as they stepped from the carriage. I was an opportunist. I knew that all eyes would be on the officers and not on the second gangplank leading to the bow section. I scurried up the gangplank, my sack secured around my back. I kept low and made no sound on the wooden plank. Reaching the deck, I paused to peer around the side. I saw that the deck watch had ceased smoking and the men were standing to greet the returning officers. The two marines had retrieved their muskets and were standing to attention. I had already decided the best place to stow away. There was an orlop deck below the places the crew slept and worked. It was used to store cables and as a hospital should the ship see action. Once the ship sailed and the cables were stored none would visit it. Apart from the inevitable rats, I would have my own quarters. The layout of the ships was similar. The open deck had guns and there were hatches which allowed access to the decks below. The cargo would be on the decks below. The crew had their quarters with the heavier main guns of the ship. There would be many cabins for the East Indiamen carried passengers. I knew, from my explorations, that only rich passengers had cabins. I had stolen from them. The other passengers would share a deck with cargo. The emptiest deck was the one where they stored the ropes and, sometimes, powder.

I waited as the officers came aboard, sheltering behind one of the guns that were secured to the deck. I was close enough to hear their words. "Welcome aboard, Captain."

I paused to peer at the captain of the ship. I recognised him as he was the first to board. I had watched the ships long enough to know the protocol. The man stopped and peered along the deck, "Is all ready for sea?"

The officer of the watch knuckled his head, "Aye, Captain Mackintosh."

"And the crew, Mr. Cunningham?"

"Due back by midnight."

"I rely on you, Mr. Cunningham, to ensure that they will all be ready for duty when we sail. I will brook none who report for duty in an intoxicated state."

I saw the officer salute as he answered, "Do not fear, Captain, they all know my right arm is ready to punish any transgressions."

"And all the passengers are aboard?"

"They are, sir. The servants and third-class passengers are in their places and all is ready for sea."

"Very well, carry on."

That told me who was the bosun on this voyage. Mr. Cunningham would rule the lower decks while the captain ruled the ship. I liked to store names. They often helped me in my thievery. I used the distraction of the arrival of the officers to slip down the ladders that led to the next deck. There were more guns here but there were also hammocks and tables secured to the low deck above by ropes. The crew would sleep here. It was empty as they were all ashore and those that remained were the deck watch. I went down the ladder to the next level. Indiamen were wider and less sleek than Royal Navy vessels and the hatches were narrower. I had been told that they could lift portions of the deck to facilitate the loading of larger pieces of cargo. This deck had cargo but I also heard voices. There were people on this deck. I remembered the conversation I had heard. These would be the servants of the passengers or those who could not afford a cabin. Like me, they would be poor. I saw that they had hammocks but that they shared their temporary home with cargo. There were boxes and crates all of which were secured by ropes to metal rings on the side. I used those as cover as I did what I did best, moved silently and like a ghost.

The next deck was packed with cargo and I had to pick a path through the chests and sacks to reach the next level. This time there was no central hatch just one at the bow and one at the stern. The cargo filled the hold but a path had been left to enable the crew to inspect the cargo and to reach the deck I sought, the orlop deck.

It was the last deck that was almost empty. It was also the lowest one and I had to bend my head. It was so dark that I waited for a few moments. There had been little light on the deck above but there was none here. I knew, from my experience as a thief, that your eyes would adjust and I waited until they did. Dark shadows appeared and as I neared them I saw that they were neatly coiled ropes. It reminded me of my home. The hatch I had used had been open and I left it so. A little light would be provided. I would not be in complete darkness. I knew, from the ropes, that this was the orlop deck and lay at the bottom of the ship. Beneath the wooden deck would be ballast and then the mighty keel. At least it was a newer ship and would have been solidly built. It would not be as empty once we left the quay for they would store the ropes used to tie us to the land. I had to find a nest. I made my way to the bow. I had to do so by feel and touch for it was almost pitch black. I felt my way to the bow. There the timbers of the ship were closer together as the hull narrowed. When they came together I knew that I was as close to the bow as I could be. There were cross braces and supporting struts. I found that I could store my sack on one side and make a home on the other using the timbers that were designed to make this part of the ship as strong as possible. The wood was not finely finished but they were reassuringly solid timbers. This was a well-made ship. As I had to climb up I knew that it would not be used for storing the cables. Sailors were neat by nature and they would store the looped cables on the wooden deck and closer to the hatches. My home, hopefully, would be ignored. It was so black I could not see anything but I did not mind the dark. Darkness was my friend because it hid me. I saw the dim glow from the hatch I had used and that was all. I took my ale skin out and found a niche where it would be safe. I took out my cloak. As a thief, my cloak was my disguise. Now it would be a blanket and a protector against the damp. I left my clothes inside the sack but took out the food I had brought and tucked those provisions with my ale skin. I had eaten well at the inn and I had enough food for three days. After that, I would become a thief again and steal what I needed. I would not remove my treasure belt. Until we reached the place I would leave the ship it would be as a second skin.

I settled down to wait for the movement of the ship that would tell me we were heading down the river when the tide was high. I was too excited to sleep as well as feeling more than a little nervous. I had left a home where I knew every entrance and exit. I had exchanged it for a potential trap. It was a compromise. If I stayed in Blackwall then I would be a dead man. Alfred had made that quite clear. Here I could still be in trouble but the worst that might happen would be that I would be put ashore somewhere. I had wanted a new start and this one had been sent my way. It might not be the start I wanted but it was the one I had been given. I would take my treasure and start a new life with a new identity. William Smith would be my name. I had been born a William but not a Smith. My father had been Bill. I wanted an anonymous name. I did not know how much effort Ralph Every would put into finding me but I would make it as hard for him as I possibly could. Looking for William Joseph Hogarth would not help him.

I did not hear as many rats as I had expected but then I realised that the ship was relatively new. More would inhabit the ship before long. Rats did not worry me. I had a sling and I had killed many rats in my den. They would learn to avoid me; I was a predator. I heard the crew coming aboard not long after my eyes had begun to adjust to the darkness. Above me, the muffled noise of men who had been drinking and whoring drifted down to me. When the hatch above me was thrown open the light seemed almost blinding. I knew it was an illusion. The light showed me that there were more ropes and hawsers than I had thought. One was particularly large and I guessed that would be employed to tow another vessel. All the ropes were new. The noises above me became clearer. I heard snippets of conversations as men worked on the deck above me. When I heard the sound of the gangplank being withdrawn and the calls of the bosun then I knew that not only was our departure imminent but that men would be descending into the orlop. I pushed myself back into the corner.

The song from above me told me that men were moving around the windlass to haul the anchor up to the cathead. The muffled thumps I heard were the ropes that secured us to the quay as they were thrown aboard. Soon they would be brought down and I would have company. I still had time to leave my hidey hole and return to the land but what was the point? I would be hunted and killed. I had to leave if I wished to live. It was at that moment I realised that there was nothing left for me in London. I would make a new start. I would land at the first port of call and head inland. Captain Every plied the seas. In a different part of the land and away from the sea I could make a start and the coins I had would make that easier.

The light from above as part of the deck was removed felt blinding. I knew it was not as bright as it appeared. It would be a candle inside a glass. The ship carried powder and fire could be disastrous. I tried to get further into my cubby hole but I knew I would not be seen. There were too many shadows and, besides, the crew would just want to deposit the ropes and then close the hatch. I heard their voices before I saw their shadows near the hatch. Even as I saw them placing the ropes in their designated places I felt the motion as the ship began to move.

"Come on you lollygaggers. There is work to do."

I heard muttered cursing and then partial darkness was returned to me. They had left both hatches open. I did not realise until much later that all the hatches were only closed in heavy seas. I had never been on a ship when it sailed but I knew, from what I had heard in the inns and from my father, that the passage down the Thames took time. I snuggled down and slept. The motion of the ship rocked me into a deep slumber. It was the need to make water that woke me. The movement of the vessel suggested that we were at sea but I would not know until I reached the deck. This would be a gamble but it was, perhaps, a good place to leave my place of concealment. I had to do it at some point and this early in the passage I might escape scrutiny. I took my jacket and donned it. I knew that the crew had a uniform and while the jacket I wore did not look like their uniform, it did look like the clothes of a servant. I had seen enough ships being loaded to know that those who travelled on the Indiamen went with servants.

I headed for the hatch and peered through it cautiously. I had no right to be where I was and getting in and out of the orlop deck would always be fraught with danger. I turned my head slightly and listened. There was silence. I slipped out and stood. It was a mistake. The decks were low and I banged my head. I would have to learn to crouch. I made my way to the light I could see from the far end of the deck. This was one of the cargo holds. The cargo was secured by ropes but the crew had left gaps so that they could inspect it. I saw a light from the end of the hold and that suggested a hatch. When I had descended I had seen that the hatches all had covers but I doubted that they would be closed unless the ship had to endure a storm. This was the time for confidence. If I skulked, then I would be noticed. I made my way down and climbed the ladder to the next deck.

This time there were hammocks slung and a couple were occupied. This was not the crew for I heard the sound of women's voices. I had passed them when I had descended into the bowels of the ship. Now I saw that they were occupied by servants. I knew that from their dress. I was lucky when I emerged for I did so without attracting attention. I went up the ladder to the next deck. When I passed through the deck, I saw neatly folded hammocks and the deck was empty. I saw guns and knew that these were the crew's quarters. The deck appeared to be empty. The tables I saw were hanging from the deck above and swung with the motion of the ship. I made my way along to the next ladder which lay at the far side of the deck. I slipped up it unseen. I found myself at the cabins of the paying passengers. There were cabins but this time I spied fine clothes and the man who emerged from his cabin saw me. It was then I realised that I had come up at the bows of the ship.

I knuckled my forehead and said, "Good day, sir."

He frowned and then said, "Did you see Hargreaves down there, boy?"

I was quick thinking and I said, "I am afraid I have not learned all the names of the other servants, sir."

He nodded and went to the hatch, He shouted down, "Hargreaves."

I heard an answering voice, "Coming, sir."

I said, "If you will excuse me, sir."

"Of course." I was anonymous, a nameless servant.

I headed towards the bow and just below the bow castle. I knew from watching the ships that the better cabins were to be found there. I came out into the daylight and it almost blinded me. We were at sea and it was, from the position of the sun, mid-morning. I had slept longer than I had planned. I looked up and saw that the sails were what they called reefed. They were giving us just enough motion to make progress. As I stood to get my bearings I observed the crew. Some of them were attending to the tackle on the guns that lined the deck. When I had descended, I had seen more guns, larger ones.

I spied a young man, he looked to be in his early twenties. He was tanned and his hair was neatly tied behind his head. He was coiling a rope and when I approached him he smiled. I said, "Excuse me, sir, I am one of the servants." I lowered my voice, "How do you take a piss on a ship? This is my first voyage."

He grinned, "Aye, well, you are in for a treat young man. The gentry and officers can use the wooden toilets in their cabins but the crew and you servants have the delights of what we call the heads." He laid down the rope, carefully, and pointed to the port side of the ship. "If you walk your way along there to the bows,

22

then you just pee over the side. Hold on though. That is what we call the leeward side as the wind is coming from the starboard quarter. Always test the wind." To demonstrate he licked his finger and held it up.

"And if I need to do anything else?"

His smile became broader, "Ah, well that is always exciting. Drop your breeks. Grab hold of the ship and stick your backside out over the side."

It seemed daunting but I nodded, "Thank you, sir."

"I am Ned, and who might you be?"

Once again, my quick mind came to my rescue. I would no longer be William or even Bill. I needed a new name and I used my mother's father's. "It is John."

"Aye, well, John, I daresay I shall be seeing more of you once we head south."

"South?"

"Aye, these are the Downs and we are waiting here to meet the other Indiamen. Once they join us we head south for Madeira."

"Thank you, Ned." I now knew the port where we would land. I had never heard of Madeira. I had hoped that we would call at another English port but I was resourceful and Madeira would be the start of my new life. I made my way to the place Ned had said.

The bows curved and was the place that the crew and servants used for their toilet. There was a gap between the cabins and the rail, the crew called it the gunwale. I moved along it and I saw another servant, for he was not wearing the uniform that Ned had, he was squatting and hanging on. I waited for him to finish. He looked over and said, "I shan't do this too many times."

Just then the bow dipped and water showered him. He looked at me in terror. "Are you alright?"

He nodded, "And now I have finished." With his breeks still around his knees, he made his way back toward me. I moved backwards to allow him to use the space I had occupied. He pulled up his breeks. He shook his head, "Good luck!"

Warned by what I had seen I made water but timed it so that I was not showered by the sea. I made my way back to the main deck. There were more people there. I saw huddles chatting to

23

each other as they pointed to other ships and the distant land. I
saw at least four groups. I made my way down the deck towards
the stern. I knew that there was a ladder there and this would
give me the chance to explore the ship.

It was as I neared the hatch that was near the quarter-deck
when I heard the lookout shout, "Sail Ho."

The officer of the watch asked, "Where away?"

"South and west, sir."

I looked where he pointed and saw the sails of the slightly
smaller Indiaman as it headed towards us. With the attention of
the crew on the ship, I slipped down the hatch. It was there I
spied the galley. There were cooks preparing food. I waved and
smiled. One of them waved and smiled back. I walked further
astern to the hatch that led down to the next deck and it was there
I struck gold. It was what passed for a pantry on the ship. I saw
loaves of bread and I snatched one and slipped it beneath my
shirt before heading down the ladder to the next deck. It was as I
made my way down the deck towards the bow that I realised I
should have looked for water or ale. I had a waterskin but it
would not last long. I decided to go back to my nest with my
treasure and then seek the water barrels. I cursed my
overconfidence. I should have found the water first. I decided to
return to my place of concealment. I had ale for at least two days,
three if I rationed myself, and there would be better opportunities
for me when it was dark. I chose a different route back. I needed
to know the ship like the back of my hand. There were three sets
of steps that led down to the deck below close to the stern, the
bow and in the centre where the great mainmast dominated.

When I had gone down to the last deck with the guns, I had
worked out the number of decks with guns. The main deck had
the smaller ones. I counted twenty-eight on the two decks. It was
as I prepared to go to the deck occupied by servants and cargo
that I heard the order given for all hands. I thought that I was
alone on the deck, which housed the crew but when a handful of
men suddenly rose like wraiths from their hammocks I realised
that I was wrong. They raced past me as they hurried up to the
main deck. The arrival of sails meant that we would be sailing
again soon. Descending to the next deck I passed some of the
other servants. In a way, it was a good thing. They would see me

as just another servant, one they had not yet met, but a fellow passenger. I smiled and nodded as I headed to the bows and the ladder leading down to my nest. The hammocks close to the ladder were empty. Most of the servants would be working. I wondered why there were some still below deck. I glanced around and seeing that I was unobserved went down to the orlop deck.

I found my home and made it comfortable. I was hungry and I was thirsty. Until I had found some way to replenish my supplies then I would be on rations. That last meal I had enjoyed had been a good one. I took out the bread I had pilfered. My other food was some cheese, a couple of onions, an apple and some salted pork. They would last longer than the bread and so I ate half of the loaf and washed it down with a mouthful of ale from the aleskin. I had with me a leather cup. The next time I went on deck I would use that to drink from the water barrel. That done I settled back. I would have to wait until dark before I ventured out. Even this far down I was aware of a different motion. The sails were set and we were sailing south to wherever Madeira was. My adventure was beginning, and more importantly, my life was now, marginally, safer.

Chapter 2

I must have dozed off. I was woken by light and voices. I froze. There were men on the orlop deck. I could smell beer and sweat. I saw four men and they were sitting on one of the large hawsers. I dreaded them turning for they would see me. Then I realised that I was hidden by the dark and the small candle they were using barely lit them, let alone me. It was just that its lighting, in the dark, had woken me.

"Come on, give me a six."

I heard the clicking sound and knew they were playing with dice.

"Got it!"

"Keep your voice down, you fool! If Cunningham hears us, then it will be a flogging."

"You worry too much. The passengers above are making enough noise as it is."

I relaxed a little. They were breaking the rules and would be more worried about being caught than anything. I learned their names and that Mr. Cunningham was the bosun. I had worked that out already. The bosun was the one who was in charge of the crew. The captain commanded the ship.

It was the distant cry of, "All hands on deck!" that made the game end and I took my chance. As they hurried up to obey the command I left my new home and, when they had climbed the ladder, made my way to follow. I would be regarded by anyone who saw me as one of the crew.

It was as I climbed that I felt the stronger motion of the sea. Passing the servants, I heard weeping and a voice said, "Alice, we have thousands of miles to go. I expect that we shall have worse storms than this. We are a new ship and the captain, so Master William tells me, is the best in the company. Show courage girl."

"Yes, Mr. Hargreaves."

I climbed up through the empty crew deck and passed the cabins. I heard the conversation and saw lights from under cabin doors. Once I reached the main deck it was a frightening sight that greeted me. The crew were swarming up ladders as rain pelted down and, glancing to the side I saw waves that looked big enough to swamp us. The ship was rocking from side to side as well as moving up and down. Either I had not noticed in my nest or it had become more violent as I had climbed the ladder. I grabbed hold of the gunwale. I was lucky. The crew were too busy fighting nature to worry about me. I had the chance to locate where the water barrel could be found. I saw that there was a barrel fastened to the base of the foremast. In the cacophony of shouts, the crack of the sails and the sound of the storm I could not be heard and I moved like a shadow to the barrel. I lifted the lid and used my leather cup to draw some water. I drank four cups and replaced the lid. I saw that I was close to the place where they cooked the food and stored their supplies. I took my chance and slipped down the ladder. I was soaked to the skin. I should have used my cloak. Then I realised that my cloak would have marked me. The crew wore no cloaks.

The deck was lit by a candle suspended from the deck above and contained in glass. The galley was empty. I saw that the crew had simply abandoned it. The storm had necessitated all the crew, including the cooks, to work the ship. I saw then that were was a pot of something. I went over and saw that it was a stew. I knew that it would be mainly vegetables and grain but as the pot felt warm it would sustain me. I found a wooden bowl and a spoon. I quickly ladled the food into the bowl and, after eating a few spoonfuls headed down to the next deck. I found a quiet corner and ate it all. I tucked the bowl inside my damp shirt and searched the shelves. They were all secured by a piece of wood I later learned was called a fiddle. I found a small crate containing apples and I took four of them. Hearing returning voices I headed down to the crew's quarters. It was as I passed the hammocks that I saw the small seaman's jacket. It had fallen from the hammock. I was a thief and I took it. It would help me as a disguise.

I made my way, unseen to my den. I now knew that it was used by others but, so long as I made no sound when they came down I would be safe enough. I stripped off my clothes and stored my treasure, the apples, bowl and spoon, with my belongings. I had spare underwear, breeks and a shirt. I donned them and laid my clothes on the timbers. I hoped that they would dry. The ship seemed watertight. I knew, from my father, that older ships tended to be damp and leaked. The jacket I had stolen would be as a disguise. The next time I went on deck I would appear to the servants as a member of the crew. What I would need was a hat. I had learned that hats afforded the best of disguises.

I could hear, as the night progressed, the effects of the storm. I heard the retching and the screaming from above me as the passengers endured the wild seas and skies. I felt cosy and safe. Like the man I had heard speaking to the servant, Alice, I did not believe that we would be wrecked, at least not here. I had lived long enough by the river to know that ships which were well out to sea had less chance of being wrecked than ones that were close to shore. I did not know where Madeira lay but I knew that between the south coast and the south was open ocean. I slept.

I had slept too long as I woke when it was almost dawn but the motion of the ship was calmer. I needed to, not only make water, but to risk the lurch over the side too. I knew that the crew would be exhausted and I might not be noticed. I rose and donned my newly acquired jacket. My clothes were still damp. It would take time for them to dry. I took off my boots. When I had spoken to the sailor, Ned, I had noticed he had bare feet. I needed to look like a sailor. Before I left the darkened orlop deck I used a piece of string to fashion my hair into a tidier tail behind me. It would add to my disguise as a seaman. The servant's deck was silent except for snores and one low moan. On the crew deck, all was silent but for the creak of the hammocks. It was the galleys where I was almost undone. The cooks were there already. The smell of cooking bacon made my stomach ache. Salted bacon would last a longer time aboard a ship. The porridge that I saw bubbling away in the pot would be seen as less attractive to sailors. Once the bacon was gone then they would endure the oaty gruel.

One glanced up as I passed and shook his head, "There's nowt for you, yet."

I shook my head, "I have the squits, cook."

He laughed, "Aye, well that will end soon enough."

I had passed the test. The next time he saw me he would assume I was one of the crew. If, however, I saw Ned, then he would wonder at my seaman's jacket. I was making problems for myself. The sooner I could leave the ship the better.

I saw that the sails were reefed when I emerged on deck. I had come out close to the quarter deck and a voice shouted, "Where are you off to?"

I deepened my voice and, saluting, pointed towards the bow, and said, "The heads, sir!"

A blue-coated arm waved and I hurried forward. I did not need to hold a wettened finger to determine the wind direction, I could feel it and I went to the leeward side. I was alone. I made my way along, grateful that the motion of the ship had eased. Although a terrifying experience the first time it was not as daunting as I had expected. The downside was that my breeks were dampened by the spray. As I headed to the stern hatch I saw the sails of the other ships. We had two consorts but we were clearly the leader. To the east, I saw the first faint glow of dawn. There was a water barrel by the mainmast and I took the opportunity to drink four mugs of water. No one seemed to think anything untoward and I walked as leisurely as I could down a deck that was shifting beneath my bare feet.

When I reached the galleys the cook spied me and said, "Still have the squits?"

"I think they have gone, sir." I had learned that using the word 'sir' was the best way to win friends.

He nodded, "Here, this might help you. Don't tell your messmates." He took two of the pieces of bread that were piled already for breakfast and dipped them into the pool of fat that lay beneath the bacon. He slapped three pieces of bacon on the bread and handed me the unexpected meal.

"Thank you, sir."

He smiled and shook his head, "Cook, will do. I am no officer. Now be off with you and join your messmates."

I fairly skipped down the ladders and I was so quick that the bacon was still warm and the fat still oozed down my chin as I ate the unexpected treasure.

I was becoming used to the dark. The open hatch threw a weak shaft of light and I was able to make out shapes. I wondered how far we had to sail. I hoped it would be days rather than weeks but I had made a start. I consoled myself that if I was discovered as a stowaway they could not return me to London. It would be Madeira. I was, for the moment, safe from Ralph Every.

Over the next few days, my life developed a pattern. I worked out the best times to go on deck. I avoided the galley, using that ladder only one day in three. I chose the times when the passengers were either eating or sleeping to pass them and whenever I heard the crew called to duty I headed up to the deck. It was on those occasions when I donned my jacket, I noticed that many of the male servants had also shunned shoes and I left my boots safe in my den. At other times I left the jacket in the orlop deck. As I passed servants and passengers I was acknowledged. The servants would all assume that I worked for a master they had not seen and the masters and mistresses would not care who I was. They would think that I was a solitary soul who did not make friends easily. I was a servant and therefore unimportant. I even engaged in casual conversations with one or two of them which was normally as I waited at the heads.

I learned, from what I had overheard, that it would take ten days to reach Madeira where we would reprovision and then another six weeks to reach Jamestown on St. Helena. I also learned, much to my surprise, that only four or five of those I had thought to be servants were, actually servants. The others were employees of the East India Company and were heading to Calcutta to begin new lives there. I stored that information. It was during the hours of daylight that I saw the red coats of the marines. The ship had armed men to protect the ship from pirates and enemies. It was the cook who told me of their purpose one morning when I passed the galleys. Breakfast was over and he was smoking a pipe. He poured me a mug of ale and chatted to me. I used the name John. He seemed like a friendly man. It was from him that I learned of the VOC. They were, it seems, the Dutch equivalent of the East India Company. As rivals, there was no love lost and while to the west of Africa, the ships of the two companies behaved themselves, once in the vast Indian Ocean then they would often engage in attacks on one another. It explained why we were in the company of two smaller ships. Our twenty-eight guns were a good deterrent.

I knew that we were close to port from the excited chatter of the passengers. Madeira was Portuguese but there was, I knew, an English presence. The English controlled the wine trade and I saw a chance for me to land and find some means of employment until I could take a ship back to England. I was not a lazy youth and I did not mind hard work. I made sure that I vacated my home before the crew came down for the ropes that they would need. I packed my bag.

The shouts of the crew and the noise of the passengers told me that land had been sighted and with my bag slung over my shoulder, headed up to the deck. I slipped up the ladders as secretively as I could. I followed some of the lower deck passengers and reached the bows unseen. I pressed myself against the rear of the cabins at the bows and watched. The smells of the exotic Portuguese island drifted over to me and the gunwale was crowded as all the passengers strained for a sight of land after ten days of ocean. I saw then the marines. They marched to the side and after the ropes had been thrown to secure us to the shore and the tumblehome was removed, they stood guard. There were three privates and a sergeant. I watched.

The gangplank was fitted and, peering along the shoreside, I saw a second one lower down. The flash of red told me that it was guarded too. I knew then it would not be so simple as a walk off the ship. I saw that the provisions were being loaded at the lower entrance. The blue-uniformed officers, three of them, and two of the passengers, both well-dressed gentlemen, left the ship. They were saluted.

Two of the lower deck passengers, seeing this, headed for the gangplank, "Where do you think you are going?" It was the stocky sergeant with the bulging waist and scarred face who spoke.

The two men were in their mid-twenties and one said, "Ashore. There must be an alehouse we can use."

The swagger stick came across the tumblehome, "No one leaves the ship."

The other said, "But they did." He pointed at the officers and gentlemen.

"They are allowed to. You are not. Now scarper."

Muttering the two men went back to the huddle of men who were standing to look at the teeming port that promised so much. I would have to find another way off the ship. I shaded my eyes to look at the sun. It was mid-morning. I spied some hope when two of the crew left the ship. If I donned my jacket then I might be able to leave too. My hopes were dashed when they returned just moments later with barrels. They went to the water barrels and topped them up. It took them two hours to finish their task. It was late in the afternoon when the officers and gentlemen returned. All of them had the rosy glow of men who had enjoyed Madeiran wine. As the men came aboard the bosun ordered the gangplank removed and the tumblehome replaced. The crew were called to prepare to leave the harbour. While the rest of the passengers stayed to watch us leave I headed back for my cell. I could not leave and the next port of call lay six weeks away. The cheese I had brought aboard and the other foods were gone. I had not starved hitherto but soon I would. I wondered, as I descended into the gloom, if I should give myself up. It was looking like an attractive prospect. I wondered what they would do. Perhaps they would incarcerate me in a cell. If they did that I would be no worse off. I would be fed and have more light than I did now. I would not have to sneak around. However, the villain in me wanted freedom and not shackles. Besides, they might find a passing ship heading for England and put me aboard. That was the worst of all endings. I would be sent back to where Ralph Every could get his hands on me.

I had to take more chances. The cook would soon grow suspicious of my visits. The last time that I had passed through he had asked me who was the captain of my watch. I had pretended I had not heard and since then I had avoided the galley. It meant that I was forced to steal from the larder. Each time I did that increased my chances of getting caught and the easiest things to take were fresh fruit and vegetables. That meant I had to visit the heads more regularly. I was also stinking. A combination of dampness and no opportunity to wash meant that I knew I was leaving a smell when I passed through the decks. Although the crew were also pungent, my smell seemed worse.

It was three weeks after Madeira and I had just spent an unpleasant time with my rear hanging over the ship when I was discovered. It was the middle of the night and I had thought myself safe. I pulled up my breeks and was heading back to the stairs when a voice said, "John, isn't it?"

It was Ned, the sailor I had met whilst at the Downs. I nodded, "Aye, Ned isn't it?"

There was no smile, "You are a stowaway."

I tried bluster. If this had been on land I would have run. The problem with a ship was that there was nowhere to run. "No, I am a servant."

He shook his head, "I saw you with Harry Perkins' jacket. He thought he had lost it. He had his pay stopped to have it replaced. I have seen you disappearing below the decks." His face softened, "Come on, son, a problem shared and all of that."

My shoulders slumped. The game was up. I had no choice and I came clean, up to a point. I told him that I had fled London because of a man who wanted to hurt me. He was persistent and I found myself telling him how I had stolen coppers to feed myself. It was a lie but, I hoped, a believable one, He pressed me for a name. Surprisingly he had heard the name of Ralph Every.

He shook his head, "You were right to run but I am not sure the sea was the safest choice. He has tried to take company ships. From what I have heard he managed to capture three Mughal ships each carrying a fortune. They were well armed too."

That did not make me feel any better, "Then why worry about the coins I took from him? They would have been as a drop in the ocean."

He gave a cynical laugh, "Have you never noticed that the ones who have the most are desperate to cling on to what they have."

"So what now, Ned? Do you hand me over to the bosun?"

He shook his head, "I wouldn't give Bosun Cunningham my own worst enemy. No, where is your hidey hole?" I hesitated, "John, if that is your name, you can trust me. I am a decent bloke."

"The orlop deck."

He laughed, "You must be a mole then. Go back there and stay hidden. I will have a word with Rafe McTeer. He is my watch captain. He will know a way out of this."

I nodded, "Thanks, Ned."

He smiled, "I had a little brother. He came to sea last year as a boy sailor. He fell overboard. You remind me of him. I can't bring him back but perhaps I can help you."

I scurried back to my little hole. I had no idea what my fate would be, yet I knew I could not go on as I was.

Chapter 3

The ship stopped. I knew it because of the motion. It was an uncomfortable movement from side to side. I had felt it when we had stopped at the Downs. What was going on? I heard feet moving above me and the sound of a bosun's whistle. There was murmuring and then silence. I heard a splash and then the whistle sounded again. There were mumbled words that drifted down to me but I could not make out what they said. I heard the collective, 'Amen'. Was it Sunday? I had heard the singing and the 'Amen' on Sundays but that had been just a couple of days ago. Even before the feet began to move on the decks above me I felt the ship start to move again, albeit slowly. Above me, I heard the familiar chatter as the lower deck passengers returned to their deck. I knew they had held services on Sunday but they had not stopped the ship before. Perhaps it was a special Holy Day. I found myself fretting and worrying. That was not like me. I was the one who always did things, made things happen, and shaped my own world rather than waiting for the world to change me. I was in the hands of another and I did not like it.

It seemed like forever but, eventually, I saw a light appear at the hatch and Ned's voice called, "John, bring your belongings. I will take you to Rafe."

I wrapped everything in my sack and wrapped it in my cloak again making my improvised bag once more and, as I had done at Madeira, left my den. Was this to be the last time? As I wound my way past the coiled ropes I knew it was. No matter what happened I would not have to endure solitude and darkness.

Ned was smiling when I emerged. I had learned to look down when I came up and stare at the wooden deck until my eyes adjusted. I saw some of the passengers staring at me. My disguise had disappeared. We headed up to the crew deck and I saw an older man, a petty officer, seated at one of the swinging mess tables. He was alone and the rest of the men I saw, perhaps fifteen of them, sat at another table, mugs of something in their hands. They all studied me as Ned led me to the officer.

He had a pipe going and he used the stem to point first at me and then at Ned, "Sit. Ned, give him a mug of ale and then he can tell me his tale himself. I would like to hear it from his own lips before I take him to the captain."

My heart sank. I had hoped, nay dreamed, that the sailors would help me to hide until we reached St Helena. Those hopes were dashed. My quick mind began to work out that I would be placed in a cell and fed bread and water until we reached the distant island. Somehow that eased my mind for it would be little different to my existence hitherto. The ale when it came tasted like nectar. It probably wasn't but as it was the first ale I had enjoyed since that fateful night in the inn, it was wonderful.

I had decided on the truth, or a version of the truth. I told him the same story I had told Ned, that I had stolen from Ralph Every but I made out it was because I was starving and orphaned. I made suitably sad eyes. The attack by Jacob became a pursuit and fight with half a dozen of them. I told how I had stowed aboard and existed. When I spoke of stealing the pea jacket I saw hatred burning in the eyes of one of those at the table. The pipe had gone out and the officer tapped the ash out in his palm and crushed it before putting the pipe in his pocket.

He nodded, "From what you say, you are a veritable Hercules or a Robin Hood. I think that there is a nugget of truth in your tale. I have heard of Ralph Every but there is no reason why you should. However, I cannot see him wasting time over a few coppers, as you told us. Ned here likes you." He gave a sad smile, "We all know why but you are a thief and we do not like thieves."

"I was starving."

He leaned forward, "Son, you are neither haggard nor drawn enough to be starving. You have lived on short rations since you stowed away. You were not starving." He paused, "No matter what the captain says, if you thieve from us then there will be no court to decide your fate. It will be the tiddly oggy and Davy Jones' locker for you if you do." He stood. "Leave your belongings here."

"Where are we going?"

"To see the captain." He shook his head, "I am sorry, son, but you didn't think that we were going to hide you, did you?" I glared at Ned and then stared at my belongings on the mess table. "Ned did the right thing and your whatnots will be safe enough. We have no thieves in this mess. Come on, you come along as well, Ned."

It felt strange to be walking openly but it felt to me as though it was the walk I had always dreaded in England, the walk up the stairs to court and a judge. That was what the captain would be, my judge and jury. There were two marines outside the captain's cabin and Rafe said, "We have a stowaway for the captain."

They both stared at me as though I was some strange sea creature fished from the ocean. One nodded and entered. He was away but a few moments and when he returned, he said, "Captain Mackintosh will see you now."

I noticed both Ned and Rafe took off their hats as they ducked beneath the lintel. There was a second door and Rafe knocked upon it.

"Come."

We entered and I saw not only the captain, I recognised him from Madeira, but also one of the other gentlemen who had gone ashore. There was a servant in the cabin and what looked, from his inky fingers, like a clerk.

"Well, Mr. McTeer, is this the mysterious ghost that men have seen flitting around my ship, stealing jackets and food?"

My heart sank. The captain sounded like a judge already and he did not have the rosy glow I had seen at Madeira. He had the stern face of a judge about to don a black cap.

"It is, Captain. He says his name is John and he joined us in London. He says he was fleeing the wrath of Ralph Every for he had stolen from him." I noticed that every time he used the word, 'say' he emphasised it making it sound as though I was lying.

"The pirate?" Rafe nodded. "Then the boy is clearly not only a thief but a foolish one too." He shook his head and waved the servant over. The man topped up the glasses he and the gentleman were using. "What to do with you, eh? What we cannot do is to turn around and take you back to England. Nor can we simply drop you overboard." My face fell and he smiled. "Aye, my thieving friend, out here I am the law. I suppose we could leave you with the Governor at St. Helena and let him take you off our hands." He sipped the viscous liquid and drummed the fingers of his left hand on the table. He put down the glass and patted the Bible which lay on the table. "I am a God-fearing man, John, if that is your name. Today we buried a young man. He died when his appendix burst and he was in great agony. It was sad for he was a good boy sailor. It is strange but his name was John too." He suddenly looked me in the eyes, "How old are you?"

"Er, seventeen, I think, sir."

"The same age as John. I don't know why, perhaps it is because John's corpse now lies at the bottom of the Atlantic Ocean and he was an orphan too but I would offer you the position of Boy, Second Class. We need the position filled and I am not sure of the quality we could expect to find in St. Helena. It is filled with ex-slaves and the like. John will be a hard boy to replace. He was hard-working and popular. It would not be a permanent position. When we reach Calcutta, you will be paid off and landed. It is a chance for you to redeem yourself for theft, even from a pirate, is still a crime and a sin." He glanced at the gentleman.

"I am James Wintersgill and a senior partner. If you impress me on this voyage then when we reach Calcutta there may be a position for you. There are tied men there and you could work hard to earn your freedom. Perhaps this long voyage might be a way for you to redeem yourself and change your ways. India is a place of opportunity. Most of the passengers here are going to start a new life in a land run by the East India Company."

There was silence. The captain broke it, "Well, are you struck dumb? We have made an offer. What do you say? Will you serve on this ship or shall I cast you in irons and leave you in St. Helena?"

My wits returned to me, and I adopted a grateful look, "Captain, I was just dumbfounded by your kind and forgiving nature. Of course, I will accept and I will change my ways. Thank you, Mr Wintersgill, I think the chance of a new life in India is one that I will embrace. You are right, I took the wrong path and now I have the chance to take the right one."

"Very well. Mr. McTeer, John was in your watch and I leave this John in your hands. Take him to the purser to sign him on officially." I saw that the clerk had been scribing and he handed a piece of paper to the captain who signed it with a flourish. "Give this to the purser." He smiled, "Of course, the pay will have the cost of the pea jacket he stole deducted and that money will be repaid to Harry Perkins."

Rafe said, "About turn. Now you will learn how to take orders." I was marched out.

I was philosophical about the pay. I had not expected it and I still had my fortune about my waist. I would have to work, I knew that, but I would be fed. There would be ale and once I had the chance, I knew I could steal ashore. There would have to be places we would stop that might offer me opportunities. I grew in confidence.

The purser was a fat florid fellow. He had the red nose of a drinker but he was a pleasant enough chap. I was made to make my mark. I could read a little but I thought to keep that from those around me. If they thought I was illiterate I might be able to use that to my advantage. Rafe pointed out that I had a pea jacket already but I was given the rest of what passed for a uniform. I said my name was John Smith. I am not sure any of the three believed it, but they didn't seem to care. I was also given what Rafe called eating irons.

We left and headed down to the mess. I was learning the terms used on the ship already. Rafe said, "We go on watch in an hour. We have a four-hour watch. We will be off for four hours and then back on for four hours. There is the first watch, middle watch, the morning watch, forenoon watch, afternoon watch. They are all four hours long. Then comes the two dog watches. They are just two hours long. Ned, here, will tell you your duties. I don't use the rope very often but I will if I have to. Mr. Cunningham, on the other hand, the bosun, uses what he calls his starter on everyone. Lazy sailors get a double dose so you have been warned." We entered the mess deck and all faces turned to me. Rafe said, "John," he paused, "Smith here, is joining our mess. Harry, you will be reimbursed for your pea jacket so no hard feelings eh? You have a nice new one and Smith here will have to wear the one you had for two years."

Harry, as I came to realise, was not the sharpest knife in the drawer. It took some moments for it to sink in and then he grinned, "Aye, I have. Welcome, Smudger."

It was Harry who gave me my nickname. It was the one normally accorded to those named Smith. As the name was made up and I would be discarding it when I left I didn't mind, I said, "You are welcome, Harry."

Rafe walked over to a rolled-up hammock, "This is your bed and here," he went to a row of small chests, "is where you store your whatnots." He opened one and I saw that it was almost empty. "They also make do as seats. This is yours."

I looked down and saw that the only thing inside was a neckerchief.

Ned said, "That was the only one of John's belongings that no one wanted. He died an orphan and we shared what he had. If you die, we will do the same with you." He reached down and took out the neckerchief. It was white and blue striped, "Here is a present from the grave."

I could not help but shudder, however I took it and donned it.

"Now put on the rest of your uniform and sort your stuff out."

I was, thankfully ignored as I placed my belongings in the chest. Although tiny it held all that I had. I had to be clever when I changed my clothes. Before I took anything off I surreptitiously moved the money belt under my arms then I took off my breeks and underwear and pulled on the new underwear and the trousers that came to just below my knee. As I fitted the belt, I slipped my money down a little lower so that it was hidden by my new leggings. I took off my shirt and donned the new one. The rest of my messmates were taking the opportunity to rest and I was able to study, properly, my new surroundings. I saw that there were oilskins neatly hanging from pegs. Everything was neat. The hammocks each had a blanket but the blankets were folded. I learned that not only Rafe but also the rest of the officers regarded neatness as a necessity. The mess table that swung from the metal rings had a wooden rim. I learned it was called a fiddle. It was there to stop things from sliding off. There were also two greasy ropes that hung down.

"Ned, what are those? Are they to help you to get up?"

He laughed, "They are to wipe your hands on when you are finished eating. The food can be greasy. If we are ever becalmed or run out of food then they would be boiled up to make a soup."

I pulled a face, "Really?"

"We have never had to do that but… this is the sea and you never know. The waters to the east of us sometimes lose the wind and if we can't move…"

A bell rang. I had heard it before and now I discovered its purpose. A voice shouted, "Larboard Watch!"

"Right, lads, look lively."

Ned said, "Stay close and do everything I say as soon as I say it." He nodded towards my hands, "They will be red raw by the end of the day."

He was right. I was the one with neither experience nor skills. I was there for muscle and, looking at the others, that, too, was in short supply. While the skilled men climbed and reefed, looking like so many blue and white coated spiders, I hauled on ropes. I learned the difference between them the hard way. The bosun strode around the deck. To me, he seemed to be seeking failure. In my case, he found it all too readily. The knotted end of his rope found my back repeatedly. It was clear that he did not like me. He called me 'thief' from the off rather than either Smudger or Smith. I knew what I was but, somehow, his shouting the name each time I made the slightest error seemed to hurt as much as the knotted rope.

When the watch was changed I looked at my hands. In places, they were bleeding. Ned shook his head, "Worse than I thought. I didn't think anyone could get to your age without hard work. I was wrong. When you have eaten nip to the cook and ask him for some tallow grease. Rub it on your hands. A week or so should see them harden and become calloused."

I nodded dumbly. I had always been able to have a ready response but I was so tired that my mouth did not seem to want to work. I discovered, as I sat at the mess table, that the fetching of food was my duty but that would have to wait until the next mealtime. It was Harry who brought the food on a large tray with a fiddle around it. There was a jug of ale on the table too. They called the vessel, for some reason, the mess deck fanny. The food was a sort of bean stew. If there had been any meat in it then it only experienced the briefest of contacts. There were also the hard biscuits called tack.

There was an order to these matters. Ned was the senior hand and it was he who equitably dolloped the food on our platters.

He sat next to me and was kind enough to explain what I ought to do. "Season it liberally with salt. When we make the voyage back we normally have pepper to spare but not eastbound. The seasoning helps. Dip your tack in the ale. It will stop you from cracking your teeth."

I nodded dumbly and ate. To be fair it was hot and it was filling. That meal in 'The Grapes' now seemed like a lifetime ago. When we had finished Ned said, "Come on, we will take this tray back and I will introduce you to the cook."

As soon as he saw me the cook put his hands on his hips and laughed, "Well it if it isn't the lad who likes my bacon butties! I wondered about you."

"He is John's replacement, Cookie. He will come for the food from now on."

The cook became serious, "What a shame. John was such a nice, well-mannered lad. He was a credit to the orphanage." He made the sign of the cross, "God works in mysterious ways. I can think of others who deserved to die more."

I know he did not mean me but I felt guilty that I was alive and this lad, whom everyone spoke well of, was dead.

The cook saw my hands and shook his head, "Here, run this on them." He took a huge ladleful of grease and dropped it into my open palms. I rubbed it in, it stung and I winced. "Aye, it will do that at first. We will put a ladleful on when you come for food. Keep rubbing it in until it has helped your hands. A week or so and you will be like the rest." He sighed, "Let us hope we have no more storms, eh, Ned?"

"Aye, Cookie."

As we left I said, "What did he mean?"

"We can all keep an eye on you when the weather is like this. You can't come to much harm. We always lose what we call Landsmen in storms. Still, you may be the exception."

His words did not fill me with joy.

The last watch finished when it was dark. I did not envy the others as they reefed the sails. I had no idea of the time except that it was night and I was ready for my hammock. The last meal had been similar to the first but I needed it. My hands had not worsened although there was no improvement. The only good thing about the last watch was that the Chief Bosun was not on duty. It was another officer and he cracked me less often. It seemed like a sort of victory. I thought my day could not get worse but clambering too quickly into the hammock proved to be a disaster and I crashed to the deck. The rest of the watch thought that it was hilarious. That included the usually sympathetic Rafe and Ned. I am sure I cracked a rib as I fell but with so many bruises and aches already it was hard to tell.

Ned had not got into his hammock and, without drawing attention to it, he did so very slowly and I was able to emulate him. I now saw why they had all laughed because it was easy, once you knew how. With my blanket over me and the gentle rocking of the hammock, I was asleep almost as soon as my eyes closed.

Chapter 4

"Larboard Watch! Show a leg there!"

I had been woken in what seemed like the middle of the night when half of the starboard watch had returned to the mess but I soon drifted off. The hammock was the most wonderful way to get to sleep. That had seemed a moment ago but the light from the open gun ports, opened to allow fresh air through the ship told me that it was daylight. I was ready for food but it was clear that we would only eat once we had completed a four-hour watch.

The wind was fresh and whilst that meant we were moving quickly, it also tore through the inadequately thin clothes that we wore. In the odd moment when we had nothing to do, they were few and far between, I asked Ned about the watches.

"There are two mess decks. Each mess deck has a starboard and larboard watch. Some days we have a four-hour watch and a two-hour watch whilst on others it is just a four-hour one. You are unlucky. You have two long days. Tomorrow is a six-hour one and will be during the night. With reefed sails that is an easier duty. You will probably be assigned to be a lookout." He pointed aft, "Our little ducklings need to be watched. That will be interesting for you."

"Why is that?"

"You will get to meet the officers."

"What are they like?"

"They are like eggs. On the outside, they look identical with their blue uniforms trimmed with white and splashed with gold but inside…some are good but when you get a bad 'un…" he shook his head.

"And how long to port."

"St Helena?" I nodded. "Another week or so. We have made good progress but we won't be allowed ashore."

"Why not?"

"Too much temptation from the alehouses and whores. The captain doesn't want to lose any crew. Even if he allowed it, I wouldn't go ashore."

"Really?"

"The Royal Navy calls in to Jamestown, that is the capital. If they find sailors then you are pressed. I don't fancy being tied to the Navy for what might be the rest of my life. We get better pay, better food and better conditions. Another ten years and if I make rank, I should be able to save enough to leave the EIC. I can get a little pub and be well set."

"Do they pay that well?" I had not listened too closely when the purser had told me my pay. The money my father had earned would not have allowed us to buy an inn.

He shook his head, "Not bad but most of us make money the way the company does. You can buy spices in the east for coppers and when you get back to England turn the spice into gold. I save mine. My old mother has a jar in the bedroom. Ten years, Smudger, ten years and this will be all a memory."

That became the pattern for my life and the next days passed in a blur of greasy hands, carrying platters of food, suffering the bosun's knotted rope and, the most enjoyable part, was standing at the stern as a lookout. It was easy work and I impressed the officers rated and non-commissioned alike by my sharp eyes and reactions. When I was a thief it had been those attributes that had brought me rewards. Now, while I was not financially rewarded, the fact that I saw when a ship went off station quicker than the other lookout impressed them. I was also the one who could be relied upon to be alert the whole time. It was easier for me than hauling on ropes and soon I was asked to spend half of each watch as a lookout. The first time I had to climb to what they called the crow's nest, for in daylight that was where we watched, I was terrified. It was not a nest in the true sense of the word. I sat with my legs wrapped around the mast, dangling over the yard. I gripped the top of the mast, At first it was scary but soon I found that if I did not look down, I could bear it. I won't say I was frozen with fear, for I had been skilled as a climber who broke into houses at night. This was different. The tarred rope afforded me a grip. I could never have done as Ned and the others did and walked along a thin rope to reef a sail with, what seemed to me, nothing to hang on to. The rope ladders were easier to climb than the brick walls of urban dwellings.

My attention was sometimes distracted by the dozen red-coated Marines who paraded on the deck close to the bow castle.

Their lieutenant, a young man called Dunn, looked to be little older than I was yet his men were mainly older than Ned and one or two were older than Rafe. I was told that Lieutenant Dunn was the son of one of the directors. He had this position through privilege. It was cheaper than buying a commission. With their whitened belts and shining leather, they looked smart enough but all that I ever saw them do was march up and down and perform manoeuvres that would not have been out of place outside the king's palace. What I did not see was musket practice.

The other advantage of being a lookout was that you were alone. You needed to be vigilant but that apart your mind could wander where it would. I was used to being alone. I enjoyed it. I liked Ned and Rafe but there were simply too many people on the ship. My little haven in England had been lonely and quiet. I liked that. I was in the little nest on the foremast when I saw the tiny island of St Helena. I called down, "Land to the south."

I had learned that the officers liked clear messages. I received a cheery wave of acknowledgement from the deck officer for my troubles. I heard the shout for the next watch and I prepared to descend. I saw my replacement, another boy sailor, climbing the ladder. The hard part about being the sharp-eyed lookout in the foremast was getting down. I had to cock first one leg and then the other over the yard. I had discovered on the previous occasion that the easier way back to the deck was to come down a rope. It was faster but a little more precarious. My hands were still raw but not as raw as they had been. The grease was working.

When I reached the deck Rafe shouted, "Smith, coil that rope."

I had learned that skill quickly and now there was no difference between those ropes coiled by me and those coiled by Ned. The rest of the watch were waiting for their relief and I was able, once I had coiled the rope, to chat to Rafe. "How long will we be in port?"

"Long enough to take on board supplies and I think we have more passengers."

"From this little rock?"

He shrugged, "That was the rumour. It might be a little rock but ships can come from different places to reach here. Who knows? The thing is once we leave here we have the Cape of Good Hope to round and then the island of Madagascar."

"You sound worried, Chief, why?"

"Pirates, my son. The pirate fleets abound. We might be lucky. They prefer to take us when we are fully laden. If we do get past them then there is the Persian Gulf and the pirates there are even worse than the Madagascan ones. It is why we are in convoy." He pointed to the nearest mast, "See there, they are the boarding pikes we use if we have to repel boarders. The Marines will bring out cutlasses for us too. If we have to fight then everyone will have to do their bit."

As we neared the harbour I made to descend to our mess. I had learned to relish the rest. Rafe gave me a strange look. When I heard the bosun's whistle followed by the command, "All hands on deck!" the look made sense.

Rafe gave me a wry smile. "Entering and leaving the harbour needs everyone."

"But that isn't fair. We have only just come off watch."

He shrugged, "It will even out and while we are in the harbour there will be a deck watch of Marines and the rest of the watch will be made by defaulters."

I had been lucky thus far and not incurred the wrath of an officer. I knew that could change but now I was grateful that I would not have to work while we were in harbour.

There were just two ships in the harbour and they were both Royal Navy. One was, so Ned told me, a frigate, while the other was a sloop. They gleamed. I knew we kept our ships smart, Rafe had been proud of that, but the naval vessels were something else. The place itself looked like the most run-down parts of London. There were no buildings that stood out. As I helped to work the windlass and lower the anchor I was able to study both the buildings and the harbour. I also heard the cries of the men and women on the bum boats that plied their trade. The bosun's voice and fierce face failed to deter them. Once the anchor was lowered and we were tied to the shore, we were set free. We were off duty. For our watch that meant food. We had worked a long watch and were ravenous.

The cook liked me, but he was an honest man. Rafe told me of some cooks who accepted money from the mess in return for more food. As this extra food was normally spilt on the fiddle along the edge of the platter such a cook was said to be, 'on the fiddle'. As much as we all wanted more food it felt good to know that he was honest. That is not to say he didn't do me favours. He did but I didn't pay him for them. The best treat was when I went for breakfast. There was always bacon waiting for me. When we had no bread, he would soak a ship's biscuit in the bacon fat and that would soften it. I loved my breakfast.

We had some passengers who were disembarking. I did not envy them their new life. The island was small. We also loaded fresh water and supplies. It was while the meat and flour were being brought aboard that the soldiers arrived. They were our passengers. Rafe and Ned were interested in them. Rafe was knowledgeable about such matters. "These are East India Company soldiers. It looks like a platoon. See, there is a captain and a sergeant and a corporal." He nodded, seemingly satisfied. "If we have any bother they will be of more use than the toy soldiers we carry aboard."

They looked like real soldiers. The officer had a scarred face and the sergeant had white flecks in his thinning hair and his stomach suggested he liked his food. They marched aboard and stood easily while they were allocated their quarters. They would occupy half of the space where the servants and lower deck passengers resided. It had not been full and with some disembarked, they would be easily accommodated. With their red coats and tricorn hats they looked splendid and more like soldiers than our marines.

The afternoon wore on and I bored of the loading of supplies, necessary though it was. I went below deck. There was a domino game going on while three or four sailors were busy with scrimshaw work. I had learned this was the name given to the intricate carving of bone. When the cook had extracted every morsel of goodness from them, he gave dried, marrowless bones to sailors who would happily spend their free time carving. I admired their work but there was no way I would waste my time with it. Nor did I want to gamble away my coppers in games of chance. Instead, when I wasn't sleeping I would use my mind to plan my future in India. I would not return to England. Ned and Rafe had told me, not only of the wonders of the place but the opportunities for profit. From what they had said it was like legal thieving. Apparently, in India, the poorest clerk from England enjoyed servants. That would be the life for me.

Being in port meant that, for the first three days after we left, we had bread. The first day, of course, was the best as it was the freshest but even that on the third day, whilst stale, still soaked up grease and the juices from stew much better than tack. I was now used to the dull diet and it was those little things that enlivened what we ate.

I was now the lookout for our watch. I could scamper up to the mast easily. Each day that I did it improved my skills. My hands were now harder and rougher than they had been and they afforded me a good grip. I also learned to read the sea better than I had. I listened to Rafe and the experienced sailors when they talked around the mess table of the storms that awaited us when we rounded the, apparently misnamed, Cape of Good Hope. From what they said it was anything but. The watches I preferred were the night watches. Sometimes I would be the lookout on the bow and at others I would be at the stern, by the wheel with the officers. I was naturally still and silent. I was also a good listener and I picked up nuggets of information as the officers of the watch chatted as though I was not there. The officers of the night watch tended to be the more junior officers. If the weather was rough then the senior ones would be there but it was the Master's Mate on the wheel with his assistant. The petty officer was Rafe and the officer of the watch was the Fourth Mate.

Our first night watch was two days after leaving Jamestown. It went from eight o'clock at night until midnight. "What do you think of our new passengers, Mr. McTeer?"

"They seem like tough men. They seem a little more martial than our marines." Rafe was able to be so open as the two marines on night watch were by the mainmast and were asleep. It marked their casual attitude to their duty. The Fourth Mate allowed it as, being in the middle of the ocean, they would only be needed if one of the lookouts spotted anything.

The Fourth Mate's voice lowered as he said, "Mr. Wintersgill is not happy about them. They were recruited from Newgate Prison."

Rafe's, "Aah," spoke volumes.

"They were on the *Hindostan* but Lord MacCartney, when he discovered their origins, had them put off the ship at St Helena. As his lordship works for the government he has that power but Mr. Wintersgill does not have the influence and he has concerns as he has his wife and daughters aboard."

"Someone must have thought that they would not be a danger."

I saw the Fourth Mate shrug, "Mr. McTeer, I care not if they are thieves and murderers. God knows our enemies employ such men but Mr. Wintersgill does not live in our world."

I turned to watch the lights on the two ships that were following us and they were still on station. Our youngest boy, Matty, came aft with mugs of ale for the others. There would be none for me. Matty was just ten years old and as scrawny a boy I had never seen. He had come from the Marine Society, a charity that found orphan boys positions on ships. Although it was mainly there for the Royal Navy, the company also benefitted.

When he left Rafe said, "The officer, he is from Newgate too?"

This was gossip and the Fourth Mate moved further away from the helmsman. It was as though he did not see me, just eight feet away. He spoke conspiratorially, "No, he was in the British Army. He wounded a Guard's officer in a duel and was dishonourably discharged." His voice became even lower, "Sir James Cockburn, he is an old man now, but he is still very powerful and very rich. He is one of the directors. This platoon, well there are just twelve of them so platoon is the wrong word, but, anyway, they are his idea. He knew this officer and he gave him carte blanche to pick his own men from the prison."

Rafe said, sagely, "Well they have rules they have to follow now and fighting a duel just seems to me the way the nobs have punch-ups. We have them all the time on the ship don't we, Mr. Richardson?"

"I suppose."

Just then I spotted that the next ship in line, '*Canton*', was no longer in direct line astern. "Mr. Richardson, 'Canton' is off station."

He turned and lifted the 'bring 'em near,' "Well spotted, Smith." He placed the valuable instrument back in its net and lifted the speaking trumpet. "'*Canton*', back on station if you please."

There was a slight delay and then we saw the lantern at the bow covered and uncovered twice. A moment or two later the ship was back on station. Rafe and the Fourth Mate returned to the wheel.

Gossip and rumour were rife on the ship. I suppose it was inevitable for we were a crowded community. There were people who were liked and those who were unpopular. There were others who were mysteries. I knew that I fell into the latter category. The soldiers had come into our world and it meant they were the object of wandering tongues. For my part, I began to take more notice of them. The first thing I noticed was that, unlike our marines, they did not wear their red uniforms or their round hats. Their white overalls were replaced by more workaday grey ones. They also went barefoot. On their heads, they wore forage caps. Unlike the marines and the rest of the crew, when they could they spent time in the open on the deck. If there was a storm or rain then they vacated it but for the main part, the officer and the sergeant apart they kept in the open air. I asked Rafe about it.

He cocked an eyebrow, "You have sharp ears, John, be careful how you use them."

"I was just wondering why they stay on deck even when it is cold."

"You heard that they all came from Newgate?" I nodded, "Well, if you had spent a long time in a prison without sunlight, what would you do?"

I realised he was right. I had only been denied the sun for a short time but once I left my little darkened den I enjoyed the sun.

Gossip took second place when we reached the southern tip of Africa. We kept well to the south of it for it belonged to the Dutch. We were not at war with the Dutch but the Dutch East India Company, the VOC, regarded these waters as theirs. The captain decided that caution was the watchword. The problem was that the further south we went the colder it became and with it came attendant storms. Keeping on station became a nightmare and the cry of 'All hands on deck!' became a regular occurrence.

When I was called from my hammock and ascended to the deck I often passed the soldiers who knew to vacate the deck when the full crew was called. They would be in the way. Although Ned and I smiled and greeted them their faces remained impassive. They seemed an unhappy group of men.

It was on one such occasion, with a fresh storm threatening to tear the canvas from us, that the crew were ordered to their stations. I was deck crew and joined Ned to replace the rope that had sheared. It was a common occurrence. The stay was close to the forecastle. I was there with the new rope. I had seen Ned do it many times and although I might have had a stab at doing it he did it so deftly that I was just the labourer. It was as Ned hung from the rope above and I held the end of the rope up to him that I saw the young soldier emerge. He was heading for the heads. He had to be desperate for the ship was pitching so violently that there was no chance of avoiding a soaking.

I shouted as he passed, "Alright, friend?"

"Gut rot, I…" he began to vomit.

I was hanging on with one hand and the soldier tried to hang on too. The wave that struck him caught him at the wrong time and took his legs from under him. He screamed and clung on with one hand.

I shouted, "Ned!" I shifted the rope I held to the hand holding the forestay and reached down with my other. "Grab hold!"

His arm flapped around as he tried to grab my hand. I saw the fear and terror on his face. "Oh God, I don't want to die. Don't let me die!"

Ned shouted, "Grab his hand. I am coming." It would take time for Ned to reach me and it would be up to me to save the youth who looked to be almost my age. Our fingers touched and I leaned out a little more. The stay I was holding allowed me a little more flexibility and I managed to grab his hand. I gripped it as tightly as I could.

"Got you!" Ned's hand came to hold my waist and I thought we had the soldier. The sea can be cruel and the next wave smacked into us so hard that the soldier hit the side of the ship and he lost his grip. He banged his head too and even as my fingers squeezed around his hand it started to slip from my grasp.

"Nooo!" His dying cry echoed as he slipped from my hand. His head hit the bulge of the keel and his cry stopped.

"Man overboard!"

"Where away?"

"Larboard bow."

I stared at the body that was face down and slipped along the side of our ship. I saw faces lining the gunwale. Ned said, "I think he was dead before he hit the water. If so that was a mercy."

"Will the captain stop?"

As he pulled me back aboard, he said, "That is why I said it was a mercy. If he had lived he would have watched us continue sailing and drowned anyway. We never stop for men overboard. The best he could have hoped for was that he stayed by the side of the ship and one of those closer to the stern would throw him a rope." He shook his head, "That is rare. Come on John, you did all that you could. Now let us get our work finished or we will be feeling the rope of Mr. Hargreaves."

I did not know the soldier but for the rest of the watch, I could not get him from my mind. When we returned to the mess I dried and changed into clothes that were merely damp rather than soaked. The whistle went for food and I went to the galley.

The cook slopped food on the tray and Matty had the fanny filled and took the platter with the hard tack. The cook said, "I heard you tried to save that soldier boy, Smudger." I nodded, "That was brave but foolish. Look out for yourself, son. Only a fool goes to the heads in a storm."

"It just seems harsh, Cookie, to die because you have a gut ache."

"The sea is a cruel mistress. From what I heard it was a quick death."

I took the food back to the mess. The rest of the mess did not know the soldier and his death was just a topic of conversation. They meant no harm but their comments seemed callous and cold to me. I did not take as much food as I normally did. After we had eaten the others sat and either played dominoes or resumed their scrimshaw. I went to my bunk. I had my eyes closed but all that I could see was his face as he fell. I heard his cry in my ears. I opened my eyes and concentrated on the wood just above my head.

"Over there, in his hammock."

I turned and saw the officer, wearing just his shirt and overalls, come towards me. I had only seen him from a distance before. I knew he had a scar, I had seen it but close up I saw that it was still a little red and that meant it was recent. When he spoke I heard a north country accent.

"Lieutenant Crozier. You the lad who tried to save young Besty?"

"The soldier who drowned?" He nodded. "I tried but I failed, I am sorry."

"No, son, thank you. You held out a hand and put your life at risk. I don't think anyone did that for Besty in his whole life. Fate is a cruel mistress but you tried. Thank you and if you ever need a favour, just ask. We don't like losing one of our own."

I desperately wanted to ask about Newgate but I was afraid that the smile on the grim face might disappear and I had the impression that an angry Lieutenant Crozier was not a man to be crossed. "I am sorry I couldn't do more."

"You are a young lad and you will realise, soon enough, that life is not fair and the lower down the ladder you are the more injustice there is. Anyway, I just wanted to thank you." He turned and strode off.

Ned came over with a beaming smile on his face, "It has changed you, John."

"What has?"

"Being part of a crew. When you came aboard, sorry, stole aboard, you only thought of yourself. Today you thought about another and, more than that, you put your own life at risk. When you leave this ship you will be a different person."

One immediate change was that I gained respect from most of the crew. The exception, of course, was Mr. Cunningham whose only comment was that it had almost cost the ship a member of the crew. It was not a compliment. He thought I was about as much use as a barnacle on the hull but I would have to be replaced. The other effect was that the platoon all took to not only smiling when they saw me but also speaking to me. It was

never about the drowned soldier but just ordinary conversation
and I found I liked it.

Chapter 5

The storms stopped and the weather improved once we turned to sail northeast. Within a few days I missed the rain, for it was replaced by a sun which grew hotter and hotter as we headed closer to the equator. The passengers complained of the sun and the captain had canvas awnings rigged so that they could sit in the shade. The breeze from the sea made life more comfortable sitting out of the glare of the sun. For me, squatting atop the mainmast, it was hell. The sun beat down on my head so that it felt as though my brain was boiling. Rafe procured for me a straw hat. I had to tie it to my head using my dead predecessor's neckerchief. It became more bearable but the exposed parts of my body became red, burnt by the sun. I was given another neckerchief by Ned and that stopped my neck from burning. The rest of the men in my mess were less than sympathetic. Harry Perkins pointed out that eventually my skin would adapt and I would be browned by the sun. As I spent each night scratching the itchy skin his comment did not help.

Our marines were more vigilant now, and instead of marching were placed close to the lookouts on the stern and bow. Harry Perkins had been derisive about them, "If they were in the proper navy then they would be aloft with the likes of you, Smudger. God knows what would happen if pirates did attack us. This shower would be as much use as a one-legged man in an arse-kicking contest."

Perhaps the captain agreed for, when the coast of Madagascar appeared on the starboard beam he ordered the crew to practise with the cannons. As Ned told me, this was a private company and not the Royal Navy. It was all about profit and wasted powder and ball reduced the profits. On a day when the wind seemed sluggish and the sea was flat, we stopped all three ships and a rowing boat took out some old crates and barrels to use as targets. Our consorts would also try out their guns. I knew why the captains had chosen this day for we had the least wind I had experienced. We were not quite becalmed but it was a close call. It would give us a flat sea and, I reasoned, the chance to see the fall of shot better.

I found myself assigned to a gun on the main deck. Ned was the gunner and the other older, more experienced men used the rammer and sponge. Harry was in charge of the choosing of the balls and the rest of us just hauled on ropes. Rafe had four guns under his command. The guns were 6-pounders and the smallest guns on the ship. As we ran through the routine Ned explained that while we were the smallest, potentially we were the most accurate. The balls were all stacked on what was called a monkey. Matty had the job I did not relish. He had to bring the powder charges from the magazine. It was a self-contained room with no windows and he had to wear slippers to avoid sparks. If we used grapeshot then he would have to bring that too. The magazine was on the deck above the orlop. Matty would have to be very nimble in a real battle and he would have ladders and decks to negotiate. As it was we had a leisurely time. Harry was able to choose the best ball that was available. He did not choose the roundest, they were saved for when we used the guns in earnest, but they were the smaller balls. Someone had made money by selling balls to the company that were not a full six pounds in weight.

"Won't that make a difference, Ned?"

"Aye, it will. There will be windage and we won't be anywhere near as accurate but we are only going to fire one ball. It is just to show the new hands, like yourself, how to do it and," he nodded towards the watching passengers, "to let them know the sound."

When we were all ready, he blew on the linstock and raised his arm. Two of the other gun captains had already done so but most had not. When Rafe shouted, "Main deck ready, Bosun," then Bosun Cunningham nodded.

Bosun Cunningham acted as Master Gunner and while we were slow, the ones on the other deck were even slower. "If you want me down there with my starter, then I will happily oblige.

"Mess deck ready!"

I had seen the others tie their neckerchiefs around their ears. Ned nodded for me to move my feet. I was in danger of having them crushed by the gun carriage.

Bosun Cunningham shouted, "Fire!"

I was not ready for the foul, sulphurous pall of smoke that filled my nose. Even with hands and neckerchief about my ears, the blast was painful. The column of flame shot out and the gun carriage rolled back. Had I not been warned I would have been crippled for life. If I had expected the flotsam and jetsam to be demolished, I would have been disappointed. Rafe had told me that most of the balls would miss. He was right. I could see the majority bouncing, like stones on a village pond, across the water. A few did hit, more by luck than skill, and that brought a cheer. I knew every gun crew would claim to have been the ones to make the hit.

I think I was disappointed as we passed the northern edge of the pirate stronghold and we had not had the chance to use the guns. When I mentioned this Ned shook his head, "If I never get to fire the guns in anger then I shall be a happy man. If we fire them then it means that there are pirates close by and they are all mad buggers. I have no idea what makes them so but when they come at you then they care not if they live or die."

"You were attacked by pirates?"

He shook his head, "When I came to sea for the first time I met an old timer with one eye. It was his last voyage and he told me the tales."

"Perhaps he was exaggerating. We all like to dress up our tales."

"Not old Joe. You can tell when someone is lying or stretching the truth." He grinned and ruffled my hair, "Like you when I found you. You are a natural storyteller and liar, I could tell that but Joe, he told the truth."

"How did he survive?"

"A Royal Navy frigate happened upon them. The Navy knows how to deal with pirates. They sank their ships and hanged the lot of them. No, bringing the guns out once a voyage and sending a ball at a barrel will do for me."

Of course, the danger was not over. The pirates of Madagascar were almost like businessmen. Their aim was profit. It made more sense to risk their ships attacking fully laden ships that were westbound. We passed their lairs as we were eastbound. As we neared the Persian Gulf, we faced a different kind of danger. The place abounded with Arab pirates although, according to Rafe the word Arab could mean anything. It was just the term for the people who lived at the edge of the Turkish Empire. They were not organised. The men just bandied together and when there were enough of them, they would attack any ship, regardless of size. They would attack using many ships of different sizes and crews. For them, females were treasure and could be sold in their slave markets. The muskets used by the marines were highly prized and they were sought, too. Ned was, once more, the expert thanks to his mentor, Joe.

"They sail smaller, sleeker ships than the Madagascan pirates. They are faster and harder to hit. Some are small and some have crews of forty or fifty. Once they make the side of one of their victims then they swarm all over slaughtering everyone. They strip a ship like rats do a corpse."

I shuddered. How could you fight such an enemy? It seemed we just hoped that they would not know we had females on board.

The closer to the Gulf we came so the weather became hotter. It was not just during the day but the night, too. There was less wind here and life became unbearable. It was worsened when the captain put the crew on water rations. The passengers, of course, had no such privation but we did. The water was not particularly pleasant to drink but having finished the last of the beer, the water became a more attractive prospect.

I woke one night needing to make water. It was the middle watch, the quietest of all the watches. Normally I would have held it in but the night seemed particularly airless and oppressive and the chance to walk the deck seemed attractive. With reefed sails, we were barely moving and there was little air moving through the mess. I left the mess deck. Even with all the gun ports open, there was no relief from the heat. I was shirtless. My treasure belt was below my breeks. If I was seen then I might be punished for being half naked but I was too hot and I risked it. The officer of the watch was the Third Mate. Albert Wright was an easy-going officer and his watch, were, perhaps, the laziest in the whole crew. I doubted that they would even see me. They tended to gather in clumps and, as Ned said, 'natter.' With the ship barely moving there was little for them to do. Even so, when I emerged onto the main deck I crouched and looked astern, to where the officers and helmsman were. They were chatting and would not see me. It was as I turned to look for Erik, the lookout at the bow, that I saw a hand come over the head and then another. Erik was a nice young man but lazy and he had his back to the rail. I think his eyes were closed. Before I could shout a warning or alert the rest of the crew a hand wrapped itself around his mouth and a knife slipped across his throat. I saw the blood spurt.

I froze for a heartbeat. I did not know what I ought to shout but I had to give the alarm. At the top of my voice, I roared, "To arms! Pirates! All hands on deck! To arms! Pirates! All hands on deck!"

The weapons were all stacked either next to the gunwale or attached to the masts. The longest weapons were close to hand by the mainmast. I grabbed a boarding pike and ran at the assassin. I had never used one but just doing nothing would not help me and the only result would be an earlier grave than my mess mates. Even as I ran at the half-naked men who had boarded us more pirates swarmed over the side. I knew that the officers at the stern could do nothing. There were two marines there, however, and I heard their boots as they thundered down the deck to my assistance. I was lucky that the Arabs who first climbed over the gunwale had just a scimitar and a dagger. One of the two was still climbing over the gunwale. My pike was longer than the scimitar and dagger the assassin bore and I was bigger. He was, however, fast and perhaps the man saw fear in my eyes and thought I would freeze. He darted towards me and I swashed the pike from side to side. I was lucky. The edge, which I knew was razor sharp, sliced across his face, ripping it open. The other pirate had made the deck and, more alarmingly, had been joined by another ten or so. Just then the two marines' muskets opened fire and black smoke surrounded me making an impenetrable fog. The pirates took advantage and rushed us.

I braced myself and swung the pike. The tactic worked a second time or maybe I was just lucky. I ripped open the stomach of one man and cut the arm of a second to the bone. The mass of men who had been before me now split and as I lunged at another pirate, I heard the screams of the two dying marines behind me as they were hacked to pieces by the pirates. I felt their blood spatter on my cheeks. I would soon follow them. I was doomed. I was so terrified that I had no thought of running. If I exposed my back I was dead and the only thing that stopped them was my pike which I waved before me. The pirates spread out and it was inevitable that they would get behind me and that would be the end.

I heard a voice shout, "Present!" and then, "Smudger, drop to the deck!" It was not a pirate voice, it was Lieutenant Crozier and even though there were half a dozen men before me I obeyed. "Fire!" This time there was the crack of more than half a dozen weapons. I was shrouded in swirling smoke and then a voice behind me shouted, "At them!"

Lieutenant Crozier, pistol in one hand and a sword in the other led his platoon as they charged the line of pirates who were less than three feet from me. Only my pike had kept them at bay. None of the soldiers wore their tunics but all were armed. As they passed me and slammed into the second wave of pirates I stood and followed them. Unlike the two marines, these soldiers had bayonets fitted and they used them to great effect. They were longer than the pirates' weapons and, so far as I could see the swarthy Arabs had no firearms. The muskets with the bayonets flicked away swords and raked bodies. They lunged at unprotected flesh and the deck ran red with blood. The lieutenant used his sword and pistol together. His pistol was empty but he blocked blows with it and then slashed with his sword. He seemed invincible but I knew that it was an illusion. The pirates were swarming over the bows and would soon overwhelm us.

Lieutenant Dunn was brave. He was late to the battle but he led his men from the bow castle and, immaculately turned out in red tunics and blackened hats, they ran at the rear of the pirates. As I swept my pike into the side of a pirate I saw the difference between what were, in effect, professional soldiers, and ones better placed to be painted toys. While Lieutenant Crozier and his men used every trick they could to fight the pirates, Lieutenant Dunn tried to organise his men into a line to fire. Even as he waved his sword to straighten the line, he was hacked into by a boarding axe. His sergeant lasted a heartbeat longer; he was an older, fatter man with slow reactions and did not see the sword which came at his head. Their leaders gone, the marines began to die. In their dying, however, they slowed down the advances made by the pirates. They were still confined, by me and the soldiers to the front third of the ship. That would soon change.

I heard the crack of a pistol from behind me and saw the smoking gun in Rafe's hand as he slew Lieutenant Dunn's killer. The crew had been issued with cutlasses and pistols. The officers had joined them and with Bosun Cunningham wielding a boarding pike, they poured into the pirates. It tipped the scales in our favour. Had the pirates gained the main mast then they would have controlled half of the ship. As it was, they only had the bow section and we outnumbered them. Ned's stories had inflamed the men of my mess and it was the same with the other messes. They knew what would happen if the pirates gained a foothold. We would all die. They fought as though there was no tomorrow. Pirates knocked to the deck were hacked and stabbed until they no longer moved. As the survivors were driven to throw themselves into the sea there was a cheer.

Captain Mackintosh roared, "None of that! Run out the guns and kill the bastards!"

The soldiers and marines, now under the command of Lieutenant Crozier, went to the bows and poured ball after ball at the men still trying to ascend. I ran to our gun and grabbed a rope. This time there was no leisurely loading. We did everything at twice the speed of the practice. Such was the haste that none of us had time to protect our ears. When we fired at the small triangular sailed ships that seemed like a pack of sharks, I could hear nothing. It was as though I had been instantly rendered deaf. We just obeyed hand signals. The pirates' boats were so close to us that we did have success. I am not sure if there were cheers. If there were I could not hear them. I saw at least two ships totally destroyed as balls smashed them in two. A third was set alight and when a fourth ship began to sink the others fled. Our consorts were adding to the weight of shot. The pirates had tried surprise but thanks to the heat of the night, they had failed. Another ship was sunk before they were out of range and when I saw the fins of the sharks circling in the moonlight, I knew that there would be no survivors.

We did not cease to be vigilant and watched until the sun rose in the east. By then some semblance of hearing had returned and I was able to hear the orders that were shouted at me. Rafe and Ned had no idea that I had been the first on the deck. They had assumed I had followed Lieutenant Crozier. I was under no illusions. I owed my life to Lieutenant Crozier and his Newgate convicts. He and his men were scouring the decks seeking any feigning death and taking whatever treasure they had. The four surviving marines, in contrast, just sat in shock. Their old, grizzled sergeant lay separated from his head and close by the butchered lieutenant. Their endless drills and polished weapons and leather had availed them nought.

The captain sent water around for us and I drank not greedily but savouring each mouthful. The smoke from the muskets and cannons had dried my mouth even more. Captain Mackintosh and Mr. Wintersgill came from the stern towards Lieutenant Crozier. The captain held out his hand, "Lieutenant, you have saved us."

"And I must apologise for misjudging you."

The soldier flashed a contemptuous look at James Wintersgill and then shook his head and pointed at me, "It's not me you should thank but this little bantam cock. When we arrived, he was holding off the pirates with a boarding pike, the two marines already dead. He is either a brave lad…" he winked, "or too stupid to know the danger he was in."

The captain and the company man looked at me as though I had two heads.

"It's right, Captain Mackintosh. It was Smith there who shouted the warning. He was the one who shouted for all hands to come on deck." Albert Wright added his praise to that of the soldier.

They looked at me as though a magician had waved his wand and made a miraculous transformation before their very eyes. "Then we are in your debt, young man. I am glad that you stowed away. When we reach Bombay I shall be in a better position to reward you. For the present we have to make up for lost time and," his voice became sad, "to bury our dead."

As they moved away, Bosun Cunningham approached. His face was as black as thunder and his bloody hands were on his hips, "So, you think that you can give orders? Who do you think you are, the Chief Bosun?"

I cowered and shook my head, "No, Chief Bosun. Sorry."

The scowl turned to a grin and he put an arm around me. I confess I flinched, "I underestimated you. You'll do young 'un and if you want to stay aboard this ship then you have a bright future."

We had been lucky. The doctor might not have been able to save John with a burst appendix but he sewed up the cuts the crew had suffered at the hands of the pirates. While he tended to their wounds, we washed as much of the blood from the deck as we could. The passengers had been kept below deck and the captain did not want them to be offended. We would have to get the holystones out to completely eradicate the evidence.

I had not witnessed the funeral of John, the man who had died of a burst appendix and whom I had replaced. I was present for the funerals of the ones who had died in the fight. They were mainly the marines. Poor Erik had died and another of the deck crew, Peter, had also perished. As we waited for the service Ned told me that in the Royal Navy, the dead were sewn into their hammocks and slipped over the side with a cannonball to weigh them down. This was the East India Company and hammocks were too expensive to waste. They were sewn in their blankets. Cannonballs were used to ensure that the corpses did not float but they were the ones pitted with rust or clearly misshapen. Lieutenant Crozier and his men, along with the surviving marines, came on deck in their uniforms. They would be an honour guard and would fire a salute, so Rafe told us, when the bodies were consigned to the deep.

The passengers emerged and stood a little apart. They had seen nothing of the horror of the night battle but they must have been terrified as the screams, shouts, and sound of gunfire had filled the night. Captain Mackintosh spoke the words and I heard the names of the dead men. It was Mr. Wright's watch that held the wooden boards on which lay the corpses.

When the captain finished, he nodded and Lieutenant Crozier said, "Honour Guard, present. Fire!" As the muskets exploded into the air the boards were tipped and we heard the splashes as the dead went to the bottom of the sea. No one would visit their graves and few, passing above them, would even know that men had died here. The tale would be told in port and the crews of other ships passing this place might wonder about the battle with the pirates, but they would not know for certain where the dead lay. It was a sombre thought and terrified me. I did not want to die but if I did then I wanted a grave. I hoped that, sometime, long in the future, when I did die, there would be someone who would wish to tend my grave. They could not do that if I died at sea.

As luck would have it, we were the watch that was on duty. I did not mind as the rest of the crew, the night watch apart, would be set to work with holystones to clean the deck. I climbed the mast to my lofty perch. I would be alone with my thoughts.

I knew, as I scanned the seas, that the pirates were still out there. The smudge to the north was the coast. I would ensure that I shouted a good warning. I could not, however, as vigilant as I was, escape the thoughts that crowded in my head. I had killed, not just once but many times. I had not enjoyed the luxury of being able to count but I knew that at least half a dozen pirates had either perished or been wounded at my hands. I was a thief but I had never been a killer. Did killing in battle make me a murderer? I doubted it but one thing was clear, I could never go back. I could not undo the past. I consoled myself that if I was a real killer then I would have ended Jacob the Cooper's son's life in that alley in London. I had killed because I had to. It had changed me. I knew that it had altered the way that men viewed me. I was no longer 'the thief', I was the hero. I quite liked the change. When men like the bosun smiled at you and others like Rafe and Ned patted you on the back it felt good. For the first time since my mother had left, I felt wanted and welcomed. It was as I sat there, with my straw hat on my head and my arms now tanned and brown, that I knew I would never return to England. My life would be lived far from the grubby streets of London. The East India Company gave me a lifeline to a better life and I would grasp it with both hands.

Chapter 6

There had been some damage to the ship which necessitated minor repairs and we were kept busy, when on watch, completing them. We had learned that the pirates had come from the little island of Socotra. Rafe said that when we reached Bombay that information would be passed to the admiral in charge of the East Indian flotilla that patrolled those waters. The threat would be eliminated and the nest destroyed. Cannonballs would destroy their boats and their home. They would pay a high price for their boldness.

It would be a further two weeks before we reached Bombay where we would finally be able to drink as much water as we wished. There, half of our passengers would disembark and we would reprovision. What we would also need was to take on more marines although, as Lieutenant Crozier and his men were bound for Calcutta, that was not a problem. Those two weeks saw my life change dramatically. I became even more popular with my messmates and when I was on deck I found that other crew stared at me. The story of my defence of the ship became exaggerated, not by me, but by others who told it. Mr. Wright, in particular, did so. I think that was out of guilt. Had he been a better officer then Erik would have been more vigilant. He might still have died but others might not have. After a few days, my notoriety made me uncomfortable and I yearned for the anonymity I had enjoyed before the fight. I tended to stay in the mess where I endured the heat. As we had two night watches the last week was almost a return to normality.

The day my life changed again, Bosun Cunningham fetched me from the mess. We had just come off watch and eaten. The mouthful of water had not been enough but as Bombay was just a few days away, I knew that the drought would soon end.

"Smarten yourself up. The captain wants to speak to you. Look sharp now."

I quickly fastened a piece of cord around my unruly mop of hair and wiped my hands on the ropes hanging above the mess table. I was about to leave when Ned thrust my pea jacket at me. I was hot enough already but I donned it. We made our way to the captain's cabin. I saw that the two men on duty were not marines but Lieutenant Crozier's men. One of them winked at me as I entered.

There were three men seated at the captain's table: the captain, Mr. Wintersgill and Lieutenant Crozier. The clerk was at a tiny folding table just behind the captain. I was not sure if it was the presence of the company director but the captain seemed to like a record kept of everything he did.

There was a seat and Captain Mackintosh said, "Sit, Smith."

As I did the bosun, behind me, growled, "Hats off!"

I whipped off the straw hat and the captain, smiling, said, "That will be all, Mr. Cunningham." When he left and closed the door the captain said, "This might seem a little formal, Smith, but I want an official record of your service to the company. Since the attack I have questioned everyone, yourself excepted, and learned that you are the reason we still have this ship. Your visit to the heads was most propitious." He smiled, "Even the bosun thinks highly of you and that is a rare accolade. I was going to offer you a permanent position on the ship. We would have paid you as an ordinary seaman rather than a landsman." I said nothing for I could tell that there was more coming and I was not sure if I wished to be a sailor. The captain continued, "However, you have impressed Lieutenant Crozier. He has lost a member of his platoon and the company is expecting twelve men to arrive at Calcutta. He would like to recruit you as a member of his platoon of soldiers. You need not accept either offer. You have done more than could be expected of you and if you choose to leave, either in Bombay or Calcutta, you shall be paid the money that is owed."

James Wintersgill leaned forward, "Not to mention a five guinea reward from the company."

I was genuinely taken aback. Five guineas was a substantial amount. That was the reward for my capture offered by Ralph Every. Ned had told me that a guinea could last a man half a year in India.

The lieutenant said, "You are a soldier, Smith, I saw that on the deck. You wielded that pike like a veteran and not someone who had picked it up for the first time. You have natural skills and it would be a shame to waste them. We would all like you in

67

our section. Your pay would be greater than that of an ordinary seaman."

I did not know what to say. To give me time to think the captain poured me a mug of ale. They were drinking wine. I was happy to be offered the ale. I needed to be refreshed. When I had swallowed the much-needed beer, I left half in the mug to savour later, I had a question. "Lieutenant Crozier, I confess that your offer is attractive, however, I know from the regular forces in England that they serve for seven years. If I took you up on the offer, how long would I serve?"

"The same, seven years and, before you ask, the pay is not the same as a British regular battalion. Here you are only paid two shillings a day. That is eleven pennies less than in England." He smiled, "But, life is not as expensive here as it is in England."

I looked at the captain, "And that pay is greater than as an ordinary seaman?"

"It is but a bright lad like you could be promoted."

He had glanced at Mr. Wintersgill when the lieutenant had been speaking. I knew that he was being pressured by the company man to let me join the soldier side of the company. If he was going to be based in Bombay then he wanted the best of soldiers serving the company. There I might make a difference. On a ship, I would not. I had almost made my mind up before the offer was made. If I was on the land then, if I did not like the life, I could always run. India seemed to me, from what I had heard, to be a land of opportunities for a man such as myself.

"Thank you, Captain, I appreciate your offer but I think that I might like to try the life of a soldier."

I saw the nod of disappointment on the face of the captain but I was taken aback by the lieutenant's next harsher words, "Don't think it will be easy, Smith. My men are tough men but they obey my orders and Sergeant Grundy makes your bosun seem like a children's nanny. If you become a soldier then you will have to work twice as hard as any of the others as they are trained already. We have from now until we reach Calcutta to turn you into a soldier."

"I leave the mess now?"

The captain shook his head, "Tomorrow morning. I believe that your watch has a dog watch this afternoon. Tomorrow will be soon enough, Lieutenant. Smith can say his goodbyes to his messmates and then don the red uniform."

The company director said, "You will be paid off tomorrow morning. I believe, Lieutenant Crozier, that there is a bounty for signing on?"

"Yes, sir, two guineas."

"Then you will be well off, Smith. I pray you do not waste your money as some others do on gambling."

I shook my head, "Gambling, sir, is not one of my vices."

As I drank the last of the beer, I almost choked when the lieutenant said, quietly, "Just thieving, eh, Smith?"

"If that is all, sir?"

"It is. Thank you, once again."

Every eye turned to me when I entered the mess. "What did the captain want?"

"I am being given a reward of five guineas for what I did." They all cheered. I think it was a genuine reaction. They would not expect anything for themselves but I was one of their own and I had been rewarded. "And I am to join the soldiers. This is my last night in the mess. Tomorrow, I join Lieutenant Crozier and his men."

The faces went from joy to sadness. Ned shook his head, "Are you sure, John? I mean life is hard enough on a ship but in India…"

I shook my head, "Both choices are hard. I have tried one and the other has an appeal." I owed it to Ned and Rafe to give them my real reasons but not the others.

Rafe nodded, "Well you make your own decisions and live by them. We will give you a send-off tonight after we come off watch."

The rest went back to the mess table but Rafe and Ned followed me when I went to the open gunport. I sat on the wheel of the gun. They looked at me expectantly for an explanation and I gave them one, "It was the pirate attack. It was just as bad as you said, Ned. We survived but it was luck that saved us. You said that going back we will have those pirates and the Madagascan ones too."

Rafe said, "The bosun told me that the captain will ask for the Bombay Squadron to destroy that little nest."

"But it isn't the only one, is it? You might survive. I pray that you do but this ship was a means to escape a certain death in London. Ralph Every is a pirate. I might run into him in London or at sea. India is far enough so that he can't get his nasty fingers on me."

They could tell, from my words and my tone, that I would not change my mind. Ned shook his head, "I wish I had kept my big mouth shut now and never mentioned the pirates."

"If you had, Ned, then we might all be dead. Your stories kept me awake that night. You can't go back in time and change things. I know only too well that a man has to live with his decisions for good or ill. It is a fool who thinks that he can change the past."

As I stood my last watch, I wondered if I had made a mistake. I stood at the bow, in the same place Erik had met his untimely end, but I did not feel as though I was in any danger. I watched to the fore and, as it was daylight, Matty was in my normal position on the cross trees. He was being promoted. With a fresh breeze from the sea keeping me a little cooler and the sun setting behind me, sending its rays to illuminate the sea ahead, I thought that I might return to the captain and ask to be kept on. What made me change my mind was the spot of blood that had escaped scrutiny. It was not on the deck but on the wood just below the gunwale. I had seen Erik die. I had watched his blood flow. I would become a soldier, for the East India Company.

There was always illicit drink on the ship. Rafe ensured that no one abused its use. That night we had a small celebration; I sipped the drink which would have cleaned the blood from the deck far faster than a holystone. They told tales of sailors long gone. These were not the cautionary tales as told by Ned but reminiscent ones told with fondness and humour. Some of them were about sailors still on the ship. I learned that Harry had actually fallen from a yard when he had first come aboard the ship but, amazingly, had struck the sea and been rescued.

"You can bet I have never fallen since."

I shook my head, "But how could you face climbing up again after the fall? I could not have done that."

He looked at me as though it was I who was the slow one, "It's life, isn't it Smudger? You learn from the things that might

70

hurt you. If you are dead it doesn't matter and if you are alive it shows you how to keep on living."

It was a good night and we celebrated until the first watch was called at midnight. Our watch were not needed until the forenoon watch. As I had learned, that was a luxury. I rose when the others did. Matty now fetched the food and I had my last breakfast with my messmates. As they prepared for the day I gathered my belongings and wrapped them in the cloak that had lined my chest. I would not need it and so I gave the pea jacket and straw hat to Matty. The jacket would be a spare in case another one of the mess lost theirs. I waved farewell but we all knew that we would see each other again and I went to the deck with the lower deck passengers. The soldiers were using their own mess table and looked up as I approached. None wore the red tunic. I saw that the lieutenant was missing. The sergeant was smoking a stubby pipe. He nodded to a chest that stood against the mast. "That was Charlie's. You can use that for your whatnots."

"Thank you."

"Thank you, Sergeant." He corrected me, "You are in the army now, son, and rank is everything. That is Corporal Neville and you call him Corporal."

"Yes, Sergeant, sorry Sergeant."

He smiled, "Don't worry, you will get used to it. You have shown me that you have a backbone. Keep your nose clean and we won't have to see it."

I frowned, "See it?"

One of the others, I later learned his name was Seamus and he was an Irishman said, cheerily, "Aye, if we see your backbone it is because you have company punishment and are going to be flogged."

The corporal came over and opened the chest for me. I saw that it was full already. "Poor Charlie left this world just wearing his underwear. That has saved you the expense of having to pay for this lot. Regard it as Charlie's payment for you trying to save his life." He took out the items as he described them. "Two pairs of breeches, grey, two pairs of pantaloons, white, two gaiters, black, two pairs of stockings, one pair of boots." He shook his head, "If they don't fit then you will have to buy yourself a pair.

Two shirts, one waistcoat, one stock, one tunic and one hat." He then took out the belts, bayonet frog, knapsack, ammunition pouches, canteen and the like. "We will show you how to wear the webbing and the like." He smiled, "This is old fashioned uniform. When we get to Calcutta we shall be given more modern uniforms. These tricorn hats are a relic from the past." He nodded to the sergeant who was approaching, "The muskets we use are the only decent piece of equipment we were given." I learned as I got to know the men, that the men who issued such equipment were often little better than thieves. If they saw a way to make money then they would take it. The sweepings of Newgate Prison did not merit the best.

The sergeant came over and handed me a musket and a bayonet, "This is the India Pattern musket. It is thirty-nine inches long. These are new and made by the East India Company. The lieutenant insisted on being given them. You keep this clean. Every day it needs to be serviced." He handed me a little leather pouch. "This piece of kit is probably the most important you will have. Don't lose it. There is a picker to clear the fouling that comes with using the back powder, a brush and a needle and thread. You might need that if you are to make the uniform fit."

I looked at the array of uniform and equipment. It looked daunting. I was aware that the rest of the men were staring at me. I had worked out that only the lieutenant was missing. I was desperate to ask their names but felt intimidated by their close scrutiny.

"First things first. Eddie, fetch me the shears." As the soldier went to a chest the corporal approached me. "Your hair is too long. That might be alright for sailors but not for the lieutenant. He likes short hair, the shorter the better. Eddie is a dab hand with the shears. Sit on my chest and he will give you a shearing."

The sergeant said, "I will introduce the men who will be closer to you than any family. As you know most were recruited from the prison. Better you hear their story from me than wonder. They are all good men now, despite what people like Mr. Wintersgill might think. The man with the shears is Eddie Lowe. You should get on well with him for he was a thief too."

As Eddie cut the first hank of hair he snorted, "Not as good as this one, Sergeant Grundy, I got caught."

"Albert Wishart over there is also a thief." Albert, who did not look much older than I was, nodded and smiled. "George Mainsgill was inside for vagrancy." The man nodded but did not smile and I wondered at his story. "Now Dai Evans is our Welshman." The short, stocky soldier had curly jet-black hair and he grinned. "He was in prison for violence as was our Irishman, Seamus Hogan. They are both a little too handy with their fists."

Seamus grinned, "Ah, but thanks to the good lieutenant, Sergeant Darlin, I am a reformed character." When the others all laughed I knew it was a lie.

"Bob Cathcart is our Jock. He is a thief like you."

Bob was young and had a mop of bright red hair. He shrugged, "You will have to tell me how you avoided getting caught."

"John Williams there was also a thief. You are in good company."

"Aye, but I stole to get food for my family."

"And last, but not least, is Edmund Byers, also in prison for violence."

The last man was older than the corporal and had the broken nose of a pugilist. When he spoke I saw that he had lost teeth. He grinned, "Aye, but I was paid to fight. I kept the alehouse free from trouble."

Seamus shook his head, "The judge didn't think so."

Byers shrugged.

"All done."

I looked at the floor and saw my hair. The sergeant said, "Clean up your hair and then let us try on your new clothes."

I had hoped that I could dress privately but that was not going to happen. My hesitation brought a cynical snort from the corporal, "Come on, son, you haven't got anything we haven't seen before."

It was not embarrassment about my body but the fact that I would have to reveal my money belt. I took off my shirt and then my breeks. The sergeant came over and took off my belt, "Well, well, well, a walking bank." He shook his head and dropped the belt in my chest. "You don't need to hide this on your person, Smith, you can trust us all. We don't care how much you have in there. We have all had a new start. If you are lucky enough to bring a few bob with you, then well done but it will not make any difference here. You can keep this in your knapsack and it will be safe. Now, let's make you look like a soldier."

Part Two

The Soldier

Chapter 7

The whole section, I learned that was how they viewed themselves, were like mother hens as they helped me to dress. There were buttons and fastenings that bewildered me. The boots and hat both fitted me. The shirt was a little loose but as that was covered by the waistcoat and woollen jacket it did not matter. I was hot enough before the jacket was fastened but I felt the sweat pour from me.

Corporal Neville laughed, "Aye, that is why we just wear shirts and overalls on deck. These jackets might be fine in England but out here…"

They helped me to fit the belts and adjusted the buckles so that it was comfortable. Sergeant Grundy handed me the one-foot-five-inch bayonet. "This fits on the end of the musket. It gives you a weapon that is as long as a pike. The trouble is that it is heavy and weighs the end of the musket down. We only fit it when we know that we have to get close to an enemy."

They all stood back and nodded. A voice from behind me said, "Well, you look like a soldier, Smith. We have just fifteen days or so to make you into one."

The lieutenant was standing there. I felt embarrassed, "Do I salute, sir?"

It was as though I had told the funniest story for they all, the scarred lieutenant too, laughed. "When we are on parade we salute. Until we join the rest of the East India Company ranks, we just stand to attention when ordered and say, sir, sergeant or corporal. Now get your gear stored and wear just your breeches and shirt. It is time for musket practice. Byers and Hogan, you are on duty. Relieve the marines."

Seamus groaned, "That means four hours of sweating like a pig. Do we have to wear these hats and tunics, sir?"

"Of course you do. When we reach Calcutta, I will see if we can get some straw hats. I believe that they are considered acceptable but here, with a company director watching, we do it properly."

I was soon ready as were the two sentries and we trooped out together. I had my musket, powder and ammunition but I had no idea how to use them. We went to the bows of the ship. The lieutenant just observed. It was Sergeant Grundy and Corporal Neville who took me through the drill. The corporal had the musket and the sergeant had the words.

"Take the cartridge from the ammunition pouch. Bite off the ball, put the paper charge in the barrel and spit the ball into the barrel. Take your ramrod and ram the cartridge down. Replace the ramrod. Lift the musket and pull back the hammer." I watched everything that the corporal did very carefully. "Present." The corporal did all that he was told and then raised the musket to his shoulder. "Take aim, Corporal." I could not see what he was aiming at as there was nothing on the sea. However, the corporal obeyed. "Fire".

The noise hurt my ears and the flash, not to mention the smoke, obscured everything until the wind took it away.

Sergeant Grundy smiled, "There you are, easy eh? Now you have a go."

The corporal had made it seem easier than it was in reality. For one thing, I did not like the taste of the powder. He gave me the same instructions but I seemed to take an age to do what had seemed moments when the corporal had performed the same actions. "Present". When I lifted the musket, it felt too heavy. "Move your left hand further down the barrel." I did so. "That's it. Now keep the stock pressed hard against your shoulder and lean into it. Find a target. I know there is nothing out there but look for a white tip, anything and when I say, 'fire', squeeze the trigger."

"Yes, Sergeant." I was aware of all the eyes on me and I pressed against the stock of the musket and waited for the command.

"Fire!"

I was not prepared for the kick of the musket nor the flash of powder. I had no idea where the ball went. I felt like a failure.

Corporal Neville said, "Not bad for a first attempt. I reckon that you have the makings of a soldier but by tonight your shoulder will be black and blue."

The sergeant then took me and the rest of the men through the drills and commands. We all fired together. We did not always fire, I think the lieutenant was aware of the need to conserve cartridges and powder until we reached Bombay but we fired enough times to confirm the corporal's opinion. We had a rest at noon and ate on the deck, in the shade of the foresail.

Seamus and Dai sat next to me and I asked the questions that had been racing around my head all morning. "How do you remember to do all that?"

"It's not as hard as you think. We were all in prison until four months ago. We have not had much more training than you. The two soldiers are the sergeant and the lieutenant. They were both in the regular army. The sergeant served for twenty years."

"Why did he leave, then?"

Dai lowered his voice, "He didn't leave. He was dishonourably discharged."

"What for?"

"We didn't ask."

"So, we are all in the same boat, so to speak? We are all new to this game."

"Aye, better than spending the next years in gaol. The seven years we signed on for is less than our sentences."

By the end of the day, I was weary but I began to think I could be a soldier. As we ate our evening meal the lieutenant and Sergeant Grundy explained a little more to me. "When we get to Calcutta we will join a regiment. Things will change then. We will live in a barracks, unless we are on campaign in which case we will have tents. We will also have a ration of beer and whatever passes for spirits. I must warn you, Smith, not to abuse that. They flog in the company just as they do in the regular army."

I nodded. I had never succumbed to drink. I enjoyed a drink as much as the next man but I could take it or leave it. "And what is it that we do, sir?"

The lieutenant smiled. With his scarred face it was a cockeyed one. "Do, Smith?"

"Yes, sir, do we fight battles or what?"

Realisation dawned, "Ah, battles. Possibly. We are soldiers, not of the king but of the company. We are here to protect the interests of the company. We may well fight those who are allies of England. Mr. Wintersgill spoke very disparagingly of the Dutch East India Company and I believe that they are seen as enemies. It will be interesting, eh?"

Sergeant Grundy said, "And when we reach Bombay we have to be as smart as paint. Mr. Wintersgill will be leaving us and we will need to present arms smartly. Our uniforms will have to be spotless and everything well-polished. I suggest you spend as much time as you can between now and then practising the movements we showed you and then ensuring everything is clean."

I wondered at the wisdom of joining the platoon. It seemed like a lot of work. I consoled myself with the thought of the guineas I had been given and the knowledge that once we reached Calcutta and I got to know my way around, I could always run. Sharing a mess with Rafe and Ned had opened my eyes to the possibilities of life away from England. There were islands, they said, where a man with even a single guinea could live like a king. I began to imagine my life as the ruler of some island where I had servants and power. The drills and the polish were a small price to pay for that.

Bombay came as a shock to me. St Helena had been a tiny little watering hole in comparison to the bustling waterway that was our first port of call in India. Sergeant Grundy inspected us closely. We had to fit our bayonets. It was extra weight and I said, "Why, Sergeant? I mean we aren't going to be fighting anyone are we?"

He sighed, "You are new, Private Smith, and I will exercise patience. One, you don't question orders you obey them, I tell you to fit your bayonet and you say, *'Yes Sergeant.'*" I saw the others grinning. "If you want to know why we are fitting bayonets it is to make a good impression. The light will shine off them and the civilians like a show. As soon as they leave then we can go back to an easier life."

The lieutenant called him over and Bob came next to me, "The sergeant was told by the lieutenant to go easy with you for a few days. If you want to ask anything then ask one of us. It is new to us all but we've had a little more time enduring the sharp end of Sergeant Grundy's tongue. The lieutenant likes you and is making your life a little easier."

Standing in the heat, wearing a woollen tunic and hat not to mention holding a musket and bayonet, I could feel the sweat pouring from me. The civilians were gathered on the deck too but they had servants with umbrellas shading them from the sun. The crew had the easier time of it. They wore just a shirt and breeches. Coming into the harbour was easier for them than working at sea. They just had to obey the orders of the officers who had the trickier task of negotiating the bum boats and other vessels as we headed for our berth.

After we had tied up Sergeant Grundy roared, "Present arms!"

I was new to this but thanks to my new comrades in arms I knew the drill well and we all performed it perfectly. Certainly, the company director beamed and the others clapped as we did so.

Lieutenant Crozier said, "Would you care to inspect the section before you leave, sir?"

"I would be delighted to." He walked down the line nodding and smiling at each of the men. I think his view of them changed following the pirate attack. When he came to me he leaned in and said, "I have high hopes for you, Private Smith. I can see a man of your enterprise rising through the ranks. I am pleased that I gave you the first step on this ladder. I look forward to watching your progress in the Honourable East India Company."

I said, "Thank you, sir. I will not let you down." Even as the words came from my lips I knew that as soon as I had the chance then I would run. The young hero they had seen in action was an illusion. I was still the same chancer as I had been in London.

Our work was not finished when the passengers left the ship. We were given duty. We had to watch the quayside of the gangplank as well as the ship side. As there were two gang planks it meant eight of us were on duty at any one time. The other four would relieve us two at a time but it meant we would have at least a four-hour duty baking in the Indian sun and wearing wool. My first duty was on the quayside with Albert.

Sergeant Grundy came down to support us as well as Bob and Edmund. The locals, so the sergeant told us, loudly, would steal anything that they could. He used his swagger stick to sharply smack any who came close to him. We still had our bayonets fitted as the sergeant thought that would discourage any with criminal intent. I could not help thinking that we were the perfect men for such a task. We were all thieves. The difference was that these were Indian thieves and we had been English ones.

Bob and I were relieved after four hours. As soon as we reached our quarters, we took everything off except for our underwear and drank as much as we could. The first provisions that had been brought on board had been beer and water. We drank the beer and when I had drunk enough to satiate my thirst I lay down on the hammock. It had been warm, not to say hot, on the voyage east but now it was like a furnace. It was new to us all.

Bob said, "I never thought I would miss the movement of the ship, Smudger, but at least we had a breeze. The air here feels heavy. I am not sure I can cope."

"I know what you mean. Why do we have to wear such heavy jackets?"

"Someone must think it looks smart but see, the red dye is already seeping into our white breeches. I can't see them staying white for long. Then we won't look as smart."

He was right. One thing the voyage had taught me was to sleep while you could. Even though the ship was tied up I was able to fall asleep quickly, but it seemed like moments only before Eddie and Dai woke us.

"Right, me lovely lads, you two are on the main gangplank but on the ship this time."

Before I dressed I went to the pot in the corner and rid myself of the beer I had drunk. When in port we had piss pots to avoid civilians seeing us urinate over the side. Sergeant Grundy's bellowing voice from the deck made us both move sharply, "You pair, on deck now or there will be company punishment."

I had no idea what that meant but I wanted no punishment of any kind. We dressed in damp clothes and hurried on deck. Lieutenant Crozier was with the sergeant and he said, as we moved to our allotted positions, "You can take off the bayonets. You won't need them here."

He and the sergeant left us to check on the other sentries. The locals had realised they could not get aboard and were at the other ships that had docked after us. It meant an easier duty. It was better on the ship as we were afforded some shade from the masts and furled sails. It was little enough but you did not feel as though you were baking. The duty continued as night fell. The difference was that we just had four men on duty and we had four hours of sleep. As much as I had looked forward to Bombay, now I could not wait to leave. Life at sea was much easier. We learned that there were no marines to replace the dead and we would have to continue to act for them until we reached Calcutta.

We left the next day on the afternoon tide. We had a few more passengers, company officials this time, and we sailed south. Whilst it was a relief to be back in shirts and breeches, the temperature rose as we were heading for the equator. My former messmates spoke to me when we were not on duty and they told me that I could expect the temperature to stay the same for the rest of our time on the ship.

Rafe pointed at the coast which was never far away, "The land keeps the heat, see, and that is the problem. When we are out on the ocean, it is always cooler. Here we are too close to the land."

"Will we stop again?"

"Nah. We pass close to Ceylon but we have one more stop and that is Calcutta."

"How long?"

"It is two thousand miles and the winds can be unpredictable but a good estimate would be eight to ten days."

We had taken on more powder and cartridges in Bombay and we began to use the muskets more. The fresh fruit we had taken on came in woven baskets. The cook was happy for us to throw the empty ones overboard to give us a target. I enjoyed the challenge for the wake of the ship allied to the waves made it hard to aim. When any of us managed a hit it was greeted with raucous cheers. I took the view that this was a good thing. If we could hit a small moving object at sea, then a man-sized target would be easier.

One change was that we were issued with new hats. Perhaps our performance against the pirates or Mr Wintersgill's words had an effect, for our new uniforms and equipment were brought on board. The tricorns that had seemed so smart to me when I had first seen them were now floppy and shapeless. The lieutenant handed the new hats and uniform out. He smiled as he handed me the hat. "These are new to us all. They are called a shako." He tapped the side of it and it sounded firm. "They won't always be this hard. When they get wet they might well lose their shape but not as badly as the tricorn. Look after it and the rest of your equipment."

Sergeant Grundy frowned, "They are new to me too, lads."

The lieutenant nodded, "We are the first to be issued them. It will, I am afraid, make us stand out until every battalion is given them."

After one training session, as we cleaned our muskets, I mentioned my thoughts about our musketry skills to Sergeant Grundy. His derisive laugh told me what he thought of that idea. "These muskets, Smith, can send a ball a long way but at anything further than ninety paces any hit is pure luck. All we are trying to do is get you to aim at something. When we do open fire, we will all do so together. Even the lieutenant will use a musket. Twelve muskets all fired at the same time have the chance of hitting one or two men."

That did not sound much. "But, sergeant, if we all fire together, won't whoever we are firing at have the opportunity to get closer to us?"

He smiled, "When I was in the 68th we could get five rounds off in a minute. When we get on dry land, at a proper range that is what my aim is. We will train you so that you can reload so quickly that we will put a wall of lead before us." He held up his musket and said, "In the heat of battle we don't bother with a ramrod. If you bang the stock the ball will go down. I have seen at least one dozy bugger fire his musket with the ramrod in the barrel! Jogging the musket is quicker."

I was sceptical. Although I could now load faster than when I had first been given my musket I doubted that I would ever be able to get off more than three shots a minute. I did take the cleaning of the weapon seriously. When I ran, I planned on

taking the musket. It would be a useful thing to have. I quite
enjoyed the discipline of cleaning the weapon and removing
every trace of powder. That it pleased the office and sergeant was
of no matter but I could tell that they were pleased. Similarly,
with the bayonet, I kept it honed sharp enough to shave with.
Back in London, my knife had been my weapon of choice and I
knew how to use mine. What I did not like was the washing. We
had to wash clothes every two days. It was important, so
Lieutenant Crozier told us, as it prevented disease. I was not so
sure. Back in England, I was lucky to wash my clothes once a
month and I had suffered no illnesses.

Chapter 8

Calcutta would be the first time I would step on land and walk since I had sneaked on board the Indiaman. I had come close in St Helena but as we gathered our belongings and lined up next to the tumblehome, I was both excited and fearful. Both St Helena and Bombay had smelled different to London, but this was an even stranger smell. The wooden houses close to the stone buildings of the company seemed to teem with people and the noise assaulted my ears. As we waited, I realised that my plan to run almost as soon as we landed was doomed to failure. I would have to be a soldier for a little while longer. I sensed that the others were as nervous as I was.

Bob shook his head, "I thought English was hard to understand but that din from the shore… it's like a foreign language."

Seamus laughed, "You dozy Scotsman. It is a foreign language. Did you think they would all be speaking English?"

He shrugged, "Something like that."

Ben Neville, the corporal, had been left in charge while the lieutenant and sergeant had gone ashore and entered the white stone building with the company flag flying above it, "We will all have to learn some of the language. The lieutenant says it is Bengali."

Rafe was coiling a rope nearby and he said, "You will find they understand some English but they are sneaky buggers. They start jibber-jabbering in their own language and you have no idea what they are saying."

Ben nodded, "And that is why I intend to learn as much of it as I can. Who knows, seven years from now when I get my discharge I might settle out here."

John Williams shook his head, "Here? When my time is up it is back to England for me."

"What is there for the likes of us in England? What happens to old soldiers in England? They end up as either drunks or beggars. I don't think it will be any different in this company. You have a chance out here to make a new start."

That was the moment I realised that the others, or some of them, at least, felt the same way as I did. It confirmed my decision that I would bide my time for a while. I would see how the land lay and only when it was the right time would I run. My guineas and the coins I had brought from England were safe in my money belt. That would stay around my waist. I had no need to dip into it for I would be paid and I was still a thief.

Rafe came up to me as we saw the officer and sergeant leave the building, "Well, whatever your real name is, good luck. You have the chance for a new life. You seize it." He held out his hand and I shook it. "We all liked you and thought you might join the crew. Take care, eh? Give up your thieving ways."

"Thank the lads, Rafe, all of them."

"Aye, I will do."

"Pick up your necessaries. We are off." Sergeant Grundy's voice set us off and I followed Bob down the gangplank. My bag and musket were slung over my shoulder and we moved down the gangplank. It seemed to bounce as we did so. When we reached the stone quay it felt strange. It was as though I was still moving. The corporal saw my face and smiled, "We all felt the same, Smudger, when we landed at St Helena. It will take some time to get your land legs."

"Attention!"

We all snapped to attention. I did it without thinking.

"Three cheers for the ship. Hip, hip, hooray. Hip, hip, hooray. Hip, hip, hooray."

As we cheered I looked back and saw the gunwale lined by the crew. They were cheering. I had not missed my family but as we turned to follow the lieutenant I found myself missing Rafe, Ned, Harry, Matty, the cook, and even the captain. They had looked after me. They had changed me. As we marched in a red line into the heart of Calcutta, I knew that the men around me would change me again.

"Where we off to, Sergeant?"

"No talking in the ranks, Byers, you will find out soon enough."

The red file cut through the sea of humanity that swarmed all over the streets. I had thought that London was busy but it was empty compared with Calcutta. The first thing I noticed was that we seemed to tower over the people we passed, even the men. They stared at us and I saw that we were of as much interest to them as they were to us. Had they never seen redcoats before? We walked for a mile or more and sweat was oozing from every pore. The interest in us seemed to diminish the further from the port we walked. The sound of our boots was regular. We were all marching. It was as though we had ceased to be individuals and had become a single red entity.

We passed through increasingly mean-looking buildings and the stink of human and animal waste made me almost vomit. We seemed to be heading for a stockade. I saw the flag flying above the wooden walled building and saw that there were soldiers there and they were wearing red coats but they were not white men. They were locals. I was confused. I had thought that we would be joining Englishmen but clearly, that was not the case.

The sentries at the open gates saluted as we entered. There was a parade ground and I saw two artillery pieces. Inside there was a stone building and then a series of tents. My heart sank. We would be camping.

"Section, halt!"

We stopped and waited for the next command.

"Drop your bags, lads, while the lieutenant and I go and find out which are our tents. Corporal, take charge."

"Yes, Sergeant Grundy." Ben might have been in gaol for violence but he had adapted to the military life quickly. He seemed at home as a non-commissioned officer.

I don't know what I expected but it was not this. It felt almost deserted. Apart from the two sentries on the gate, I counted just six more on the walls. They wore red tunics but had sandals rather than boots and their heads were covered in a broad soft hat. It looked to be more comfortable than our shako and afforded shade from the sun.

Eddie Lowe snorted, "This looks worse than the gaol and the stink…"

Seamus said, "Not as bad in here as out in the street though."

Bob waved a hand to swat away the flies. They had swarmed all the way from the ship, growing in numbers but standing still we seemed to attract them. "And these flies are worse than the midges at home."

Seamus chuckled, "And like me, you will all start to smoke a pipe."

Bob said, "Why?"

"Keeps them away."

I remembered that some of the sailors on the ship had smoked pipes and they had told me the same. I had forgotten that information until that moment. I splatted one that had landed on my neck. Perhaps I would invest in a pipe and tobacco. Anything that would keep these flying devils from me would be useful.

Eddie said, "Aye, but will a pipe keep away spiders, snakes and the like? I hear that this land is filled with them."

The thought of sleeping in a tent where any creature could creep and slither made me shudder.

I saw the lieutenant, sergeant and an older officer emerge from the stone building, They were followed by a native wearing a red tunic.

Ben snapped, "Attention!"

We all came to attention although the bags lying on the ground made it look less smart than was intended.

Lieutenant Crozier said, "This is Colonel Coleman and Havildar Singh. We will not be here for long but the Colonel would like a word with you."

I studied the officer. He wore a white wig. I had seen some older men wearing them in London but they were rare. He also had a red face which suggested he drank a lot. As soon as he spoke I knew he did not like us. It was his tone, his words and his manner.

"You are here but briefly. This is the headquarters of the 1st Bengal Infantry. You are merely attached to it. I am less than happy that the company has chosen to send thieves and vagrants to my command. You will be leaving and heading up country. The rest of my command will be returning from manoeuvres at the end of the week. You will be gone by then. Any indiscipline will be rewarded by the lash and Havildar Singh knows how to wield a whip." With that, he turned on his heel and like a faithful dog, the havildar followed him.

I saw the sergeant and the lieutenant exchange a look. Lieutenant Crozier's voice sounded weary, "Right lads, we aren't here for long but let us make the best of it. We have been allocated five tents. One for me, one for the sergeant and corporal and the rest of you have the other three. Choose your own tentmates. You have an hour to settle in. I will try to get more suitable attire for us but I am not hopeful."

We followed the sergeant who put his bag and musket in the second tent. He stood at the next one and Seamus, Dai and Eddie Lowe entered. The next one was taken by George, Edmund and John Williams. That left the last one for Bob, Albert and me. I saw that, as we entered, there were four cots. At least we would be off the ground. You could only stand up in the middle. The other two took the cots furthest from the tent's flap and that left me by the opening. We put our bags down and then went back outside to stack our muskets. I had learned the system on the ship although we had not used it. Four men stacked their muskets together so that they all supported each other. You had to both stack and remove them together. It prevented damage to the weapon and made the guns easy to grab in a hurry. We all knew our own weapons. The muskets stacked, we returned to the tent to unpack. There was a reason to unpack. Dampness and mould were a danger.

Albert said, "Let us use the spare cot, eh? It will keep our clothes off the ground. God knows what creepy crawlies will come at night. I don't fancy waking up to a spider in my drawers."

I removed the sheet and blanket from the spare cot and began to lay out my spare shirt, breeches, and underwear. I placed my blanket on my cot. I doubted I would need it to keep warm and it would make the canvas cot more comfortable.

"What do you reckon he meant by up country?"

Albert shook his head at Bob's question, "Away from here?"

I had laid out my things and I sat on the cot. I wanted to take my boots off but I was not sure if I would be able to get them back on quickly. "If we do leave here then I think we will have to take food and tents with us. How will we manage? It is bad enough carrying our knapsacks and muskets but tents, food, pots and pans…"

The other two had not thought of that and they stared at their knapsacks.

Ben poked his head through the tent flap. "Follow me, there is food."

We took our plates, mugs, spoons and forks and followed him. I had not realised that the tent had protected us from the sun's rays. It had been hot in the tent but once we left it was as though our heads were seared by the sun. I felt as though we were being cooked ourselves. Life was going to be different in India.

We headed for a wooden building. The smells that emanated suggested food but the smells were not what I was used to. Bob said, "What is that stink, Corporal?"

"I think that is our dinner." Ben sounded unhappy at the prospect of eating something he did not recognise.

Inside the building, mercifully out of the sun's rays, I saw that there were long tables flanked by benches. It looked large enough to accommodate a hundred and twenty or more men. There were cooks, three of them, standing at one end. Havildar Singh stood glowering at us as we entered. Sergeant Grundy was already there and he gestured for us to line up behind him.

"The food is not what we are used to but it is all that there is. When we are on the road we will cook for ourselves but here we eat what is placed before us. Just chew and swallow, eh boys?"

He held out his plate and the three cooks dolloped items on it. There looked to be a stew, thin bread and a yellow blob of something I did not recognise. The bread wasn't a loaf as I was used to but a thin circle, like a pancake. I doubted I would enjoy it but the sergeant was right. Food was food. There was an urn at the end and I guessed and hoped that it was tea. That was something familiar at least.

We all sat on one table. We plopped down our cutlery and food and then went to fill our mugs. It was, mercifully, tea and there appeared to be plenty of it.

I smiled for all of us drank first. It delayed having to try this new and strange-looking, not to mention smelling, food.

Albert asked, "Sarge, what is a havildar?"

Sergeant Grundy tapped his stripes, "Same as me, a sergeant." He looked at the food, "Well, best get this over with."

He took his fork and speared what looked like a piece of meat. He looked at it suspiciously before popping it in his mouth. "Salt beef but they have used too much pepper. The thing is as hot as Hades."

I took my spoon and tried some. It was hot. I then tried the yellow stuff. It was bland by comparison. I tried a mixture of the two and it was less hot. I had a sudden thought and taking a piece of the flatbread, smeared it with the stew and the yellow blob. It took away some of the heat.

I said, "Try mixing the three, it is not as hot that way."

They all did as I suggested and the sergeant grinned, "Well done, Smith. You are a clever blighter, eh?"

We ate and I found that the more I ate the less peppery it became. The tea, sweetened and milky, also helped.

When we had finished Sergeant Grundy and Seamus took out their clay pipes and went to the brazier used to keep the pots warm. They took a spill and lit it from the coals. They soon had their pipes going.

The sergeant looked at me, "I know Smith is not your real name but it will do. What is your real Christian name? I am guessing it is not John." A few times John had been used and I had not reacted.

I realised that I would be giving away one of my secrets but I could see no harm in it. "William."

The sergeant spoke my name, rolling it around his mouth to get used to it, "William, William. You are not a Bill. How about Billy?"

I shrugged, "I am happy with Smudger."

From then on, I had a mixture of Smudger and Billy. I answered to both. After I had left the company they would only have that to identify me. I could invent a new identity.

The lieutenant arrived and he had the same food as us. We moved down the bench so that he could join us. No one said anything. He did not seem to mind the heat of the food. When he had finished and Ben had brought him a cup of tea he took out a thin cigar and lit it from the brazier. He nodded to his empty plate, "Get used to the heat of the food. They use hot peppers. It masks the taste of meat that might be going off."

"Don't they have proper bread here, sir?" Dai liked his bread.

"It is as rare as hen's teeth. When we join up with the rest of the battalion we might be lucky and find they have an oven and yeast."

Ben asked, "The rest of the battalion, sir?"

"Yes, the 1st Bengal Battalion. They are hundreds of miles away with General Cornwallis, at Mysore. I am afraid we won't be seeing them for some time. Colonel Coleman is sending us on a little expedition first. We will be leaving to travel up country in the morning."

Sergeant Grundy was the experienced soldier, "Tents sir? Our own food?"

The lieutenant nodded, "I have managed to get a horse, more of a nag really and a cart. The horse is supposed to be for me to ride but it seems prudent to use it to pull a cart. The food will be salt beef."

That made us all smile. We were used to corned beef as we termed it although how long it would last in this heat was anyone's guess.

Sergeant Grundy tapped out the ash from his clay pipe and replaced it in his tunic. "Upcountry, sir?"

The lieutenant nodded, "There is an English missionary and his family. They live in the foothills almost two hundred miles to the north of us. Deoghar is a holy place for the Hindus and a local warlord objected to the missionary preaching Christianity. He and his family have been imprisoned. We have to get them out and bring them back here. They want a ransom for them so his story sounds a little bogus to me."

Seamus said incredulously, "Twelve of us?"

The lieutenant threw the stub of his cigar into the brazier, "I think it shows how highly the Colonel regards us, Hogan." We all heard the cynical tone. The colonel was making a gesture. If we failed, and it looked likely that we would, then it would have just cost twelve criminals. The powdered wig had told me all I needed to know about the officer.

Corporal Neville asked, "How do we get wherever we are going, sir? Have we a map?"

Lieutenant Crozier snorted, "Of course not, Corporal. We are just going to wander over north India aimlessly and hope we find them."

"Sorry, sir."

"I have a map and a compass. In addition, we have a sepoy with us. He can speak English and knows the country and customs. We do not."

"Sepoy, sir?"

"A Bengali soldier in the East India Company. We will meet him this afternoon after we have the horse and the cart." He smiled and said, "Until then your time is your own. If you wish to go back into Calcutta to buy whatever necessaries you might want then do so. Sergeant Grundy will issue this week's pay."

I knew what I wanted; a pipe and tobacco. In the short time we had been ashore the insects swarmed. The pipes and the cigar had kept them at bay but they would return.

The coins handed over, I went with the others back to the market we had passed. There was safety in numbers. Once again, as we neared the market my ears were assaulted by the noise and my nose by the stink. Cows had defecated on the road and no one appeared to have cleaned it up. Dogs had done the same. Around the fort, there had been none and I guessed that Colonel Coleman liked things to be clean. What I was not prepared for was the bartering that took place. I kept at the back when we approached the first stall. Ben wanted some material to fasten to his shako to keep the sun from his neck. He picked up a piece. The stall holder held up his fingers to indicate the price he wanted. Ben shook his head and one finger came down. He shook his head again and another finger came down. It went on until there were two fingers. This time when Ben shook his head the stallholder nodded. Ben handed over the coins and took the cloth. As it had only cost two coins and seemed a good idea the rest of us all sought the same. This time the stallholder held up two fingers.

Ben, Albert and I had decided to buy pipes. There was a shop which sold such things and we went there. The owner spoke English. That was, perhaps, no surprise as the English would be his best customers. The clay pipes were cheap, just two pennies but I reasoned that they were a false economy. If they broke they would be of no use and as we were going to be travelling it seemed more than likely that there would be breakages. Instead, I bought a short, stubby, rosewood one for six pennies.

The owner asked me if I had smoked a pipe before and I shook my head. "You need to season the pipe, sir. Soak it in vinegar. When you first light it do not overfill it. This is a good pipe and will become better with age."

The others bought clay pipes and then the owner selected our tobacco. For an extra penny, he supplied a small piece of oilskin to keep it from drying out. We left with our purchases and headed back to the fort. We were at the edge of the market when Seamus called out to us, "Here boys! We have found a pub!"

We wandered over and saw the rest of the section sitting on barrels and tree stumps outside a house.

Ben said, "Pub?"

Seamus shrugged, "What passes for a pub in these parts. They sell beer. It isn't porter but it is stronger than the piss they gave us on the ship and it is cheap."

I was still not much of a drinker but I did not want to look odd and so I bought one. It was refreshing. I detected some kind of fruit in it which made it cleaner somehow. Seamus, John and Dai were heavy drinkers. They were drinking two to everyone else's one. I sipped mine and made it last. If they thought I was saving money I did not mind. By the time Seamus had spent all his pay, we were all ready to return. We felt hungry. We made our way back. Seamus and Dai seemed unaffected by the drink but John was staggering a little.

Ben said, "Billy, you are unaffected by the drink, help me to support John. The last thing we need is for the havildar to have him on a charge."

"Can he do that?"

"It is the rank that gives him the right. I suspect that he is the colonel's man and he does not like us already."

With Ben and I on either side, we kept John walking in a roughly straight line. As Ben had suspected the havildar was at the gate and his eyes were seeking any infraction. Ben said, "Attention!" and we all saluted as one. Even John Williams did so and the havildar and the sentries waved us through. We put John on his cot and he began to sleep. Ben said, "We will have to watch him if we find anywhere else that serves beer. He was trying to keep up with two serious drinkers, Seamus and Dai."

I found some vinegar. We kept a skin of it to use on wounds. I put some in my mug and placed the pipe in it.

The bugle blew for the evening meal and this time the rest of those in the fort, the colonel apart, joined us. I took the pipe from the mug of vinegar and left it on the bed to dry. Williams had sobered up enough to be able to walk a straight line. There were twice as many of us as there had been when we had eaten lunch. The food was much the same although there was little meat this time. It was filling but the heat of the food made us all drink more tea. The sergeant and the lieutenant joined us and we ate together. Ben told them about the cloths we had purchased. Lieutenant Crozier said, "I have managed to get us some straw hats. We will save the shakoes for when we need to look the part."

Just then a small sepoy came over to us and saluted, "Lieutenant Crozier?"

"Yes."

"I am Private Aadyot Ganguly and I am honoured to be your guide."

He had an engaging and eager smile and, as we came to know, was desperate to please us. His English was understandable once you became used to his sing-song delivery.

"Good. You have a musket?"

"Yes, sir."

"Then we leave after breakfast tomorrow. Meet us with your equipment at our tent."

"I shall endeavour to be of service to you, sir." He saluted and then turned around smartly to rejoin his comrades.

Sergeant Grundy glowered around at the table, "And he is of more use than any one of you so look after him. The last thing the lieutenant and I want is to be stuck somewhere without the means to talk to anyone."

Ben looked puzzled, "Sarge, aren't there more of our soldiers up there?"

The lieutenant shook his head and answered, "The company has soldiers at Madras, Calcutta and Bengal, Corporal Neville. Most of the soldiers of the company are heading towards Mysore where the Governor, General Cornwallis, is finishing up mopping up the company's enemies. We are on our own. Most of the land is ruled by allies but that doesn't mean a great deal."

"And if we do rescue them, sir, what then? Bring them back here?"

"If we can, although we may have to go to Madras with them. That is a longer journey. We shall see."

Even the lieutenant sounded despondent. My heart was in my boots. All my plans were now in ruins. I had wanted to find my feet and learn some of the language. I had hoped to find out how things worked and then sneak off quietly and disappear. That was clearly not going to happen and, even worse, it looked likely that we might fail and, at best I would be a prisoner and at worst, dead.

"Right lads, early night. Make the most of it. From now on we will all be losing sleep at night. Here we have walls and sentries. On the road, it will be just us.

The three of us trudged to our tent. Just walking from the mess hall to the tent meant a battle with the flying creatures that swarmed from everywhere. Even when we closed the flap they were still there. Bob said, "Get that pipe of yours going, Smudger."

Albert nodded, "I should have bought one too."

I took it out and the tobacco. I remembered the instructions of the tobacconist but I knew I hadn't been able to season it for long enough. I half-filled it, as he had suggested, and then realised I had no means to light it. I would need a flint. I remembered then the sentries and their brazier. The coals burned not to keep them warm but to keep away the flies. I went outside and was attacked immediately. They filled the air before me and I hurried to reach the brazier. The two sentries grinned unsympathetically but moved aside to allow me to get close. Putting the pipe in my mouth I took a twig from the ground and lit it from the brazier. I held it over the bowl of the pipe and sucked. I had seen other pipe smokers and knew that you simply blew out the smoke. The pipe seemed to draw and I dropped the twig back into the brazier. I kept sucking and blowing all the way back to the tent.

"Thank God, we were being eaten alive." I sat on my cot and the other two flanked me, using their hands to flick away the flying devils. The pipe was drawing but I was beginning to feel nauseous. I did not know if it was the pipe or the food which also appeared to be rumbling and gurgling in my stomach. I slowed down my rate of sucking and blowing.

Bob patted me on the back, "It is working. Keep going, Smudger, while we get undressed."

I did so but I realised that, for the first time in my life, I was doing something for someone else. I benefitted but not as much as they were. The snores from them told me that they were asleep within minutes. The pipe went out. I looked in the bowl and the lack of a glow gave me the reason, I had smoked the half bowlful. It had worked. The air in the tent was still filled with the smell of the smoke and I was able to get undressed. It was as I undressed that I discovered another effect of the food. The other two began to make noises other than snores and the smell that rose would have been enough, without the smoke, to drive away the insects. It took longer for me to get to sleep than them but that was because I worried I might be sick.

I woke while it was still dark and before reveille. My guts had woken me and I knew I had to get to the latrines. They were on the far side of the compound and, in my underwear, I ran as fast as I could to reach them before I had an accident. They were simply boards over a cesspit. The stink brought back my nausea before I reached them and when I arrived, I saw that Albert and Dai were there already.

Albert's teeth glowed white in the dark, "You too, eh?"

"Aye, just made it!" I sat and I was just in time. The relief was a joy.

Dai had finished and as he washed himself he shook his head, "I will be glad to eat proper food again."

Albert said, "God knows what we will get for breakfast."

By the time I got back to our tent, Albert was dressing. "It is almost dawn. I thought I would dress." I nodded. "At least the insects have found someone else to annoy."

Our dressing, especially the jingling of the equipment, woke Bob. He had to do the race to the latrine too and by the time he returned we were dressed and the bugle brought the fort to life. Thankfully the breakfast was more familiar. There was porridge as well as the flatbreads. I stuffed a couple of the flatbreads in my tunic. The old thief in me knew that I should hoard food while I could.

We had all barely finished when Sergeant Grundy bellowed, "Well, my lovely lads. Your life of leisure is over. Pack your kit, take down your tents and bring them and your muskets to the cart."

We were about to embark on what some might call an adventure but I felt like it was a punishment. I should have jumped ship in St Helena.

Chapter 9

The cart looked too small for all our bags let alone the supplies we would be taking. There were two cooking pots as well as spare balls, some powder, the food and then the waterskins. We had all filled our canteens with the boiled water that they had in the fort but once we were on the road we had been advised not to drink the water. We would have used cold tea but it had all been drunk. Remarkably everything went in. The two pots hung from hooks at the rear. The horse that we had been given was the sorriest-looking animal I had ever seen. Back in England, she would have been ready for the knacker's yard.

The colonel and the havildar came to see us off. I think they were just keen to be rid of us as though we had polluted their world, somehow.

"Smith, you can lead the horse for the first leg of the journey." The others jeered. "And after that, the rest of you get to take a turn."

"Right, Sergeant Grundy. What is her name?"

"No idea. Whatever you name her will be the name we use."

I walked up to the horse and gingerly took the leader, "Now then, what is your name to be?" At the sound of my voice, she turned and when I looked into her soulful brown eyes, for some reason a name came into my head, "How about we name you, Duchess?" As I said the name she whinnied. I am not sure if she understood me but I took it as a sign and she became Duchess. I stroked her mane and she seemed to like it.

"Corporal, you bring up the rear with Smith and the horse."

Seamus said, quietly, "Aye, that will save us all from stepping in horse shit."

The havildar brought out a small, locked chest and placed it in the cart. He said not a word to anyone but he nodded to the lieutenant who acknowledged it. When everything was loaded the lieutenant and the sergeant led the way with Private Ganguly and we headed on the road north. The new straw hats made a difference. My head was cooler and our faces and necks had some protection from the sun. We had all tied the neckcloths we had bought around our necks and that helped. The lieutenant and sergeant did not insist we keep our tunic's top button fastened. I would not have a chafed neck.

The word road was an exaggeration. There was a layer of stones but beneath them was just hardened mud. Rafe and Ned had told me of the rain they endured in this part of the world, it had a name, monsoon and when that came we would have to trudge through a morass of mud. As we headed north, we passed fewer but meaner-looking houses. The smell was marginally better but as the trees, they called it a jungle, took over from tended fields we were assaulted by the stink of rotting vegetation. I was hot after just a mile and I knew we had thirty or so to go but I resisted the temptation to drink from my canteen. Each time we passed a puddle of water, I let Duchess drink and I envied her despite the green scum that covered it. I did eat the flatbreads regularly. They became increasingly drier and I reasoned by noon would be too stale to eat.

We were still suffering from our first encounter with the food of India and we had to stop four or five times during the day as others emptied their bowels. The lieutenant and Sergeant Grundy showed no sympathy for the men and we pushed hard. We stopped at noon at some nameless little village. We had food with us but Private Ganguly, with money from the lieutenant, bought some fruit to augment our diet. I knew from Ned and Rafe on the ship that eating fresh fruit was essential. We drank the tepid water in the waterskins. When we stopped for the night we would brew up a batch of tea and the next day have a better drink.

As we left the village Lieutenant Crozier said, "Do you need relief, Smith?"

I did not have to carry my musket like the rest and it was easier just to lead the horse. She was very docile. "No, sir, I am fine."

Nighttime saw us twenty-eight miles from the fort. Thanks to the frequent toilet stops we were not as far along the road as we might have hoped but we found a campsite. That is to say a flat piece of open ground with a little grazing for the horse. The river was never far away but we camped far enough to avoid any watery wildlife that might decide to investigate our camp. There was a clearing we could use and while I unpacked the cart and then took Duchess to be watered, the rest of the section erected the three tents we would be using. The lieutenant and the sergeant began building the fires to cook the food and make the tea. Walking to the river was the scariest thing I had ever done. Private Ganguly came with me. He would collect water for the tea and the stew we would eat. Boiling the water would clean it of impurities.

As we walked I said, "Aadyot, what sort of creepies do they have around here?"

"Creepies?"

"You know, spiders, snakes," I mimed, "stuff like that."

He grinned cheerfully, "Many spiders. Some are big enough to hunt birds. Snakes? Lots of them. If you make a lot of noise they might flee unless they are too big. They do not like smoke and fire. When we have a fire going they will keep away." He pointed to the trees, "Watch for them hanging down." We neared the water and he put his hand out to stop us. "We look. There may not be crocodiles here for the river moves too quickly but it is as well to watch for them." Seemingly satisfied he nodded, "There are none. You can let the horse drink and I will fill the pot."

His words had not reassured me and I held my bayonet in my right hand as I lowered my left to let Duchess drink. Aadyot bent down to fill the pot. When Duchess had drunk enough, we headed back. I was a nervous wreck as my eyes flickered from the canopy of trees to the ground looking for one of the myriad of creatures that could hurt me. The poor road we had used now seemed like a haven of safety. I found a patch of weedy undergrowth where Duchess could graze and I tied her up. The tents were already erected. There would be five in our tent. Without cumbersome cots, there would be plenty of room but I was wary about the snakes and spiders. I happily took the least popular place in the tent, right in the middle. I reasoned that a creature would have to slither over a tent mate before it could reach me.

Sunset was not slow here in India. One moment it was sunny and the next so black that you could barely see your hand before your face. The fire that had been built helped and the smoke kept away most of the insects. Lieutenant Crozier had a large piece of cloth and he ordered Dai and Seamus to hold the four corners over the pot. Aadyot poured the river water slowly through it. The green slime and some small waterborne creatures I had not seen before were collected. Dai and Seamus shook it clean and folded it. I went to gather firewood. I didn't care if it was green; it would not be for the heat but the smoke.

This time we were eating salted beef cut into chunks with some greens and beans. The beans would be a little hard and that was why the sergeant put in twice as many as we would need. The rest would be left for the following night's meal. Aadyot prepared his own food. The beef was against his religion. He was able to eat the greens, beans and water but he mixed it with his own spices and some rice. He looked happy enough at the choice.

As we ate, Sergeant Grundy gave out his orders, "Three watches: the lieutenant will have the first watch with Smith, Byers and Cathcart. I will take the second watch with Williams, Mainsgill and Lowe. The corporal will have the last watch with Wishart, Evans and Hogan."

Aadyot said, "What about me, Sergeant?"

Sergeant Grundy looked at the lieutenant who said, "He can be with me. Tomorrow, we change the order. It will be Neville, then me and the sergeant last. The next night, the sergeant, then Neville and last me. We rotate. It is fairer on everybody."

We all saw and appreciated the gesture. I was tired but I did not want to go to bed only to be woken for a duty. I managed to get the pipe going and sat with Aadyot, Bob and Edmund. I thought back to my plan and this seemed a perfect opportunity to put something in place I had thought of on the ship. "Aadyot, how about you teach me some words."

"Bengali?"

I shrugged, "Whatever language they speak around here. If someone is going to insult me I might as well know what they are saying."

I saw the lieutenant give me a curious look but he said nothing. Aadyot seemed happy to teach me. The lesson continued as our watch went on and by the time we were relieved by Sergeant Grundy's team, I had learned a few words and phrases. As I headed for my tent the lieutenant said, "A good idea Smith but the closer we get to Deoghar, the more vigilant we shall have to be."

"Yes, sir."

That became the pattern for the first week. I was not always the one with Duchess but when I had the duty it was an all day one while the others led her for just half a day. She seemed to respond better to me and our officer preferred it when I led her. We made better progress. Each night I would spend my time learning Bengali but I also paid attention to the noises in the jungle. As Aadyot explained, noises were a good thing. If there was silence, then that was the time to worry as it meant someone or something was hunting.

When we saw our first snake it was a huge one. The lieutenant said it was a python. It hung on a tree over the road and the lieutenant chopped it in two with his sword. Aadyot was happy for he said it was good to eat and tasted like chicken. I was dubious but once it was skinned and butchered and placed in the pot we all ate it. It did taste like chicken but I didn't really enjoy it. Aadyot also told us that if we could kill a crocodile that also made for good eating. The idea of trying to kill one of those armoured beasts terrified me. We had still to see one and the thought of it made me more terrified than had I seen one. I kept wondering, each time we neared the river, would this be the day? I became adept at smoking my pipe and it did work. I even managed to find a couple of pieces of flint on the road so that I could make a spark. Seamus said I could use the musket's pan but I was not sure.

The night before we would reach Deoghar the lieutenant gathered us around him. We had eaten and those with pipes smoked them. Lieutenant Crozier had spent a long time speaking to Aadyot during the day. I had been leading Duchess and I had no idea what they had spoken about.

"We will reach Deoghar tomorrow. The man who is the ruler there, Private Ganguly says his name is Nawab Wasim, looks to be the most powerful man in this land. Colonel told me that the title was just lord of Deoghar. It seems he has grand ideas about himself. He is supposed to be an ally of the company but Ganguly here thinks that he admires the chap they call Sher-e-Mysore or Tiger of Mysore, Tipu Sultan. He and his people are allies of the French and might explain why he has allowed this warlord to take the hostages." He paused and looked at the sepoy. "Is that about right, Private?"

"Yes, Sahib. I grew up not far from Deoghar and I know this warlord. He is what you English call a thorn in the side of the Nawab. The Nawab would have the British gone from India and this way he lets the warlord hurt them."

"For that reason, I want to keep our numbers hidden. I will go with Ganguly and one other to the palace and ask the Nawab for the return of the missionary and his family. You will all keep yourselves hidden until we return."

"Sir, isn't that risky? What if this Nawab takes you prisoner?"

The lieutenant smiled, "Sergeant Grundy, the colonel may not think much of us and might have sent us on this apparently hopeless mission without much likelihood of a return, but the danger will come not from this man but from the warlord Jahan Cholan."

"Then why go to see him at all? Why not just head up to this warlord's lair and take back the hostages?"

"Politics, Sergeant. I have a letter given to me by the company. It requests the aid of the Nawab and reminds him of his responsibilities to the company. He signed a treaty and the resident would have him honour it. No, I do not doubt that we will return but I suspect that we will be followed and a messenger will warn Jahan Cholan that we are on our way. Our target will be watching for three men and not this whole section."

Ben asked, "Sir, how far away is the stronghold?"

"Twenty miles to the north in the foothills. According to Ganguly, here, it is a sort of hill fort with mud walls."

"And how many men, sir?"

"The warlord has thirty warriors who protect him."

I looked around. We had thirteen muskets. We had no chance. Others did the same as I did.

The lieutenant threw the stub of his cigar into the fire. He had seen our looks and understood our misgivings, "We do it by a mixture of two things, gentlemen: the threat of a larger force coming and our discipline." He took a stick from the pile of kindling next to the fire, "I have a map for you Sergeant, but for the benefit of the others, here is the plan." He drew a crude map in the earth, "This is Deoghar. Here is the hill fort. Sergeant Grundy, you will have the section wait here." He marked a cross to the northeast of Deoghar. "It is on the road out of the town. You will have the section hide and when I pass you will wait and apprehend any who are following us. When we move up the road I want to travel as just three Company soldiers. You and the section are our insurance. When we reach the fort you will all hide outside and the three of us will go within. I hope that our threat will work but if not then the three of us will try to effect the rescue. The section will wait without and be prepared to fire on those who would do us harm."

I could see that the sergeant was less than happy with the plan. "Sir, with due respect, the plan is mad."

"No, Sergeant. He won't risk hurting us for he wants his ransom. The hostages are safe for he thinks that we will be bringing a chest with four hundred guineas inside. That is the chest in the cart."

Seamus asked, "With four hundred guineas in it, sir?

"No, with twenty guineas. If warlords think that they can kidnap and demand money we will have more such incidents. I have no intention of handing over the chest too quickly. The money we carry is grudgingly given by the resident who has instructed the colonel to send us and recover the hostages."

"And if you do not emerge, sir? What then?"

"Then, Sergeant Grundy, you will be in command, and you must do as you see fit." The sergeant nodded. "Any more questions?"

The sergeant said, "Just one, sir. Who will be the third man? Are you asking for volunteers?"

The lieutenant laughed, "Sergeant Grundy, you know better than that. This is not a democracy. Smith, you have more of a grasp of the language than the rest and unlike the others in this section you are the most successful thief we have."

I was taken aback and I just said, "Successful, sir?"

"Aye, you are the only one who didn't end up in gaol. The three of us will not have a duty tonight and we leave before dawn."

I was stunned. I should have run long ago. Now I was walking into a place where there was little likelihood of my return and I could do nothing about it. I cursed myself for learning some of the language.

Bob said, as we went to our tent, "You'll be alright, Smudger. You are clever. The lieutenant is right. You didn't get caught."

What I knew and they didn't was that luck had been involved. I had been identified as a thief and that was why I had run. I would need all my wits about me to survive this hole into which I was rapidly sinking. The belt of gold around my waist suddenly felt heavy and, at the same time, worthless. How could I spend it if I was dead? As I lay on the blanket I contemplated running but I was hundreds of miles from Calcutta and I would not survive on my own. I was part of this section and, for good or ill, I would have to stay with them. The first time we reached anything that passed for civilisation I would run.

I was woken by the smell of salt beef being fried. I rose and dressed. Sergeant Grundy was cooking the beef, "Thought you might want a decent breakfast, son." His voice was kind. Aadyot had taught us how to make the flatbreads and use the side of the cooking pot to cook them. He wrapped the flatbread around the beef and handed it to me. "Tea is in the dixie."

I used the mug to scoop the tea out of the dixie and ate the beef. I felt like a condemned man having his last meal. We had no milk but we had sugar. It was not like the sugar we had in England, but it sweetened the tea.

The lieutenant came back from the jungle where he had made water. "Well done, Sergeant, this will set us up nicely." He seemed quite happy to be going on such a risky adventure. When he had finished he said, "Smith, Ganguly, bring your packs here."

We both obeyed.

"Smith, give your powder and cartridges to Ganguly. Private, you will carry them for him."

"Yes, Sahib."

He lifted the chest from the cart after I had handed over the items, "You will carry this, Smith." He patted my back, "You are stronger than Ganguly here." That done he said, "And wear your shako. We are here to represent the company.

We hefted our packs and slung our muskets.

"See you on the other side of Deoghar tomorrow or the day after. Good luck, lads." I noticed that he had not brought his musket. His sword hung down as his only weapon.

"Good luck, sir." The men chorused.

I walked past Duchess and stroked her mane. I would miss her.

Chapter 10

"Walk with me, Smith. Private Ganguly, take the lead and step out smartly, eh?"

"Yes, Sahib."

The sepoy happily strode ahead of us, his musket slung over his shoulder.

The lieutenant was next to me and he spoke quietly and, it seemed to me, more like a friend than a superior officer. "You think that this is hopeless, isn't that right, Billy?"

It was the first time he had used my Christian name, and it threw me. I answered honestly, "Yes sir. It is mad."

He laughed, "And that is why I chose you. I have no idea what you really did in England that made you run but you managed to evade detection for a long time on a ship. If you could do so on an East Indiaman then a village should be child's play. You are clever, not to say cunning, and that is what we need. We are walking into a trap and therein lies our hope for they will think they have three more hostages. You can speak a little of their language. Play dumb, as shall I. We let them think that only Private Ganguly can speak their language and we use that knowledge to our advantage."

"Yes, sir." We walked for a while in silence and then I said, quietly, "I don't want to die, sir."

"No one does and I have no intention of dying here. When I die it will be on a battlefield, leading men in war. I didn't want this but our little section is not wanted by the likes of Colonel Coleman. We need to impress others. When we return, and return we will, then I will go to the company offices with our hostages. Hopefully, it will get us a posting somewhere where there is action. You want action, don't you?"

I shook my head, "No, sir, I want to live."

He laughed, "And you will. Now step a little livelier. I want to be there well before dark." I felt better after our talk for I had been honest and I kept in step with the officer. We caught up with Aadyot and we marched together. It made the walk easier, somehow.

Deoghar had a wall and a double gate but the gates were open. The sentries asked about our business but I think that they had already decided to admit us. The red uniforms had that effect. I picked out enough words from Aadyot and the sentries to work out what was said. I understood more than I could speak. I had learned how to work out what was being said. I recognised the words 'Nawad Wasim' and 'Lieutenant Crozier'. I deduced the rest. The pointing arm also helped me to understand. Aadyot translated and we walked through the gates into the streets. They were not as crowded as Calcutta and here the people parted as we passed through. Red uniforms were less usual here, two hundred miles from Calcutta. We were stared at as though we were a spectacle.

The palace was not particularly grand but it was far bigger and better built than most of the houses we passed. The superior ones were close to the palace and that made sense. Those with money would want to be as near as they could to the ruler. There was a wall around it and another gate. This time I understood more for Aadyot said exactly the same thing he had before. This time one of the guards took us to the entrance and the portico that offered some shade from the sun. I heard, "Wait here, sahib." Aadyot translated and the man disappeared inside.

The lieutenant said, quietly, "Look for a way in and out, Smith. Imagine you are trying to break in. How would you get out?"

"Sir."

I casually turned and looked at the walls. They were low enough to climb and were more ornamental than defensive. The building had a large double door that looked solid enough but, I reasoned, there had to be other entrances and exits for the servants. A place like this would have many. It was always easier to use a door than a window. Getting in was harder than getting out as most doors were either barred or locked from the inside and the key was normally to hand. Windows were a fool's way out.

I had time for a good examination as we were made to wait for some time. The sentry eventually came out and with him was a grandly dressed man with a richly decorated turban. He spoke in English, "Lieutenant Crozier?"

The lieutenant snapped to attention, "Sir."

"You wish to see the Nawab?"

"I do. I have been sent by the resident from Kolkata." I noticed that he pronounced the word the same way that Aadyot did.

"I am the major-domo. Come with me." He hesitated, "If you would leave your muskets here." He gave an apologetic smile, "They are a little intimidating, you understand."

"Of course."

"And your knapsacks. You may put them over there." There was a table. Aadyot and I took our weapons and rested them there. I still had my bayonet in its frog as did Aadyot in addition to my two knives, one secreted in my boot and the other beneath my tunic. We put the three knapsacks there. I put mine so that the straps were facing the floor beneath Aadyot's. If anyone examined it then I would know.

We were led through a cool hallway with our shakoes held in our right arms and the three of us marched. It was done without thinking. We had drilled every day when I had been on the ship and it seemed, to me, the most natural way to move now. As we passed servants they bowed. I was not sure if it was for the grandly dressed major-domo or our red coats. The grand hall had been prepared and I partly understood the wait. The Nawab was trying to make an impression. He was seated on a raised dais and was grandly dressed. Two men hovered close by and they had long swords. I guessed that they were bodyguards. The Nawab was younger than I expected. He looked to be in his thirties. He had an immaculately trimmed beard and moustache and his clothes almost shone with the gold and silver threads interwoven in them.

The major-domo bowed and said, "Your Highness, this is Lieutenant Crozier of the Honourable East India Company. The other two men are soldiers in the company."

"You are most welcome, Lieutenant, although we were not expecting a visit. Will you stay with us this night or do you have to leave?"

"We can stay, Your Highness."

He turned to the major-domo, "Have rooms prepared for our guests." The fact that he gave the commands in English made it clear they were for our benefit too. "And the purpose of your visit?"

He had to have known why we were here but this, it seemed to me, was a game.

"The resident and my colonel are concerned about the kidnapping of a missionary and his family, John Hardcastle."

He adopted a sympathetic look, "Ah, yes, most deplorable." There was silence and the Nawab smiled.

"The resident would like to know what is being done to recover them?" The lieutenant was speaking calmly as though enquiring about the weather rather than the fate of English hostages. It seemed to me that he knew how to play the game too.

The Nawab feigned a look of sudden clarification and understanding, "I see. Your resident thinks that I ought to be doing something about it. The problem is, Lieutenant Crozier, that the man who took them is a holy man. He was offended by their attempts to turn his people to Christianity. I tried to explain that to Mr. Hardcastle but he was stubborn and said God would protect him. I cannot risk offending my people. Jahan Cholan is a holy man."

From what Aadyot and the lieutenant had told me that was clearly a lie.

The Nawab smiled a silky smile, "I believe a ransom was sought?"

"It was."

"Then if your resident pays it all will be well."

He was not going to help.

The lieutenant nodded, "This visit is mere courtesy, Your Highness. We came here to let you know we will be visiting with this...Holy Man." I hid my smile for the tone used by the lieutenant told everyone that he did not believe what the Nawab had told him. "We will negotiate for their release."

"The three of you?" His mask slipped and he could not disguise his surprise.

"Negotiations do not need numbers although if we have to we can send to Kolkata for more men. The resident thought that words from a handful of men were better used than muskets from a battalion." It was a clear threat and I saw the smile leave the Nawab's face.

"You do know that Jahan Cholan has a hill fort and would be able to resist an assault, even by the famed red coats?"

"I do although it seems strange that a holy man would need walls."

The lieutenant had won the battle of words and the Nawab clapped his hands, "I have rooms already prepared for you. If you would care to dine with me this evening?"

"I would be honoured."

"Your men will be taken care of." As we were led away, I thought that the Nawab's words could be taken two ways. I still had my knives if it was the more sinister one. I did not like the implication. Were we superfluous and could we be eliminated? As we retrieved our knapsacks and muskets, I saw that mine had not only been turned but opened. The strap had not been fully fastened. The contents had been examined. They knew about the chest. I said nothing. The major-domo took us to some grand rooms. A servant waited and bowed. The major-domo said, "Your room, Lieutenant."

He nodded, "See you later, Smith, Ganguly. Enjoy the sights."

Our quarters, when we reached them, were much humbler. We left the main palace and went to a row of small buildings. There was an open door. "This is your room for the night. When the food is ready you will be collected. Until then you will have to stay within." His tone made it clear he thought we were his inferiors.

I answered in the same tone the lieutenant had used, "Of course."

There was an oil lamp burning and I saw that there were two straw-filled mattresses on the floor. I took off my rucksack and placed my musket in the corner. While Aadyot did the same I went to the door and looked around. There was no one in sight. I closed the door and then opened the rucksack. The chest was still there and locked. The lieutenant had the key. I shook it and felt the coins moved. They had examined my knapsack but not removed the chest. They knew we had the ransom with us.

The sepoy watched my examination and then asked, "What is it?"

I told Aadyot. "We will need to be careful tonight. We say little and we listen. I will pretend I cannot understand anything."

After checking for wildlife below and above it, I laid my blanket on the mattress. I had barely finished when a servant came and spoke to Aadyot. Even before he had translated, I had worked out what he had said. We followed him to what passed for a mess hall. I recognised three of the guards we had seen on our way in and there were servants who were also eating. They were all male. The servant gestured for us to sit and as we did I said, quietly, "No women?"

"They have their own room, sir."

I said, "It is Billy, Aadyot."

He beamed at the invitation to use my Christian name, "I am honoured, Billy."

I groaned when the food arrived. It was the spicy kind that had upset my stomach that first night.

Aadyot said, "Billy, if you do not want it to be as hot then put some of that on it."

He pointed to a bowl filled with a green-speckled white, thick liquid. "What is it?"

"We call it rajika or raita. It is made from herbs, yoghurt and cucumber. Try it."

I did as he suggested and it took some of the fire from the stew. I also used the flat breads although the ones we were served had more substance and flavour to them. I found I quite enjoyed the food. There was also rice and that took the heat away too so that I was almost able to taste the food. Although I was concentrating on the food I was listening to the words around me. They were spoken too quickly for me to understand much but I recognised the words *'Jahan Cholan'* and *'missionary'*. I was pleased to have worked that out. The lieutenant would find it useful. No one tried to speak to me and that was unsurprising but Aadyot was also ignored and I wondered why. While fruits were brought as a sort of last course I asked him why.

He shrugged, "I am seen as a traitor to my people for I serve the British."

"Why are you a company soldier, then?"

"My father and his father both served the East India Company. My grandfather fought at Plassey and he was awarded a medal. My family are all warriors. The company is fair and some of our leaders, like this one, are not."

"Will you stay in the ranks?"

He smiled, "I hope for promotion. Travelling with you can only help my career. I would like to be a havildar. When I am then I will marry and sire sons to follow me in the company as a soldier."

I admired his dream. He had one and he would make it come true. I had a dream too although my experience thus far had made it less clear to me. I still wished to leave the company before the seven years were up but I would no longer run for the sake of running. There was little point in fleeing into danger.

When we had finished and both bowed and thanked our hosts, we returned to our humble chamber. The oil lamp would need refilling if we allowed it to burn all night so we made water and then closed the door. We laid our muskets against the door. If anyone tried to open it then the muskets would fall. I let Aadyot turn out the lamp and I lay, for the first time since England, in a room rather than either a cabin or a tent. It felt like luxury.

We enjoyed an insect free night and the muskets were still in place the next morning. We both woke early. Our bodies were in the routine of the march. After making water and washing, we headed for the hall where we had dined the night before. There appeared to be even more people there. I guessed that these were the servants who would wait on the important people. Some were leaving even as we arrived. There was no porridge but there was a rice dish with vegetables that Aadyot assured me was mild. It was milder than the food we had eaten the night before but it was still spiced. I must have been getting used to it for I found I quite enjoyed the taste and it felt filling.

I said to my companion, when we had finished, "See if we can get some tea for our canteens, eh?"

"Good idea, Billy."

Our canteens being filled, we went outside. The sun had now risen but it was bearable. The walk to the city wearing the shako had been almost painful after the straw hats. We headed back to the main building. There were two guards barring our way. There was little point in arguing with them and so we found a piece of shade and squatted on the ground. We waited. I knew that while we both had things we wanted to say it would be better if we kept quiet. Whatever we said might be overheard and I was keenly aware that we were in a hostile environment. Everyone who entered what was effectively the back door was a servant and recognised. The two guards eyed us both suspiciously. There was a time I might have worried but I had fought pirates and I was more confident. Using my fists and knives had never been a problem. When I had dealt with Jacob before I fled, I had known what I was doing. Now I could use a musket and a bayonet. Palace guards posed no threat to me. I smiled back at their scowls knowing that it would annoy them. I thought about lighting my pipe but I did not. I would reserve that as an insect deterrent. I now enjoyed smoking the pipe which seemed to make me calmer and able to let trivial things not bother me.

I have no idea how long we waited but, eventually, a servant came to the door and, pointing to us, said something to Aadyot. He said it so quickly that I did not make much of it out but when Aadyot rose I guessed what it was. We were taken to the entrance where the lieutenant awaited us.

Lieutenant Crozier turned to the major-domo, "Thank you again, for your hospitality."

"And good luck on your quest." He said not a word more and we followed Lieutenant Crozier outside.

No one said anything as we walked through the town. This time we headed north and left Deoghar by another gate. There were people entering and leaving and we had some small houses and farms to pass. The lieutenant waited until we were five miles from the gates and there was no one around before he spoke.

"Well?"

"They examined my knapsack, sir, and found the chest. They didn't appear to open it. The servants all know where we are going."

He nodded, "As I suspected Jahan Cholan will know we are coming. We can expect a welcoming committee." He smiled, "How was the food, Smith? Still have the shits?"

"No, sir, I am getting used to it."

"Right, let us step lively then. We have a fair way to go."

"I wish I had the straw hat, sir. My head feels like it is boiling."

"After today you can have it back. We are playing a part, Smith. Everything now depends on Sergeant Grundy and the rest of our section. They are our secret weapon." He smiled, "That and what I hope is your natural cunning."

We started marching and after a mile or so I asked, "Sir, you and Sergeant Grundy, you aren't like the rest of the section, are you?"

He turned and gave me a baleful look. I wondered if I had gone too far. He sighed, "No, Smith, we were both in the regular army. We were both soldiers. Sergeant Grundy did twenty years, and I did ten." He said nothing more. I wanted more information but a short while later he said, "Just leave it, Smith. Let us say we all have a past. I don't ask about yours. Don't ask me again. You have the potential to be a good soldier and this life might be the making of you. You have impressed the sergeant and me. That is no mean feat. Try not to spoil things with unnecessary questions."

The road climbed and I spied smoke in the distance. The lieutenant saw it too, "Unless I miss my guess that will be the hill fort." He glanced at the trees to the side of the road. It was no longer the steamy jungle through which we had first passed. This was more of a forest such as we had in England. I had never seen one, I only knew London but I had heard them described. The sound of the monkeys and the odd snake hanging from a branch were enough to tell me that the similarity ended in the openness of the trees. He said, loudly, "Not far to the hill fort."

I smiled. The words were intended for the section. I had not seen them but if they had done as the lieutenant had asked then they should either be hidden close by or would be soon enough.

The heavily armed men who stepped from the trees, three miles later, were most definitely not the section. They held a variety of weapons that were pointed at us and there were eight of them. With murderous-looking faces and unsheathed swords, it was not a warm welcome.

The lieutenant said, calmly, "I take it you are Jahan Cholan's men. We should like to see him."

The blank looks told us that they did not understand a word and Aadyot translated. I understood the words this time.

The one who had the best musket said, "Follow us."

What surprised me was that they did not ask for either our muskets or the lieutenant's sword. I realised it did not matter. It was not as though we could do much about it.

Chapter 11

As we were marched up the hill, passing people tending fields, I consoled myself with the thought that this had to be part of the lieutenant's plan. If he had wanted us to fight them off then we would have loaded our muskets. Slung over our shoulders and unloaded they were just ten pounds of unwanted weight. By the same token, our captors could just let us keep them and that way we carried them. They would be taken once we reached our destination. One thing the lieutenant had drilled into me was the need for me to identify the weakness of the place he had said was our destination. As we were marched towards it I did so. The hill fort was small and square and stood above the small village. Aadyot had told me its name translated to Cholan's place. His family had lived here for generations. Before the present warlord, they had all been out-and-out bandits but Jahan Cholan purported to be a holy man. The kidnapping of the missionaries showed that was a lie. The people tending the fields had stared at us when we had passed and now the villagers, working outside their homes, scrutinised us. The red uniforms were unusual.

I studied the gates and the fort. They were stone-walled but only eight feet or so high. There were towers at the corners and a gatehouse which doubled the height at those places. The gates were opened but guarded by another two men. I saw two men at the gatehouse but no one on the towers. Two old-fashioned cannons peered over the walls at the gatehouse. The ones I had seen at the fort that had been briefly our home were functionally smooth. These were decorated and intricate. I could see that better as we closed with them. When we neared the two sentries, I saw that there was a dry ditch running around the fort and that the ditch was filled with nasty-looking sharpened stakes. We passed over a wooden bridge that spanned the ditch. Passing beneath the gatehouse it was cool and dark and then we emerged into a parade ground. Built into the far wall was a house made of better stone than the fort. It reminded me of the palace at Deoghar but this one was smaller and less well-decorated. It was clearly a copy. Other buildings ran around the side and there was a fighting platform above it. I saw a small gate in the wall opposite the main gate. That appeared to be the only other entrance. Wooden ladders led to the walls. We were marched to the house and the guard held up his hand for us to stop. He left us and I took the opportunity to surreptitiously peer over my shoulder. The gates were shutting and I saw that there was a set of stone steps which led to the guns above the gatehouse. The guns were long ones and I saw an unlit brazier in the centre of the gatehouse. Next to the guns, there were small piles of cannonballs.

The lieutenant appeared to be nonchalantly calm. I was trying to be so but I was becoming increasingly terrified. I could see how to break into this fort but an escape looked improbable. I wondered where the sergeant and the rest of the section were. The tended fields had extended almost four hundred paces from the walls. The only place they could have hidden was in the trees to the south of the fields.

A man wearing finer clothes than our guards appeared with the man who had gone in. "You will hand over your weapons." He spoke in English.

We looked at the lieutenant who nodded. He said, with just a touch of indignation, "I do this under protest. We are British soldiers of the East India Company and neither bandits nor brigands." I handed my musket and bayonet to one of the warlord's men. From the look on his face, he thought it was his to keep.

The man had a smooth smile and a greasy voice, "Jahan Cholan is a holy man who abhors violence. Your weapons frighten him. They will be returned to you when you leave." The lieutenant unfastened the sword and handed the weapon and the scabbard to another bandit. "Follow me."

We entered the house which was cool and that was a relief. As the lieutenant did not take off his hat neither did we. We went down a short corridor and entered a room with couches and comfortable chairs. There were women in the room and it reeked of perfume. The man I took to be Jahan Cholan was younger than I had expected. He looked to be in his mid-twenties. He wore a turban and his clothes appeared to be silken. He did not look like a bandit. Could he be what he said, a holy man? If so he was a holy man with a good income. Behind him stood a man who was clearly a bodyguard. He had a long two-handed sword resting on the ground and he was bare-chested. He was even taller than Seamus. The scars on his chest were intended to be seen. They were a mark of courage and intended to intimidate. I was already scared enough and they merely added to my existing fear.

Jahan Cholan spoke English and spoke it well, "Welcome, gentlemen. Have tea brought for our guests." One of the women rose from her couch and left. "You are a lieutenant in the East India Company?" It was a question.

Lieutenant Crozier nodded, "I am Lieutenant Crozier, and I must object to our treatment. We have had our weapons taken from us."

He gave an innocent smile, "And why would you need them, Lieutenant Crozier, here you are safe. I do not like weapons. Sit. Your men also."

We waited until the lieutenant nodded before Aadyot and I sat. I took in, as we did so, that there were three doors, including the one we had used.

"I take it, Lieutenant Crozier, that you are here for those who would try to tempt my people from the path to enlightenment that they have chosen."

"Yes, Jahan Cholan, we are here for the missionary you kidnapped and his family. May I see them?"

"All in good time. I believe you have brought a payment for the hospitality I have shown them."

"You mean ransom?"

Jahan Cholan was smooth and his face remained the same throughout, "We are a poor people and our guests need to be fed and housed. That costs and all we asked for was the remuneration we deserved."

"Then let us see them."

The tea arrived and Jahan Cholan held up his hand to stop it from being poured. His voice lost some of its syrupy sweetness as he snapped, "Show me the money, now, Lieutenant!"

We heard the unmistakable sound of muskets being cocked and, turning, I saw a different four men from the ones who had brought us, with old muskets pointed at us.

The lieutenant said, "Smith, the chest."

I took off my pack and slowly unfastened it. As soon as they realised it was three hundred and eighty guineas short, we would be dead men. I took out the chest and handed it to the lieutenant. He took the key from around his neck and unlocked it. He did not open it, "Give it to him, Private Smith."

I handed it to him. I did not bow.

His eyes and his smile showed his eager anticipation. I returned to my couch. When he opened it the look turned to one of incandescent anger and he hissed, "What is this? Is this some sort of bad joke? There are less than thirty guineas here."

"Twenty, actually." Lieutenant Crozier's voice was as calm and smooth as Jahan Cholan's had been earlier. "A purse of twenty guineas is more than enough to compensate you for housing the family. That is what you said the money was for, didn't you or were you really after ransom?"

He stood and threw the chest at Lieutenant Crozier. The officer deftly caught it. "I will show you what I am really after." He jabbed a finger at Aadyot, "You, lackey of the English, you are as worthless as a piece of dung but you can still serve me. Return to Kolkata and tell the resident that the price for the return of the missionaries and these two Englishmen is now one thousand guineas. If the money is not here in fourteen days, then the heads of these two men will adorn my walls. A week later will see the first of the children join them. Do you understand?"

Aadyot had courage. He stood and said, "Lieutenant?"

Lieutenant Crozier nodded, "Do as he says, Private Ganguly. Tell the colonel and Sergeant Grundy that we did our best but we were defeated by treachery. Tell them not to give up hope. It is always darkest before midnight. You understand?"

Smiling he said, "Yes sir." He put his knapsack on his back and, escorted by two of the guards, left.

"You wanted to see the others? Take them to our other guests and put them together!"

As we stood Lieutenant Crozier said, calmly, "What, no tea?"

Jahan Cholan almost screamed, "Take them from my sight!"

This time we were bundled unceremoniously from the room. The guards pushed us. I tried to remain as calm as I could, but it seemed to me that the plan had failed. At least Aadyot would not suffer the same fate as we. The bright sun, after the shade of the house, almost blinded me. We were herded towards a building next to the small door in the north wall. There were two guards waiting outside and they rose as we approached. They grinned as they saw us propelled towards them. I saw that at the side of the building, close to the gate, were a table, two old chairs and a brazier. A piece of canvas shaded the seating area from the sun. The door opened and darkness hid whatever was inside but there was a stink of human waste. We were pushed inside.

The door was slammed shut and I heard the bar dropped into place. The darkness was not complete for there was a small tallow candle flickering in the middle of the room and as my eyes adjusted to the light I saw the missionary, his arm around his wife and two small girls clinging to their mother. They were clothed but filthy. I saw a pot in the corner and the stink from it told me what it contained.

Lieutenant Crozier said, "Mr. and Mrs. Hardcastle, I am Lieutenant Crozier and this is Private Smith. We are here to rescue you."

The man who was unshaven and thin gave a wry smile, "And who will rescue you, Lieutenant?"

"We will be out of here in one day, I promise you." He smiled, "Now, tell me the routine and omit nothing. Smith, examine this room."

"Sir."

While the missionary went through the way the guards operated I walked around the walls to look for a weakness. There were no windows and that explained the stink. The missionary explained that food and water were brought twice a day and, in the evening, the pot was emptied. I reached the door. It had a gap all around it but not enough to escape. I ran my hand around the frame and when I reached the hinges my heart soared. They were made of leather.

I returned to the others. The lieutenant looked at me, "Well?"

"Leather hinges, sir. We can cut them and there is enough space between the door and the frame for us to lift the bar."

He nodded, "I thought we had a chance. This was once a stable. We escape tonight."

The missionary shook his head, "You are deluding yourself, Lieutenant. I thank you for coming but two men could not hope to effect a rescue. You have doomed yourself and my family to a slow and lingering death in this dungeon."

"Just be ready to move when I say and do exactly what I tell you and all will be well." The woman and the children were softly sobbing. I think that our imprisonment ended whatever hope of rescue they had harboured, and the missionary had confirmed it. He turned to me and waved me to a corner away from the family and the stinking pot. He squatted and I emulated him. "You still have your canteen?" I nodded and took it from my webbing. I handed it to him. He took a swig. "Have a drink yourself. We can't afford to be dehydrated." I did as he said. "Now, tell me what you saw."

"By my count, there are nineteen or so men who constitute a threat. They have two cannons on the gatehouse and I think they must have a brazier there at night. As the bridge will be raised when the gates are barred at sunset then the escape route that way is not viable. That leaves the gate at the back as the only means of escape. I think they will guard it, sir."

"Sharp as a tack, Smith. You are right. Now we have three knives between us. Mr Hardcastle says there is a meal just before dark and that is when they empty the pot. I intend to cut those leather hinges after they have left us. I am guessing that they will change the guards sometime after that. The conversation we hear as they change the sentries will be our opportunity. We lift the bar together when the men have settled down. If we angle our blades and lift together we should be able to clear the restraints and then lower the bar to the ground. The hard part will be to move the door silently but as they will be next to the brazier and seated, we should be able to do it. We eliminate the guards and then…" he paused, "look, Billy, I am going to ask you to do something that is risky but if you do not do as I ask then all might be for naught, and we will be executed."

I nodded, "Sir, I can see how we get out of here. We might even be able to eliminate the guards outside. Perhaps we might make it out of the gate but those sentries at the gatehouse will see us and raise the alarm." I lowered my voice, "the hostages will move too slowly for an escape."

"Exactly. I need you to get to the gatehouse and get close enough to the two men to kill them. Then you will leave by the gate and follow me. Do you think you can do that?"

"Sneak up and surprise them? Not a problem, sir. As for killing men in cold blood... I have to be honest, sir, I am not sure."

He sighed, "I know and not many men have to do this. If it is any consolation I have never stuck a knife into a man's back but the task we were given was Herculean in nature. This was the only solution I could come up with."

"You thought of this before we got here, sir?"

"The broad strokes, yes, but not the detail. I counted on the fact that they would send Ganguly back and he could tell the sergeant the time of our escape."

I smiled as I remembered his words as the private had left, "Midnight."

He nodded, "The sergeant will be alert before then. If we can get to the tree line before we are discovered, then we have a chance. Ten muskets can fire fifty shots in a couple of minutes. Our holy man would need a larger warband than the one he has to achieve that."

I thought back to Jacob. I had baulked at killing him but if I had done so then I might have delayed pursuit. Then there had been the risk of pain and possible death. Here there was a guarantee. It was kill or be killed. I glanced at the two girls huddled into their mother. They were young, less than five years old, and this was not right. I had sisters and I would not wish for this to happen to them. I convinced myself, "I will do it, sir."

"Good man. Now get some sleep, you and I will need to be alert this night."

I used my knapsack as a pillow and, after taking a second small swig of water, I rolled onto my side and tried to sleep. It was not as easy as I had hoped but I managed. I was woken by the shaft of light from the opening door and the command, in very poor English to, "Move to the back wall."

I saw the two muskets pointed at us. One was Aadyot's. I rose and did as we were ordered. The two guns and guards remained outside the room and others brought in the food. Two pots were placed in the door and pushed towards us along with a fresh tallow candle. The other was almost spent. The door closed and Mrs. Hardcastle went to the pot and began to use a cup to pour the gruel into the four wooden bowls that they had. She looked to the lieutenant and he said, "Take as much as you want. Smith and I have fed well. We are happy with whatever is left, if any."

There was not much left but we divided it anyway. It filled, as my mother might have said, 'a small hole'. We also let them drink their fill from the pot containing tea. They left us but a cup each. If nothing else it told me that they had endured much during their confinement. It must have been an hour after we had finished when the door opened again and we were asked to move back. This time two servants came in. One took the pots and the other the pisspot. We had all used it and it was dangerously full. It did not take long for a fresh one to be placed in the corner. I saw that the sun was setting and it was getting dark.

The door closed and the lieutenant said, "I saw the brazier on the wall and from the shadows there are still two men." I nodded. The brazier would help me as it would take away the night vision of the two sentries. For once the red uniform would actually help as it would appear black in the dark. "I think the two chaps with the muskets are the sentries who guard us. We wait an hour or so. Your knives are sharp?"

"A knife that is not sharp, Lieutenant Crozier, is about as much use as a piece of parchment for a fireguard."

"Then we wait an hour and begin to cut." He turned to the family. "Use the pot in the next few hours and when I say move then do so." He looked at the girls, "They must not make a sound. You understand?"

The mother said, "Is all this necessary? Surely the company will pay a ransom."

The officer shook his head, "This is not company land and you do not work for the company. I am afraid that the East India Company is a commercial organisation."

He did not say that our presence, as criminals all, was a sign that the family was unimportant.

"But how will we escape?" I noticed that it was the wife asking the questions and not the man who had relied completely on God.

The lieutenant sighed, "We will remove the door and then Smith and I will dispose of the guards."

"Dispose?"

He nodded, "Keep your girls inside until we are done and tell them to avert their eyes. It will not be a pretty sight."

I saw her back stiffen as she realised what we intended. She glanced at me, "You are but a boy."

I smiled, "Yes, ma'am, but I will do all that I can to help you and your family escape. You can trust the lieutenant. He is a good man."

Strangely it was my words that made her smile and nod, "Girls, come here. I have things to say to you." All the time Mr Hardcastle just stared at the candle's flame as though seeking divine inspiration.

I waited until Lieutenant Crozier nodded before I rose and took my sturdiest knife from my belt. Had they searched us they would have found that one, I suspect they would not have found the one in my boot. I knelt and took the lower of the two hinges. I began to saw and cut through the leather. It was not easy but I knew I was making progress. I listened for noises outside and was reassured by the crackling of the brazier and the buzz of conversation between the two sentries. I finished before the lieutenant. I used the cut piece of leather to strop the blade. It would not sharpen it properly but it would give it an edge once more. When the lieutenant had finished his, he peered through the crack and then waved me to the back wall.

"I think we wait an hour before we lift the bar. They should be getting tired and, by my reckoning, it should be almost midnight. Put your bag on your back. When we lift the bar keep your knife at an angle to hold the wood next to the door." I nodded.

I replaced my cup, platter and spoon and took another swig from my canteen. I handed it to the lieutenant who also took a swig.

I was becoming nervous and I emptied my bladder. I realised that, if nothing else, the sound of the pee would reassure the guards outside.

The lieutenant tapped my shoulder and I took out my knife. He blew out the candle. The only light was the sliver of light around the door frame. Our eyes would soon become adjusted to the dark. This would be the trickiest part but not the messiest, that would come when I used the knife to end the life of the sentry. I placed my knife in the gap and the lieutenant mouthed, "One, two, three." On 'three' we began to lift the bar. I heard the slightest of sounds as the wood scraped along the door but the crackling of the brazier would mask it. The lieutenant nodded and we both pushed our knives so that the blade guards were against the bar. It cleared the restraining wood.

Once again, he mouthed, "One, two, three." We lowered the bar. It took an age for we had to do it together. He whispered to the family, "Stand against the back wall and when I wave then come with me." The missionary nodded.

I had the easier task for I had the side of the door with the hinges. I grabbed the leather and nodded to the lieutenant. He mouthed, "One, two, three," and we moved the door away from the opening. The gap around the side made it easier. We laid it against the wall. I saw the light from the brazier on the gatehouse but other than that there was no movement. The air felt cooler and fresher.

We both had our knives out and I followed the lieutenant as he slipped out of the door. We braced our backs against the wall and he peered around. He turned back and pointed to me and then to his left hand. I nodded. I was to take the man on the left. I had to trust the judgement of the officer. He had seen the situation. This time he held up the fingers of his left hand one at a time. When he raised his third finger, we both moved quickly. The two men were dozing. We stepped behind them and I put my left hand around the man's mouth. Without thinking I just drew the blade across the man's throat. The warm blood splashed on my hand and tunic. The lieutenant had done for the other one. We placed them so that they were leaning against the wall and would look to the sentries on the gate as though they were sleeping. The blood looked as though they were each wearing a dark scarf around their necks. Then we unbarred the gate. The lieutenant pointed to the gatehouse and I hurried towards it.

I used the walls of the buildings on the left for cover and I moved silently. I had learned when I had been a thief, that the best way to move silently was to do it slowly and without sudden movements. You avoided anything that might make a noise if you stepped on it. I reached the steps and began to climb. I was not a fool. The lieutenant would already be leading the family around the wall. He would not risk running to the trees until I joined him or he knew that it was safe. I could afford to be careful. At the top of the stairs, knife in hand, I watched. The two men were standing over the brazier. They were speaking and I picked out a word I recognised, naan. I knew what they were doing. They were cooking bread on the brazier. They had their backs to me and the man on the left was close to the gatehouse parapet. I moved closer, placing each foot carefully. My movements were so slow as to be almost imperceptible. There was a wooden fighting platform and I made sure that I placed my feet so that they did not cross the joints where it might creak. I am not sure if the lieutenant thought I would fail for killing two men silently was a tall order. I had no intention of dying. It was as I neared the two men that I saw my musket resting against one of the cannons. I knew it was mine. I had no ammunition, but someone had obligingly fitted the bayonet.

It was the man on the left beginning to turn that decided me. I hurtled at him with my head down and my knife held before me. I rammed my shoulder into his middle and then swashed my blade at the other. The man I had struck tumbled over the wall. The cry, as he hit the stakes, was more of a groan than a cry but the crack as he broke the wooden stake would tell the lieutenant that one guard was down. The other guard made the mistake of trying to grab the musket. I lunged with the knife and the tip went into his throat. It ended the possibility of a cry. I slashed to the side and ended his life.

I grabbed the musket and was about to flee when I heard a shout of alarm. The sound of the cracking stake and the partial cry had been heard. The stakes in the ditch that had effectively ended the life of one guard meant I could not use that means of escape. I had to think of something. I saw the barrel of powder and I drove the butt of the musket into it. Slinging the musket, I took handfuls of powder and made a hurried trail from the barrel. I had to work quickly for there were fiery brands appearing in the courtyard. I took the small shovel from next to the brazier and took a shovelful of coals. I hurried to the end of my powder trail and dropped the coals. They hissed as they ignited the powder, and I took to my heels. The flames raced to the barrel faster than I had expected but I was below the wall when the barrel exploded. The explosion lit up the night but I did not falter. With the musket held before me, I ran for the back gate. In the explosion-lit sky, I saw fearful faces looking up and I took to my heels.

Two men had gone into the cell when the alarm was given and one emerged as I approached. They both had swords but I had the musket with the bayonet. I lunged at one and the bayonet tore into his side. The other shouted the alarm but came no closer. I ran out of the open gate and headed for the corner of the fort. There was a path and it was well-worn. The light from the sky showed me the way and when I rounded the corner I saw that the lieutenant and the family had gone. I was alone. The explosion and alarm had decided him. Muskets fired at me from behind. I ran as fast as I had ever run. I did not look back as I passed the front wall and headed for the village. Villagers had emerged but the sight of a man with a musket tipped with a bayonet running at them made them take shelter.

I heard the crash of the drawbridge as it was lowered. The worst thing I could do would be to look behind me. Even as I heard the crack of more muskets from behind me, I ran. I had almost reached the edge of the village when disaster struck. It was disaster in the form of a villager, a brave one who just threw a large lump of kindling into my path. I tripped. I heard the roar of triumph from those who, presumably, had left the fort and were intent on catching me. Even as the villager raised the second piece of kindling to smash into my skull, I swung the musket and the bayonet slashed across the man's thigh. He screamed in pain and I stood and took to my heels. I heard the sound of feet chasing me. The edge of the trees was just fifty paces from me but the fall and my exertions had tired me. They would catch me. I could hear the shouts from behind and they seemed to be at my shoulder. I did not turn.

"Smudger, drop to the ground, now!" It was Sergeant Grundy's voice and even though it felt foolhardy I obeyed and threw myself to the ground. I braced myself for the bayonet in the back but instead, there was a roar of India Pattern Muskets and the night was lit up by the flash from their muzzles.

"Run!" It was the lieutenant who gave the command.

I raised myself to my feet and ran. The section was ahead of me with levelled muskets and bayonets but they had left a gap in the middle. As I passed it, the muskets fired again. I stopped to catch my breath and a third volley fired.

"Cease fire."

We were swathed in the fog of musket smoke. Lieutenant Crozier suddenly ran towards the bodies. He reached down and picked up a sword. It was his. One of the bodies moved and the movement was ended by a swinging sword. He knelt and picked up a musket. "Private Ganguly, your musket!" He threw the musket to Aandyot. The man with the sword was the bodyguard. Lieutenant Crozier took the heavy purse that hung from his belt. He tossed it in the air. "We have some of the money that Jahan Cholan took." He looked back at the fort. The flames were rising and there were smaller explosions suggesting that the fire had ignited other gunpowder. The fort was in disarray.

Sergeant Grundy said, "I think, sir, we have pushed our luck as far as we can, this night."

I spied Duchess and the cart and I was stroking her head when Lieutenant Crozier said, "I agree, Sergeant. Mrs Hardcastle if you and the girls would climb into the cart." I held Duchess still while they did so. "Well done, Smith. Take the lead. You deserve it."

Chapter 12

We moved all night and only stopped at dawn. We had only managed ten miles as I was concerned that Duchess was pulling too much weight. The family could go no further. Even being transported in the cart had tired the woman and two girls. I think part of the exhaustion was the relief that they had been rescued. Ben and Seamus went back up the road to check but there was no pursuit, at least not yet and we could rest.

"Right lads, empty the cart of your bags. We will let Mrs. Hardcastle and the bairns have more room to ride. Get a fire going. Cathcart, Williams, take post a hundred yards up the road. We will spell you when we have a brew going. Mrs. Hardcastle, when the cart is empty put the children in there and we will try to make you comfortable."

She nodded and then turning to me, kissed me on the cheek, "Thank you, Private Smith. We escaped thanks to your courage. We are in your debt."

I was embarrassed by the kiss and just mumbled. "It was nothing."

Seamus laughed, "He half destroys a fort and says it is nothing. Remind me to be with you when you do something that is worthy of note."

Lieutenant Crozier came over, "The explosion?"

"They gave the alarm, and it was all that I could think of. I threw coals on a powder trail and ran."

"You were lucky. You could have gone up with it as well."

Sergeant Grundy came over, "And looking at your bayonet you have learned how to use that, too."

The rest of the section also made a fuss. After the incident with the pirates and now this I was rapidly becoming the opposite of what I had been when I had lived by the docks. What had changed me?

We ate cold rations. Sliced salted beef and some of Aadyot's bread. It was filling. I was still replete after the food at the palace. That done I went to Duchess. She was pleased to see me. I was as happy about that as anything. The straw hat also made a welcome return. I took the blankets from the other men and used them to make a comfortable nest. Mrs. Hardcastle climbed in and then the two girls. With her arms around their necks they would be able to sleep and be safe for the lieutenant put Seamus and Dai next to the cart. Their huge presence was comforting.

We marched just fifteen miles that first day and made a camp close to a small village. Mr. Hardcastle looked up the road and asked, "Is this far enough? Will they not try to take us again?"

The lieutenant shook his head, "No, Mr. Hardcastle. For one thing, Private Smith's action means that they will need to rebuild their fort and we killed too many of his men, including his bodyguard, for him to have any chance of taking us. There will be no pursuit."

I tended to Duchess again and groomed her as best I could. I found some grain for her to eat and that augmented her weedy diet. That done I joined my comrades around the fire. We had erected all our tents for the family would need to use one. It meant we could not move as quickly as we had on the way north. Mr. Hardcastle had also struggled to keep up on the road which was another reason for our early stop.

After we had eaten and while the family retired to sleep, the lieutenant spoke to us all, "We have all acquitted ourselves well, none more so than Privates Smith and Ganguly." There were nods and murmurs of approval from my tent mates. I found myself swelling with pride. "We also have information which I hope is useful. The muskets Cholan's guards and the ones used by the Nizam's men were all French. I suspect that our French friends are trying to ferment revolution in these parts as well as Mysore."

Sergeant Grundy said, "But you saw no French, sir?"

"No, Sergeant, but then again ours have been the only British uniforms we have seen. I know that there are units further north but this land is ripe for the French to infiltrate."

Lieutenant Crozier was the first officer I had met and I assumed that all officers were like him. That night as I stood a watch with Sergeant Grundy, the old soldier put me right, "No, Smith, he is a rare one. Most officers would not eat with their men and certainly wouldn't share a tent with two NCOs. Our Mr. Crozier is a good officer and we are lucky to have him. Notice how he put himself at risk to rescue the hostages and the majority of the section were safe?" I nodded but thought that I had been put in harm's way. The sergeant smiled when he saw my face, "Take it as a compliment that he risked you, too, Smith. It was the lieutenant who wanted you for the section after the pirate attack. He saw something in you. He could have taken any of the section with him but he chose the one he knew could think for himself."

"What happens when we join a battalion, Sergeant?"

"Ah, then we have to deal with men like Colonel Coleman and there will be others like the havildar who look down on us. We are more likely to be asked to guard the latrines or dig ditches. Still, it has been good to be a soldier again,"

I sensed sadness in the oldest man in the section, "Why did you leave the regular army, sergeant?"

He glared at me and I thought that, as with the lieutenant, I had stepped over an invisible line. He sighed, "I suppose I owe it to you but keep it to yourself, mind. Swear." I made a cross on my heart and spat. He nodded, "I served for twenty years and we were in the Low Countries. We had a young officer, he was younger than you but his parents were wealthy and they had bought him a commission. We were fighting the Froggies and a cavalry patrol caught us in open country. He ran and I had to try to save the rest of the company. Half were either killed or wounded. When I got back, I expected him to be court-martialled but, instead, he had concocted a story saying as how it was my fault. The colonel was a family friend and I was dishonourably discharged. It was me who paid the price for his cowardice."

"But that is unfair."

He snorted, "In the army, there is no such thing as fairness. The officers do as they like. They buy their rank and most do not have a clue as to how to fight a battle. It is the likes of men like me and ordinary privates who win the day. Men like General Wolfe are rare."

"Then why join this company? I would have thought that you had endured enough already."

"I know nothing else and those who join the army, most, Smith, have no choice. The rest of the lads here, they could have stayed in gaol but they saw this as a chance to make something of themselves. At least here they are paid and if they don't get killed then at the end of their time they can start again. With a few shillings, a man can live quite well out here."

It was the same words I had heard from Ned and Rafe. England was a place where the likes of us were at the bottom. Here in India, we were already higher up the ladder. I had much to think about.

The next day we set off but not as early as we might have liked to. Leading Duchess, I was close to Mrs. Hardcastle and her girls. The three thought me a hero and they spoke to me often. I discovered that they had decided to return home. Mr. Hardcastle would seek a position in England. They had thought to do good and spread the word of God. They had assumed that the East India Company would have offered protection but they had been wrong. They were disillusioned but having been so close to death they saw their rescue as a sign that they should go home. The girls were frightened little things. The experience had made them fear for their lives. Even the rest of the section scared them. It was one reason why I was given the task of leading Duchess all the time. I was the one that they trusted. For my part, they represented the family I had lost. I did not know if my family still lived but by being kind to these two, I hoped that someone else would do the same for my mother and my sisters if they were in distress.

It took two weeks to reach Calcutta. We reached the fort in the middle of the afternoon. The battalion had returned, and the fort was full. We were told to escort the family to the official residence. There was a new Lieutenant Governor and the colonel wanted us to report to him. As we moved through the bustling city Sergeant Grundy, walking next to me, explained why, "The colonel is trying to make out that he was responsible for the rescue. I had his measure from the first. He is no soldier. He likes running a fort and having smart soldiers parade. This way he ingratiates himself to the new governor so that he can cling to his position. Probably a good thing. The last thing anyone needs is a powdered man like that leading men into battle."

Having heard the sergeant's story, I understood his venom.

The residency was guarded, not by men from the East India Company, but by regular British infantry. We were admitted and while the lieutenant and the missionaries were taken within, we were asked to wait outside.

Before they entered, Mr. Hardcastle came over to me and shook my hand and then Aadyot's, "Thank you both."

Mrs. Hardcastle pecked me on the cheek, "We shall pray for you often."

The two girls each took one of my hands and chorused, "We will miss you."

They went with the lieutenant, and I never saw them again. It was comforting to know that such people would pray for me.

We found a place sheltered from the sun and sat. I wanted to smoke my pipe but when I took it out the sergeant shook his head, "Not here, son. There will be time for that back at the barracks. You seem to have done well, don't spoil it, eh?"

A corporal came out and said, "Private Smith, Private Ganguly?" Aadyot and I both stood and snapped to attention. "Come with me. You can leave your packs and muskets here."

We dropped them and then marched behind him. His uniform looked new and smart. Ours showed the time we had been on the road. Mine was still blood-spattered from the fight at the fort. We had not had an opportunity to clean it. We both wore straw hats and, for once, I wished I had my shako. The residence was cool and the hob-nailed boots of the corporal and me echoed as we were marched down a corridor. Two sentries stood at the double doors that were at the end. They opened them and we entered. The corporal did not follow us but hissed, "Hats off."

We obeyed and marched in. The door closed behind us and I saw that the lieutenant was seated before a large desk. There were three men in the room. One was seated behind a desk and a second was in the corner at a smaller desk. The third man stood behind the seated gentleman.

The lieutenant said, "May I present Private Smith and Private Ganguly."

The man looked to be in his thirties and the old thief in me recognised expensively tailored clothes. He would have a purse well worth stealing. He smiled and said, "I am Lord Mornington, the new Governor General and I was delighted to hear the lieutenant's account of the rescue you helped to engineer. For men so young it is nothing less than remarkable. Your efforts should not go unrewarded, and I have ordered that the three of you receive a financial reward." The lieutenant had half turned and he mouthed, "Say, thank you."

We both said, "Thank you, my lord."

"My brother, Colonel Wellesley is a soldier and I know he would appreciate having such men as you with him. This continent is in danger and while we are far from Great Britain, we must do all in our power to prevent the murdering revolutionaries of France from infecting this land with their foul politics. You two may wait without while I speak to your officer. Once again, well done."

We snapped to attention, turned smartly and marched out.

As we did, I heard Lord Mornington say, "You would never guess, except for their uniforms that they were not regular army."

The door closed and I turned to Aadyot. We both grinned. The sepoy said, "See, Billy, my star is rising already. I bless the day I was assigned to serve with you and your section."

The lieutenant was in some time and when he emerged, he held open his palm. There were two guineas in it, "Here is your reward, lads. You earned it."

Aadyot's eyes widened as he took his coin, "I am a rich man, Sahib."

I said, "Did you get one too, sir?"

He tapped his nose and held up a piece of paper with his other hand, "I have been well rewarded, Smith. Now let us get back to the others as we have preparations to make." Enigmatically that was all he said. We marched back through the crowded city and headed for the fort.

When we reached the fort, we were ordered to erect the tents but keep them apart from the others; that was easier said than done. The lieutenant and Sergeant Grundy then marched to the battalion office. They had still not returned by the time we had erected the tents.

Ben said, "We might as well get a brew on." We found kindling and soon had a fire going. I knew that it would soon be time for food, although as it would be the spicy kind I worried that my stomach would soon be upset again. It was as we sat, drinking our tea and I was smoking my pipe, that we saw the corporal from the residency. He was riding a chestnut. He dismounted, spoke to the sentries at the gate and showed them something. He led the horse over to us.

"Where is Lieutenant Crozier?"

Ben pointed to the battalion office, "He is seeing the colonel."

The corporal handed the reins to Ben, "This is the horse his lordship promised. His name is Dublin. Your officer is expecting him. I am off back to the residency."

He waved and smartly marched out of the fort.

Ben handed the reins to me, "You are the master of the horse, Billy, you had better see to him."

I led Dublin towards the stable. There Duchess grazed on the food I had put in the nosebag for her. The new horse towered over Duchess. Duchess just looked at me and whinnied, putting her head close to my free hand. I stroked her mane, "I am not replacing you, Duchess, this is the lieutenant's horse. You will have some company." I took off the saddle and hung it from the hook above Dublin's head. I filled a pail with water and let him drink before I put his nosebag on. While we were here, the two horses would enjoy better food than on the road.

When they had both finished eating, I hung the bags from the hooks and then took the brush and currycomb. I knew Duchess enjoyed the attention and I discovered that Dublin did too. I had just finished when I heard the bugle call us to the mess. "Well, I shall leave you two. It is time for my nosebag." The two animals whinnied. It made me smile and I hurried back to my tent to pick up what Bob called, my 'eating tackle'.

I caught up with the others as we reached the mess hall. I saw that Aadyot was hanging back. "Come on, Aadyot, you are part of this section now."

He looked at Ben for confirmation and Ben said, "Aye, besides, you can tell us what the hell we are eating."

The grin showed that he preferred our company to the other sepoys. They let Aadyot go first and I followed. He pointed out each item and gave us a description, "This one is goat. It is hot but if you put some of the yoghurt on it then it will cool. There are three kinds of bread here. That one is a little spicy, that one is plain and that one, the one with the dried fruits in it, is sweet. This is dahl and is not hot. This is rice and is not hot." The comments about the rice and the dahl were unnecessary but showed that he was keen to impress. I made sure I had plenty of the cucumber and yoghurt mix. I also took the bread containing the dried fruit. It looked interesting.

We filled our mugs from the tea urn and sat. I saw that Aadyot had to endure glares for his choice of dining companions. I hoped that when we left he would not suffer for his decision.

The lieutenant and Sergeant Grundy entered the mess not long after we sat down to eat. I saw that the lieutenant was the only officer eating in the mess. Like Aadyot he had made his choice quite clearly.

They both looked happy. Before they could speak Ben said, "Your horse arrived, Lieutenant. Smith stabled it."

"Thank you, Smith. You are becoming quite the ostler."

Aadyot said to me, quietly, "Ostler? I do not know that word."

"It is someone who looks after horses in an inn."

"Ah."

The lieutenant took a spoonful of the goat and nodded, "Good. I like this."

Ben said, "It is goat, sir. A rum thing to eat."

The lieutenant put another spoonful into his mouth and said, "You eat mutton, don't you?"

"Oh yes, sir! I like a nice mutton pie or a mutton stew."

"Goat is like sheep. More plentiful out here, it can be tough meat sometimes but this is well-cooked."

We all concentrated on the food. I realised that I must be getting used to spicy food for I was quite enjoying it. I was sweating, it was true, but as it was hot and I sweated anyway that didn't seem to matter.

When we had finished and were drinking the tea Ben asked, "What now, sir?"

He smiled and said, "Wait until we get back to our little home from home, eh?"

We were all intrigued.

Back at the tents, we squatted while the lieutenant sat on a folding camp chair he had managed to acquire, "We are leaving here and heading for Hyderabad."

"Where is that, sir?" None of us had much idea of the geography of this huge land.

"A lot further south and in the middle of the country. We get to take a boat ride again but this time to a place called Madras. We then march," he chuckled, "actually I get to ride, four hundred miles. Lord Mornington wants the Nizam of Hyderabad to disband the French troops there."

My heart sank. We were leaving.

Chapter 13

Once again it seemed the chance for me to slip away was gone. I had barely got to know the land around Calcutta and we were leaving. We marched to the docks and waited to board the East India Company ship. The *HCS Abercromby* had just returned from England and was being used to transport supplies for the other regiments that would be following us to Madras. She was a smaller ship than *HCS Campbelltown*, I did not expect to know any of the crew but I felt a little affinity with them having served, albeit briefly, as a sailor.

The lieutenant went aboard and said, "Sergeant Grundy, take charge." He held up the papers given to him by Lord Mornington's messenger. "I have to give a copy of our orders to the captain."

"Sir." He turned to us, "Stand easy."

This time we had the problem of loading two horses. I wondered how the army would fare when it had to transport regiments of cavalry for the two horses took a long time to load. Slings were used to lift the animals up safely from the quay to the deck. We sent Duchess up first. As she was lifted I ran up the gangplank. I saw two bolts attached to the gunwale. They looked to be new and I deduced that they would be there to tether the horses on the deck. I leaned my musket against the gunwale and dropped my pack to the deck. I hurried to the pulley and the sailors hauling Duchess to view the old horse as she was raised.

It was lucky that she was a placid animal. She took the experience well. I had found some root vegetables discarded close to the kitchens. They were the type she seemed to enjoy and after she had endured the journey and while the sailors unfastened the sling, I gave her a treat. The two animals would not be placed below deck. I tied her securely to two ring bolts close to the bow castle. They were far enough apart so that the two animals would not be crowded. Two sailors were rigging an awning to afford shade. That done I hurried down to the quay. The two horses seemed to like me and even if I had not sought the position, I was their carer. Dublin, however, was not happy about his treatment and I had to bribe him to allow the sling to be tied. He was snorting and stamping his feet. As the rest of the section hauled on the ropes to pull him aboard, I raced back up the gangplank so that I could talk to him. After ten feet he became agitated. His movements threatened to bring disaster to the venture, and so I began to sing to him.

I sang the ballad, Ash Grove. It was one of the few songs I knew all the way through.

Down yonder green valley, where streamlets meander,
When twilight is fading I pensively rove,
Or at the bright noontide in solitude wander
Amid the dark shades of the lonely ash grove.
'Twas there, while the blackbird was cheerfully singing,
I first met my dear one, the joy of my heart!
Around us for gladness the bluebells were ringing,
Ah! then little thought I how soon we should part.

Still glows the bright sunshine o'er valley and mountain,
Still warbles the blackbird its note from the tree;
Still trembles the moonbeam on streamlet and fountain,
But what are the beauties of nature to me?
With sorrow, deep sorrow, my bosom is laden,
All day I go mourning in search of my love;
Ye echoes, oh, tell me, where is the sweet maiden?
"She sleeps, 'neath the green turf down by the ash grove."

It appeared to work. I knew I had a pleasant voice and I had enjoyed singing the sea shanties on the other ship but the slower ballad seemed more appropriate. He looked towards the sound and, seeing me, seemed to calm a little. By the time he was level with the gunwale he was as still as Duchess had been. I stroked his neck as the sailors unfastened the sling and then led him to Duchess. After I fastened him securely I took a bucket and filled it from the water butt by the mainmast. Dublin drank and then Duchess did the same. I placed the bucket so that it was equidistant between them.

One job I knew we would have to do would be to clean the decks. As if reading my mind a sailor came from the hold. He had a bale of straw, "The bosun thought you might need this, Soldier." The man was wary of the horses, and he deposited it ten feet away.

"Thanks." I walked over to it and dragged it closer to the horses. I took my bayonet, still keenly sharp and sliced through the string that bound it. I took enough from the bale to spread beneath their rear ends. I left most of it and it kept its shape. I knew that it would, eventually, fall apart but the longer the area around the horses was tidy the happier the bosun would be. I remembered the *Campbelltown* and the irascible Mr Cunningham.

When Sergeant Grundy came aboard, he gave me two rarities: a smile and a compliment, "Well done, Smith. That was good work."

The bosun shouted, "Sergeant, your quarters are below deck. Harris, show them."

A seaman knuckled his forehead and said, "Aye, Aye, Bosun." He stood waiting.

"Right, lads, pick up your gear."

Grabbing mine I fell in behind Bob.

"Forward, march."

I saw the bosun shake his head. Our hobnails would not do his deck any good at all. That, allied to the mess the horses would make, guaranteed that the officer would be glad to see the back of us at Madras.

Seaman Harris led us down the ladders, and we were taken to the fore part of the mess. He pointed. "There are a dozen hammocks. Your officer has been given a cabin." He pointed to a table suspended from the deck above, "There is your mess." He pointed down the deck, "That is the crew's main mess. The kitchen is in the centre, close to the main mast."

The sergeant surveyed it and nodded, "The latrine is still at the bows?"

"Aye, but Captain Barclay is a stickler. If you use it while we are in port then he demands you use the side facing the sea, the starboard side."

The sergeant nodded. We had all used the latrines at the fort before we had left. "Stack your muskets over there." We were all well-practiced now and the muskets were neatly stacked. I was not sure how they would fare if we hit stormy weather but I knew that the sergeant would have a plan of some sort. "You can take off your tunics and waistcoats."

Seamus asked, "And our boots, Sergeant?" I saw the sergeant debating and Seamus grinning, said, "We don't want to upset the bosun do we?"

Dai and Seamus were as thick as thieves and Dai added, "There won't be a director aboard this time, Sergeant."

"Aye, alright then but if Lieutenant Crozier disagrees then bosun or no, you wear the boots."

It was a relief to take off the boots. We all took off our socks. This would be an opportunity to wash them. With luck, the few days it would take to sail south to Madras would be boot and sock-free.

The sergeant climbed into his hammock, he looked tired, and the rest of us headed back to the deck. Although the gunports were open the beams from the decks above us meant that it was hot and uncomfortable to be below deck. Once we were moving and at sea, there would be a breeze but in port, this was not the place to be. I reflected that the sergeant was showing his age.

The first thing I did was to check the horses. As I had expected there was a mess already. I saw the seaman called Harris and approached him, "Is there a shovel anywhere?"

He viewed me suspiciously. Soldiers, and especially company soldiers, had a reputation for being thieves, "Why?"

I pointed at the steaming pile of dung, "Well, I could let one of you boys clear up their mess, but I thought you might want us to do it."

He nodded, "I will fetch you one." I stood stroking the manes of the two horses until he returned. "This will happen a lot, will it?"

Taking the shovel I grinned, "Oh, yes.".

I shovelled a pile and went to the starboard side. Checking that there was no one working below I dropped it into the sea. It did not take me long to clear it and then I laid fresh straw down. I held the shovel out to Harris who shook his head and said cheerfully, "No, Soldier, you keep it."

That done and the animals happy, I joined the others who had taken advantage of the awning. Seamus greeted me cheerily, "Make room for the ostler, boys."

Aadyot and Bob shifted apart. As I filled my pipe Aadyot said, "I have never sailed before." He rubbed his chin, "Nor have I ever seen a different part of India. I am Bengali."

I had the pipe going. I had learned how to light the tobacco with a flint. I said, "You live in a big country."

The lieutenant appeared from nowhere, "The thing is, Smith, that this is not a country as such, it is a sort of continent. Just as in Europe there is France, Prussia, Spain and the like, here there are lots of different states. We are going to one ruled by the Nizam of Hyderabad. It is close to another called Mysore." He looked around, "Where is Sergeant Grundy?"

The corporal said, "Taking a nap, sir."

"I think our little hike took more out of him than he cares to admit," the lieutenant nodded, "I will tell you the details of our mission when he is with us and we are at sea." He glanced down at the pipe I had lit, "You have permission to smoke, Smith."

I looked around and saw that I was the only one smoking, "Sorry, sir."

He smiled, "You have done well for a new man, Smith, but you still have much to learn."

We left in the middle of the afternoon. I recognised the calls from the bosun's whistle and knew the one for all hands. I stood, along with the others and we lined the larboard gunwale to watch as the lines were loosed, the sails unfurled and the breeze and the tide took us out to sea. We were leaving the land and would be heading south. First, however, the captain had to turn the ship which was facing north. It was a tricky manoeuvre for the harbour was filled with small boats. I smiled as the bosun roared at them in Bengali. It was clear that he had learned the right phrases to use. It took some time but when I heard the orders for the topmen to go aloft I knew we would soon speed up. With all our sails set, we would race.

After we had eaten, the lieutenant took us on deck where the passage of the ship made a natural breeze. "You may smoke if you wish." Those of us with pipes took advantage. "I have our orders. We are to land at Madras." He smiled, "That should prove interesting as there is no port as such. We land in boats, but Private Smith will have to swim the horses ashore. Can you swim, Smith?"

"No, sir."

"Then that should prove an interesting spectacle." The others all grinned. "Now when we are ashore, we go to meet the resident, James Kirkpatrick. Until Colonel Wellesley and the 33rd arrive, we will be the British presence there. They have native battalions, but we will be the only European unit." He smiled and lit a small cigar using Seamus' pipe to do so. "It seems the French have sent Jacobins to the Tipu of Mysore and the Nizam of Hyderabad. There are just a handful of French at Hyderabad and it is hoped that our red coats will discourage them."

Sergeant Grundy shook his head, "This handful of men, sir? I mean it is one thing to take on a mob of hairy-arsed bandits but French troops..."

"The resident believes that the French who are there do not pose a threat yet, but if the Nizam is encouraged then it may open the door to more. General Bonaparte is in Egypt and it does not take much imagination to see that he has aspirations in India. First, we deal with Hyderabad and then, when the 33rd regiment arrives we shall see about the Tipu of Mysore."

"Are the 33rd any good, sir?"

"Sergeant?"

"Aye, good lads. They are from Yorkshire and as reliable as they come. Can't say as I have heard of their colonel."

"He is Lord Mornington's brother."

"Ah."

Aadyot put up his hand, "Sir, not that I am unhappy to be serving with you but I am Bengali and I do not know the language of those who live in Hyderabad."

"You will have a better idea of what they are saying than we. There will be a promotion for you when you return to your battalion." The sepoy brightened when he heard the words. "It will take a few days for us to reach Madras. I doubt not that it will be hard when we are there so make the most of the time on the ship."

We all adapted quickly to life aboard the East Indiaman. For one thing, the lieutenant did not bother with drills and the wasteful expenditure of powder. We had now been blooded. We washed our clothes and cleaned our weapons. Our experience at the hill fort had taught me, especially, the importance of sharp blades and clean barrels. My other duty was looking after the horses. Each day I took them for a perambulation around the deck. At first, I led one and then the other but after the first time I tried both and they were just as happy I took two of them. The only problem was that the movement often resulted in dung. Sergeant Grundy assigned a soldier to follow with the trusty shovel.

Seamus was philosophical when it was his turn, "Back in Ireland this stuff is like gold. Put this on your potatoes and it does wonders for them."

As he tossed it over the side I said, "Then I hope it does not have the same effect on the creatures of the deep."

That prompted a discussion about monsters and the sea. It was the great unknown. A passing sailor spoke of some crocodiles that lived in the sea and he told us that they were big enough to take a shark. We had seen sharks and knew their size. It passed the time as did many of the other seemingly pointless discussions. Some of the others had taken some of the hardwoods that were found close to the fort and now spent the time carving and whittling intricate objects. Some of them were quite beautiful. The shavings were used to augment the straw which was diminishing day by day.

I had just spread the last of it when the lookout shouted, "Land ho!" We had reached Madras.

It took half a day to finally reach the settlement. As we had been warned there was neither jetty nor quay. It was not a natural harbour but it had a good beach and the captain ordered the longboats to be launched. While he and his crew ferried the supplies ashore, I saw a Sepoy battalion with wagons waiting; we had to get the horses ashore.

The lieutenant said, "Smith, strip down to your underwear. I will send half the section ashore with our muskets and bags. The rest can help you to land the horses. It will mean two trips."

I shook my head, "Sir, I find the thought of one immersion in the sea daunting enough and I do not relish two. The horses have allowed me to walk them together. If we put the saddle on Dublin and Duchess' halter then they can swim ashore and I can cling on between them."

"Are you sure, Smith?"

"No, sir, I am not sure but this is new to us all, isn't it sir?"

He nodded, "Very well. Sergeant Grundy, take half of the men and all the muskets and knapsacks." I took off my boots, waistcoat and tunic and then saddled Dublin. He seemed eager to be off the ship. I wondered how he would feel about a dousing in the ocean. I saw that the captain had taken us as close as he could to the shore but I knew that the water would still be deep. I pushed the thought of sharks to the recesses of my mind. A problem I had not thought about was how I would get into the water.

"Bosun, we need two slings."

The bosun nodded, "Harris, belay landing the cargo until we have these wee beasties off our ship."

I stood at the side as the slings were fitted. Sergeant Grundy and half the section were ashore. By the time the longboat came back, it was almost time for the horses to be lowered. I was petrified and my shaking was nothing to do with the cold. It was monstrously hot and my shaking was raw, unadulterated fear. Seaman Harris said, "Can you swim?" I shook my head. "Joe, we still got that piece of cork?"

"Aye."

"Fetch it then." Joe disappeared and Harris said, "Cork floats. When you jump in keep hold of it and make sure it is a tight grip. It is important to keep your mouth closed. Even if your head bobs under you will come up. Keep hold of this piece of cork until you can grab hold of the horses. They all swim naturally."

"How do you know?"

"These are not the first horses we have landed although they normally choose someone who can swim to do this."

The piece of cork that Joe brought looked too small and flimsy to be of any use but I had to trust the sailor. My experience with Rafe and Ned was that generally sailors were to be trusted when it came to matters of the sea.

The slings were readied and Lieutenant Crozier and the rest of the section waited in the longboat with the sailors who would row them ashore.

The bosun came along, "Ready?" I did not trust myself to speak, and I just nodded, "Right lads, haul on the ropes. You, soldier, had better get ready for your jump. Keep your legs together." I shuffled forward and saw that they had removed the tumblehome on that side of the ship. I would not need to climb over.

Seaman Harris said, "Jump well clear of the side and good luck. You do not lack courage, my friend."

Bob shouted, "You can do it, Smudger." The others all cheered and that decided me. I leapt. It was a leap of faith that the cork would do as Harris had promised. I do not know what I expected when I hit the water but it was not the icy shock that took my breath away. Had Seaman Harris not warned me I might have opened my mouth but I kept it closed and I sank beneath the water. Suddenly the cork pulled me up, I know not how and my head broke into the air. I gulped in great mouthfuls as the other soldiers cheered.

One of the sailors in the boat shouted, "Keep moving your legs, soldier, like walking but in water."

Amazingly it worked and I found myself turning circles.

"Heads below."

I looked up and saw that the horses were being lowered. The sailors rowed across to be close to where they would land and I walked. I found that if I lay on the cork and kicked with my legs I made better progress and I did so. By the time I reached them Bob and Aadyot had the two leaders in their hands. I kicked my way around the side of the boat and found myself close to the rear of both horses. I insinuated myself between them. The hardest part was to come. Bob had Duchess' leader ready. Dai leaned over Dublin's back and grabbed my shirt.

Lieutenant Crozier said, "Ready, Smith?"

Nodding I let go of the cork and grabbed Duchess' leader. At the same time, I gripped Dublin's saddle. Surprisingly I did not sink. Dai let go of my shirt and smacked Dublin's rump. Dublin began to swim as did Duchess. The sand lay just two hundred yards away but it looked an impossible distance. The cries of encouragement from my comrades helped as the longboat kept pace with us. My head boobed beneath the salty water but I remembered to keep my mouth closed. It was a relief when I found that Dublin's hooves had found the sand. I risked letting go of his saddle and grabbed his leader. I was doused again but then my feet found the sand and I walked. I had survived.

East Indiaman

Chapter 14

I handed the reins to the corporal and the sergeant. There
were people on the beach both men and women but, despite the
heat from the sun, the sea had made me shiver. This time it was
the cold and not fear. It was not the time for modesty, and I went
to my pack and took off my sodden shirt and undergarments. The
two non-commissioned officers brought the horses over to give
me some privacy and by the time the lieutenant and the others
had landed I was wearing underwear and a shirt.

A well-dressed man made his way through the crowds
towards us as I donned my boots. He glanced at me before he
said, "Lieutenant Crozier?"

The officer saluted, "Sir."

"I am James Galbraith. I am here to bring you to the
residency when you are ready."

"Is it far?"

"Less than a mile."

"It won't take us long." He turned back and said, "Pack as
many of the tents on to Duchess and put the rest on Dublin."

"Won't you be riding, sir?"

"No, Sergeant, I can walk." He turned to the official.

I was dressed and Lieutenant Crozier turned to me, "Ready
Smith? Recovered from your ordeal?"

"Yes sir."

"Sergeant."

"Put on your packs."

We all obeyed. I knew how to pack the tents so that they were
a balanced load and the others were happy to take instructions
from me. That done we donned our packs and put our blankets
en banderole.

"Attention. Slope arms. Left face. March!" I took Duchess'
reins, and I saw that Dublin was led by the lieutenant. I had not
seen many officers but our lieutenant appeared to me to be
different. Certainly, Mr. Galbraith looked surprised that an
officer would lead his own horse and not ride.

I saw men who clearly worked for the company waiting with
carts to bring the supplies that had been unloaded. I suppose we

could have put our tents and muskets with those but the lieutenant liked to be in control of events. This way nothing could be lost for it was under our close supervision the whole time. There was a mixture of European and Indian people that we passed as we headed through the streets. As with Calcutta, there were many shops. The three cities controlled by the company were prosperous places. When we had sought the hostages, we had passed mainly wooden structures in the villages of Bengal. There were temples and palaces but stone buildings for what one might term ordinary people were rare. The same appeared to be true here in the Madras Residency.

When we neared the residency, I saw that there were red coats there already. They were guarding the buildings. We learned that they were the 1st Battalion Madras Native Infantry. They looked smart enough but instead of either a shako or bonnet, they wore a turban. They had short trousers that looked to me, like underwear that had shrunk in the laundry. They were also barefoot. The havildar had them present arms as the lieutenant passed. He did not look down his nose at us as had the havildar at Calcutta. It looked as though things might change here.

Mr. Galbraith pointed to an open piece of ground to the north of the residency, a whitewashed stone building with the company flag flying, "Have your men pitch their tents there, Lieutenant, on that patch of open ground."

"Is there a stable?"

"It is to the rear of the residency."

"Smith, Cathcart, see to the horses. Take over, Sergeant, and I shall deliver my missive to the resident."

I would be glad to get in the shade of the residency. The heat had drained me on the walk from the beach, not to mention the exertions of my immersion. We were an efficient section. The sergeant barely had to give an order. We all knew what to do. We unfastened our blankets, stacked our muskets and dropped our packs. Bob and I held the reins of the horses while the rest took the tents and erected them where Sergeant Grundy marked the ground with his bayonet.

We walked the two horses along the north wall, grateful for the shade, and I saw the stable block. It was not a large building and I hoped that there would be stalls as well as food within.

There were two Indians mucking out the horses. I saw that four of the stalls were occupied. I tried my Bengali and said, "We leave the horses here?" to emphasise my meaning I pointed to two empty stables. The two men nodded.

Bob deferred to me. I had not intended to become the expert in all things equine but I did not mind the role. He waited with Duchess while I led Dublin into the first empty stall and, after securing him, took off his saddle. Duchess waited patiently. Thanks to our care the animal had improved since we had been looking after her. The rest of the section, like me, spoiled her and gave her treats whenever we could. I put the nosebag I found in the stall on Dublin's head and then took Duchess' reins.

"You have a palace here, Duchess. I think you will be happy." She whinnied and nodded her head.

"She understands you!" Bob sounded incredulous.

"They are not stupid creatures. I am not sure she understands my words but the kindly tone and the stroking of her mane help."

We found pails of water and made sure that they were full. I put on Dublin's nosebag and Bob copied me with Duchess. I said, "You can head back to the tents, Bob. I will just make sure that they have had enough to eat before I take off their nosebags."

"You sure?"

"It is pleasantly cool in here."

The two men who had been in the stable had left and I was alone with the horses. I found a curry comb and while they emptied their nosebags, I combed them both.

I had just taken Dublin's empty bag from him when a handful of straw fell from the hay rack above the stalls. I looked up and a pair of legs appeared. I stepped back as a figure leapt down. It was a European with well-made boots and a silk shirt. He grinned, "You are a rarity. An infantryman who cares for horses. Are you with the chaps who just came in?" He spoke in the tone of a gentleman.

"Yes, sir."

He walked up to Dublin and stroked his mane, "A fine animal, but I am guessing the other one is your favourite."

"Yes, sir, she is."

"I can tell from the affection you show her." He held out his hand, "Geoffrey Tucker, gentleman and, according to some, wastrel. I am pleased to meet you..."

"Smith, Private Smith." Whenever I said the word Smith it sounded foreign to me.

We shook hands and he laughed, "And I am sure that was not the name used by your mother. What did she call you?"

There was something about this man that invited confidences and I said, "Bill, sir." For one thing he had been happy to shake my hand even though he knew he was my superior and the handshake had been a firm one.

"Well, it has been a pleasure to meet you, Bill." He took his jacket and wide-brimmed hat from the hooks on the wall. I had not noticed them and donning them, he left the stables as though he owned them, humming a tune.

As I walked back to our camp I saw that the sepoy battalion had their own camp and they had their fires going and food was being cooked. I recognised the pungent smell of the spices they used. I had been so long at the stables that darkness was rapidly approaching and our campfires were lit. I was hungry.

Ben pointed to a tent, "You are in that one, Smudger, with Aadyot, Cathcart and Byers." I went into the tent and saw that they had laid their blankets out already. I took mine and placed that at the side. In the fading light, I quickly checked for reptiles and insects. There were none. I folded my tunic and laid it at the top of the blanket. That done I took off my boots. It was a relief. I emptied the sand from them and then removed my socks. The socks were placed on the tunic. They were a little damp; it was a mixture of sweat and the sea. When they dried, I would shake the sand from them. Already the buzzing insects were gathering in the tent. I took out my pipe and went outside. The others were chattering about the usual inconsequential matters: the camp, Madras, the voyage down and so on. I filled my pipe and lit a twig from the fire. I soon had the pipe going and I returned to the tent. I smoked for a few moments to allow a cloud of smoke to form and when the insects departed I went outside and allowed the pipe to die.

Seamus turned as I approached the others. Albert and George were cooking the meal and the rest were seated on whatever had been to hand. The sergeant, it seemed, was taking a nap. "Here he is, the intrepid merman!"

The others cheered. Seamus moved along the log he had commandeered and I sat next to him.

Dai said, "Weren't you petrified when you dived into the sea?" Dai and Seamus were the toughest and biggest men in the section. His tone implied that he would not have done what I did.

I shrugged, "I didn't dive, I jumped. Yes, I was terrified but the sailors gave me good advice and that piece of cork more than kept me afloat. But, let us say that I don't want to do it again in a hurry."

The other smokers had their pipes out and the conversation tailed off until all we heard was the sound of insects and the crackling of the fire. The sepoy camp was a distant hum. We could smell the food as it cooked. We had learned to judge, by the smell, when it would be ready. We would soon eat.

I said to the sergeant, "Where is the lieutenant?"

"He is dining with the resident. He might even be granted a bed."

Seamus tapped the ash from his pipe, "That is a good reason to be an officer. The privilege of rank."

Dai laughed, "Could you imagine this big Mick as an officer?" He mimicked his friend, "Right, me lads, let's charge these ten thousand men, eh, have a bit of fun?"

Seamus laughed, "Better than some Taff shouting," he mimicked the Welshman, "well, there's lovely for you. How about you open fire, eh, and then we will sing a hymn?"

That they could mock each other showed their friendship.

Bob said, "I am happy to be at the bottom of this particular pile. I don't mind being told what to do."

Sergeant Grundy had risen from his nap and he pointed the stem of his pipe at me, "There's one who could be an officer. Our Smudger can think. The lieutenant was very impressed with how he conducted himself when we rescued the hostages. He told me that it could have all ended badly but for Smith's quick thinking."

I felt all their eyes on me and I shook my head, "I am like Bob here, happy to be the one who leads Duchess and follows orders."

"Food's ready."

We rose and took our plates. We lined up in rank order. Seamus let me stand behind the corporal. Even if I did not like it, they saw me as more than a private. Aadyot was at the rear. We all took turns cooking. Some were better at it than others but the food was palatable. Aadyot had his own spices and he seasoned his own food. When he cooked the food was slightly spicy. Albert and George had added some greens they had either found or stolen to the stew as well as the inevitable dried beans. I knew that the beans would be harder than they ought to be. Albert and George were impatient cooks. The dixie of tea would be sweetened and I hoped that they had found some milk. I could drink tea without milk but I never enjoyed it. I was now used to drinking tea that had goat's milk or sheep's milk added but I dreamed of cow's milk.

Sergeant Grundy said, "Tomorrow, we will try to get some fresh food." We had been issued with more salted beef and dried beans on the ship and being natural thieves we had all managed to find the ship's hold and take whatever treasures we could find. I had taken some carrots I had discovered. They were not for me but for the horses. He nodded to Aadyot, "The lieutenant will give you the money, Aadyot." The sepoy nodded. He was now an integral part of our section and indispensable to us.

One advantage of our present camp was that we did not have to stand watch; the sepoy battalion did that. After the meal, we smoked and talked. Some of the others played cards or dice. A couple of the men, Seamus and Dai, especially liked to sing and they sang ballads from home. Their voices were good and it was soothing to hear the songs that evoked home. I sat with Aadyot at the entrance to our tent and smoked so that my smoke would clear away the insects.

"What do we do down here, Smudger?"

"I am not sure but from what I have gathered we are here to stop a war."

He nodded, "When I went to the latrine I spoke with some of the other soldiers. They said that the Tipu of Mysore hates the English and has allied with," I saw him struggling with the word, "the French?"

I nodded, "Aye, the Froggies. Back at home, there is a war between our country and theirs. If it has spread over here…"

"I do not understand. Why would these, Froggies," I smiled at the way he pronounced the word that was new to him, "wish to come to this land and fight for it?"

"They want an Empire I think."

"We are a poor country, Smudger. I know that the company has made life better for us but if there is a war then it is poor people who will suffer."

I had not thought of the people. I was so concerned with surviving and, when the time came, to escaping, that the lives of the ordinary people never even entered my head. "In that case, you can rest easy. I am sure that the Lieutenant knows what he is doing. If anyone can stop a war it is him." Even as I said it, I wondered how a handful of redcoats could do anything.

We had the luxury of a long sleep, and when the bugle sounded to wake the sepoy battalion we did not jump from our beds. We had nowhere to go and nothing to do. It was the need to make water and empty our bowels that made us leave our beds. I donned my tunic after I had made water, "Sergeant, I will see to the horses."

He nodded, "We will save you breakfast."

I wandered around the residence to the stables. The horses both whinnied and nodded their heads when I went in. I had two carrots in my tunic pockets. The two stable hands were mucking out the other stalls. I held out my hands and proffered the carrots, "Good morning. Let us have a little perambulation around the yard, eh? I do not think we will be travelling today." While they crunched the carrots I untied their leaders and led them from the stalls. The yard outside was cobbled and I walked the two of them around its perimeter. I sang to them as I walked. I sang the song sung the previous night by Seamus. He had sung it three times and I had been able to learn it. It was a song about an elf who threatened to abduct a young woman to be his lover unless she could perform impossible tasks. Bob had known the song for there was a Scottish version too and he had joined in.

> *O, where are you going? To Scarborough Fair,*
> *Savoury sage, rosemary, and thyme;*
> *Remember me to a lass who lives there,*

For once she was a true love of mine.
And tell her to make me a cambric shirt,
my plaid away, my plaid away,
the wind shall not blow my plaid away
Savoury sage, rosemary, and thyme,
Without any seam or needlework,
And then she shall be a true love of mine.
And tell her to wash it in yonder dry well,
my plaid away, my plaid away,
the wind shall not blow my plaid away
Savoury sage, rosemary, and thyme,
Where no water sprung, nor a drop of rain fell,
And then she shall be a true love of mine
my plaid away, my plaid away,
the wind shall not blow my plaid away

I found that singing seemed to soothe the horses and the song made it easier for me to march. By the time I reached the stalls, I saw that the two stable hands had cleared away the dirty straw and replaced it. After tying the horses up I did what I had seen Aadyot do when speaking to his countrymen. He put his hands together before him and bobbed his head. I said, "Thank you."

They both beamed and made the same gesture. It was a little thing but I felt as though I had communicated with them. It was Seamus and Dai who had cooked breakfast. They had made porridge and fried some salted beef. It was not a combination I would have contemplated back in England but here, sweetened with some palm sugar, it was a treat. We did not always eat porridge. For one thing, it took longer to cook and flatbread was quicker. The other reason was that the pot always took serious cleaning. We indulged ourselves because we knew that we would not be moving this day.

It was noon before the lieutenant returned. The sergeant made sure that all our chores were completed but we did not have to drill. Our camp was clean, the pots were washed and we all felt like gentlemen of leisure.

The lieutenant was in a good mood. "Gather the men around, Sergeant."

Seamus quipped, "A good night, sir? Did you enjoy a soft bed?"

The lieutenant smiled, "That I did, Hogan. I drank good wine, enjoyed a fine cigar, drank good brandy and this morning had bacon, eggs, sausages and black pudding. There was white bread and toast. Life does not get any better than that."

All of us could almost taste the food he had eaten. As much as we had enjoyed our own breakfast his was the stuff of dreams. We did not resent him his bounty. He was an officer and a gentleman. Such things came their way but the description seemed to feed us too.

We gathered around him and he waved us to sit. "We have been given an interesting assignment. Lord Mornington, it seems, was so impressed by our service in the hills that he has sent us here to do something of a similar nature." I was desperate to ask questions but I had learned that such questions merely irritated the lieutenant. "We are to head to Hyderabad. The resident wants us to intercept messages that are coming from France to the Nizam of Hyderabad. He has some French troops in his land and Lord Mornington fears that they are the start of an invasion. Until more British troops arrive it is we who have to act as spies."

Bob could not help himself, "Spies, sir? Don't spies get shot?"

The lieutenant laughed, "Aye, they do, Cathcart, so let us not get caught, eh? We are going to pretend to be Froggies. The resident has some French tunics left over from the last time we fought the French and we shall wear them. Our old tricorns and breeches are close enough to the French style to pass muster."

Sergeant Grundy said, dubiously, "Sir, can you speak French? I know I can't and these lads can barely speak English."

The officer laughed, "Not well enough to fool a real Frenchman but we have a chap who does. He will be coming this afternoon. I met him last night and he seems like a resourceful sort of fellow. Today, we go back to school and learn some French. Tomorrow, we head into Hyderabad." He turned to me, "How are the horses, Smith? Have they recovered from their swim?"

"Yes, sir, they seem in fine fettle."

"Good. You have time now until after the noon break. If you wish to go into Madras to make any purchases then do so but I want you all back here at one p.m."

I had enough tobacco, I had found some on the ship and filled my pouch, but I wanted another shirt and some socks. I still had money and I wanted to be comfortable. When I ran, and that was still my plan, I wanted some clothes that did not look military. I would also see if I could buy some treats for the horses. A few of us had similar ideas and we left just the sergeant at the camp. Aadyiot was given money to buy food to augment our supplies.

We were all more confident now. We knew how to barter and we did not need to go around the town in numbers. I went alone and sought out places where I could buy what I needed. Rafe and Ned had been right. A man could live well out here for the two shirts and four pairs of socks I bought, not to mention the breeches, cost me less than a week's pay. The others, when I met them again, were surprised at my purchases. They did not know my plans. I shrugged off their interest saying that I just wished to be comfortably dressed. What I really wanted was a decent pair of boots, a gentleman's boots. The company-issued boots would mark me as a soldier. When I ran I wanted to be anonymous. Others bought tobacco, pipes and, when we found somewhere that served it, beer. Almost all of the company now owned a pipe. The ones who had not already done so bought one at the tobacconists we found in Madras. It was run by an Englishman who had worked for the company and saw the need for such a shop. We all enjoyed a smoke in his shop as he told us more about the situation this close to Mysore. When we left, we all felt that we knew a little bit more about the threat from the corpulent ruler of Mysore. We learned that the British had fought and defeated him before but the French threat was, apparently, a very real one. The tobacconist was happy at our presence and our news that the 33rd would soon be joining us made him rub his hands together. It meant profit for him.

We made sure that we were back not long after the clock in the centre of the town chimed the hour of twelve. The sergeant and Aadyot had cooked up a spicy stew for lunch. Aadyot had managed to buy a couple of animals from the Madras Battalion as well as some fresh food and spices from the market. None of us enquired what the beastie had been. It was better not to know. The handful of spices that were used would disguise the taste in any case. The lieutenant had returned to the residency and we had begun to eat when he came back accompanied by the man I had met in the stables, Geoffrey Tucker.

He grinned when he neared the almost empty pot, "I say, that smells appetising. I can see that serving with you chaps I shall be well fed." He was one of the most affable men I had ever met. With his lazy, laconic drawl and easy smile, he made you feel his friend, which clearly we were not for he was a gentleman and we were the sweepings of the gutter.

The lieutenant said, "This is the Honourable Geoffrey Tucker."

The man shook his head, "I would be obliged if you would refrain from my title. My cousin uses it but I fear that many of the things I have done have been far from honourable."

"Very well. We will be following Mister Tucker," he emphasised the word, '*mister*', "when we head into Hyderabad. We have this afternoon to learn as much French from him as we can. You don't need to be able to speak it but you should be able to understand French commands. We will masquerade as Frenchmen. This afternoon the uniforms will be brought over. We will not try them on until dark. The fewer people who know of our disguise the better. Just as we shall spy on the French who knows if the French will be spying on us."

"Quite. To that end, I shall be wearing the uniform of a captain and so you can all address me as Capitaine." He pronounced it in French. "Now let us all try saying, "Oui mon capitaine." He smiled, "It means yes, my captain. You will find that oui and non, yes and no, are very useful. Let us try it."

We all did so with varying degrees of success.

He smiled, "Not bad but most of your accents are atrocious." He nodded towards Bob, "You, my friend, are doing a wonderful job of massacring French! Would that our armies had the same success on the battlefield. Now let us begin." He went through all the military phrases such as attention, stand easy, slope arms, quick march and so on. After each one he had us say, 'Oui mon capitaine.' He taught us the French for lieutenant and sergeant. Thankfully, they were quite similar. Then he looked at me, "And you, young Smith, you need to know a few more phrases, for you are the ostler." I inwardly groaned. I had to learn the French for horse, reins, saddle, hooves and the like. It was much to take in. he smiled, "You have done well and when we are on the road I will continue your lessons, Private Smith, and those of the lieutenant and sergeant." He stretched, "Any chance of a brew? I don't know about the rest of you but I feel as dry as the Sahara desert."

Bob said, "I might be no good at French 'mon capitaine', but I can make a good pot of tea."

"Splendid fellow."

Sergeant Grundy had also been struggling and he asked, "Sir, Captain Tucker, what exactly are we supposed to do?"

"An excellent question. We will set up position on the road to Hyderabad and wait for the French messengers to bring their weekly communication to their commander in Hyderabad and the Nizam. We are going to take the message from them. The French send men from Goa which lies to the south and west of Hyderabad. We will wait on the road from the south as close as we can to Hyderabad. We intercept messages and gather intelligence for General Harris, who is on his way here with the troops who will impress upon the Nizam the need to remain loyal to Great Britain and the East India Company. He is, shall we say, wavering in his loyalty."

The old soldier persisted, "Then why do we need to know French, sir? I can understand the uniforms but why don't we just surround them and take the message?"

"And suppose there are more than a couple of them? What if they manage to destroy the message? No, Sergeant Grundy," he pronounced it in the French manner, "we need them to think that we are French so that their guard is down. We may have to wait for some time and if the locals think we are French then they will not report our presence to Hyderabad."

Sergeant Grundy nodded. What our temporary new leader had said made sense, especially to me. My life had been one where I had lied and deceived people. I liked this man who had called himself a wastrel.

The tea was served and as we drank it Ben asked, "Sir, what about our weapons? As far as I know the French use a different musket."

"You are right, the Charleville musket is different from yours. I am hoping that they won't notice them. We have a few French pistols for you to use. If most of the muskets are carried in the cart that is being provided then we shall have weapons that will seem appropriate and the means to overpower them. Sergeant Grundy, some French sergeants carry a short sword. You will have one such weapon and, I believe, you still have the tricorn hats favoured by the Jacobin soldiers. We also have four tricolour rosettes and they will add to the illusion that we are French soldiers."

By the time the gentleman had finished, we were all exhausted and yet we had done no physical activity. "I will see you all in the morning. We leave before dawn. We will be noticed but not by many. Once we are closer to Hyderabad and in French-influenced land we will change into French uniforms and, once we do, then nothing will be spoken in English." His face and voice were serious, "That is the most important thing to remember."

He turned and left. I said, "I had better tend to…" I tried to remember the words Captain Tucker, as I now thought of him, had said, "Les chevaux!"

The lieutenant grinned, "Well done, Smith!"

I strode off to the stables. When I reached it I found Geoffrey Tucker speaking to his horse, he turned at my approach, "As you can see, Bill, I too will be riding and not walking. In the absence of anyone else to look after Caesar, I would appreciate it if you would. You seem to have a way with horses."

"Of course, sir."

"And now, while we tend to our chargers, let us continue with the French lessons."

He began to teach me the words for the saddles, reins and leaders. By the time I returned to the camp and food I was even more tired but I felt more confident, not only about understanding French but also speaking a little of it.

The uniforms, rosettes and weapons, when they were delivered by four sepoys, were wrapped up. The men did not know the contents of the packages. As soon as it was dark enough we took them into our tents to change into. There was much swapping until we were all happy with what we had. The sergeant, corporal and lieutenant had no choice in the matter. The rosettes were also distributed and, like the uniforms, were given to the men that they fitted. Ben, the sergeant, Dai and I were given the pistols along with a small pouch of balls. I had never fired a pistol but the mechanism looked to be like our musket.

"Now pack your uniforms, hats and pistols in your packs. Get a good night's sleep. Smith, when we rise, fetch my horse and Duchess. The cart we are to use will be delivered first thing."

I nodded, "Sir, what do the other soldiers think we are doing?"

"They have been told that we are to head into the hinterland and scout out a new fort. Captain Tucker has been assigned as an engineer. When you see him tomorrow his uniform will be that of an engineer." I nodded. "The resident is a clever man, Smith. He and his cousin have thought this plan out well. This should be safer than setting fire to a bandit fort, eh?"

Before I retired, I cleaned the pistol and fitted a new flint. I realised that I was in a privileged position. After I had fired my musket I would have a second weapon to fire immediately. The memory of the firefight at the fort was still fresh in my mind.

Chapter 15

I had discovered that rising before dawn made the day easier. It was cooler then to wash and dress and the horses responded better to the cooler air. I went directly to the stables and found that I was the first one there. I fitted the nosebags, "Eat well, for after today, like us, you will endure hard rations." As they ate I surreptitiously filled a sack with feed from the residency's supplies and took it back to the camp where I planned to hide it until we loaded the cart. The others were rising as I neared our camp.

John Williams was livening up the fire ready to heat water, "You are up early."

I shook the bag, "It is the early bird that gets the food for the horses." I put the bag beneath the cot in my tent. I would pack it where I could easily reach it on the road.

I hurried back to the stables and filled the two pails with water. When they had finished their nosebags I let them drink and then led them from the stable. The movement helped them to empty their bowels and to make water. The two stable hands came out and I bowed to them. They bowed to me. One of them handed me a couple of what looked like apples. They had clearly practised for one said, "You leave today. For horses."

I said, in Bengali, "Thank you." I did not know if I would ever see them again but I had learned, since I had fled my home, to make friends when you could. It had made my life much easier in the Indiaman.

I put the fruit in my waistcoat pocket and led the horses back into the stable. They drank some more. I knew that this was good water and who knew what awaited us on the road? I put the saddle blanket and saddle on Dublin, but I just laid them there. I would put the saddle on properly just before we left. I found it was easier to tighten his girths if he had worn the saddle for a little while.

I said, "Goodbye," over my shoulder and we clip-clopped across the cobbles.

When I reached the camp the cart had been delivered. I had driven the tethering spike into the ground before I had left, and I now tied the two horses to it and put the saddle cloth, blanket and saddle in my tent. That done, and in the light of dawn, I examined the cart. It was well made and the axles of the wooden wheels had been greased. As with most of the carts I had seen, it had solid wheels rather than spokes. It was not pretty but I knew it would be sturdier than one with spoked wheels and, more importantly, we could easily repair it. It was larger than the one we had used in Calcutta. It looked big enough to take a man. I knew that Duchess was stronger now and I hoped she would be able to bear the extra weight. I saw that there were two leather pails hanging from two hooks. They would be handy. There were hooks around the side and I began to work out what would be attached and where. When I was satisfied that there were no defects in the cart, I used the log we had sat upon to prop up the shafts and said, "The cart is ready for loading, Sergeant."

He shouted, "The ones loading their muskets on the cart bring them here. The rest of you, get the tents down. Remember we wear the blankets en banderole today." They groaned knowing that we would be even hotter that way. When the muskets were brought, we stacked them alongside the cart, mine included. There was an order to the packing. The food would go at the bottom followed by the tents. Then we would put the water and muskets on the top. I had worked out that we could hang some knapsacks from the side. By the time the food and tea were ready, the cart was packed. The cooking pots, when cleaned, would be hung from the back. The cart felt heavy and I hoped that Duchess would cope. I hung my contraband horse food from the back so that it would be a buffer between the two pots and stop them from clanging together.

I saw the lieutenant coming from the residence along with our new officer. Captain Tucker looked splendid in his uniform as he led Caesar towards us. It was tailored and looked almost brand new. He had a long sabre hanging from his belt. It was not curved like that of the lieutenant and I guessed he had chosen it because he was comfortable with it. I saw that he had two holsters attached to his saddle and they each held a pistol. Lieutenant Crozier had also acquired a holster for his French pistol.

"Good morning."

We all snapped to attention, "Sir."

After we had eaten I saddled Dublin and then asked Bob and Edmund to help me with Duchess and the cart. They took the strain of the cart while I removed the log and I backed Duchess into the shafts. I made sure that she had a blanket to stop the harness from chafing and I did not let my two companions let her take the weight until I was satisfied that she was ready for the road.

Edmund rubbed his arm, "She is a horse, Smudger."

I nodded, "And the way you are rubbing your arm tells me that the cart is heavy. If anything happens to Duchess, then we have to carry all this gear or pull the cart. What do you think?"

"Aye, I suppose."

We had been supplied with an axe and a small saw. I hooked those on the sides, too, reasoning that we might need to use them on the journey and the last thing I wanted to do was to unpack the whole cart. The axe meant we would not have to blunt our bayonets cutting kindling. The axe would do it far more quickly.

When all was ready the two officers mounted their horses. "Forward, march!"

As we set off, I glanced towards the balcony at the residency. I saw a figure there, smoking a cheroot. I did not recognise him but I guessed it was the man who was setting us forth on this mission, James Kirkpatrick. I took comfort, as I urged Duchess, that he had sent his cousin and he did not regard our mission as a forlorn hope. The sergeant had told me that a forlorn hope was a group of men who volunteered to attack a breach at a siege. They would often be rewarded for such bravery but as few of them would survive it was always made up of volunteers. We had not been offered the chance to volunteer.

We were heading north, as we had done from Calcutta, and as with that journey, we could see in the distance the ground rising up. It was, the captain said, the Deccan plateau. Poor Duchess would need help to carry the heavy load that she had on the cart. We would have to attach ropes and pull her when we reached the steeper sections and, if we descended, use them as brakes. The outskirts of Madras seemed to go for miles but eventually, as at Calcutta, the homes thinned out and the tended fields disappeared, replaced by forest.

"Can we sing, Lieutenant Crozier?" asked Seamus.

I had become used to singing when on the ship. Sailors used songs to give a rhythm to their efforts and I had discovered it also cheered them.

"Why, Hogan?"

"It cheers a man, sir, and helps us to march."

We still, naturally, directed our questions to Lieutenant Crozier. I had no idea if the captain's rank was a real one. The uniform looked real enough but, like the French uniforms, it could simply be a costume, a disguise.

"I suppose so."

Unlike me, Seamus knew hundreds of songs as did Dai. The two began to sing and, as we learned the words, we joined in. The big Irishman was right. It did cheer the spirits and made the threatening jungle of trees seem less threatening and oppressive. It evoked memories of home. I found that I was increasingly missing what we had left behind. I yearned for cold and rain, fog and sleet. I wanted the smoky smell of wood fires and the calls of costermongers. It might pass but I was not so certain. It might have been the smells I disliked in this land. I did not know. Perhaps, when I ran, I could make more money and then return home, re-inventing myself so that Ralph Every would not even recognise me with a new name and a new identity. As we sang the road songs I became more cheerful. I had hope of a return to England.

That night as we camped close to a small and apparently nameless village, the captain told us a little more of our mission. "We have over three hundred and fifty more miles to cover. If we can make thirty miles a day then I shall be happy. The biggest obstacle, the plateau apart, will be the Krishna River. My disguise as an engineer may be called upon." I could not tell if he was serious or not. "We may well have to build a raft. Once we have crossed the river we will change into French uniforms." He lit a cheroot, "And with that in mind, it is time for another French lesson."

There were groans although to be fair to him, he tried to make it fun. His best two students, the lieutenant apart, were Ben and me. Each day we understood more and whilst our accents, so the captain said, were atrocious, we began to understand more of what he had said. Poor Aadyot was all at sea. The captain said that would not matter. The French, he told us, despite their apparent Republican views, regarded Indians as unimportant. Aadyot seemed quite happy that he would be overlooked.

As we ate our supplies the journey became easier for Duchess. When we used all the water in our skins we boiled up more from the many rivers we passed and just kept those topped up. The lieutenant had been given money in Madras to pay for supplies and whenever we passed a village, we bought whatever they had. At one village we bought the hindquarter of a goat. Aadyot skilfully butchered it so that we had the meat and were able to boil the bones to make a soup. We became skilled at varying our diet.

When the French uniforms had been delivered so, too, had our pay. Annoyingly it was too late for us to be able to spend in Madras but it allowed those who enjoyed gambling to either increase or decrease their coins in games of chance. I had known enough tricksters to know that such games of chance often did not rely on luck but dexterity. It rarely came to blows and the sergeant was always on hand to defuse an angry situation. Life on the road had, like the songs we sang, a rhythm to it. I rose first and took the horses their food and drink. I checked their coats for wildlife. There were, so the captain told me, parasites that sucked the blood of horses. When they were fed and watered I would eat my breakfast and, while the tents were taken down, I packed the cart. Sometimes we did not erect all the tents and three times, when we reached a village, we did not use them at all. Those days saw us make more miles. We sang as we marched behind the two officers who chattered away. One thing I noticed was that Sergeant Grundy, whilst he never fell behind, was struggling more than the rest of us. When we had the chance he sat more than the rest of us and, if we had the chance, he enjoyed a nap. It was no surprise. He was much older and a little portlier. None of us minded and we made sure that he was not disturbed. He was the most experienced soldier that we had and we wanted him looked after. When we camped at night I had my equine duties to attend to and that was when men, with time on their hands, would gamble or use the time productively to carve and whittle. When I thought about it, my life was completely different to that of the Blackwall thief. There my life had been lived from moment to moment as I took my chances when they came. Here I had structure. There I had been alone and here I was part of a unit. I was not particularly chatty but I was comfortable with these men and their companionship.

When we reached it, crossing the Krishna River necessitated the building of a raft and this time there was never even a question of swimming the horses. I was relieved. The sea was one thing but the murky waters of this Indian river were terrifying. We would build a raft large enough to fit us all. There was plenty of timber and after an afternoon of hewing, we had enough logs which we would bind together, using lianas and creepers, to build the raft. We rose early and by mid-morning had built a raft and we also made eight long poles.

Captain Tucker had to have had a most interesting past for he knew how to make a steering board for the rear. He did not construct it himself but Lowe and Byers followed his clear and simple instructions. He also had them make two posts at the other end. As he said, we would need one at both ends if we were to use it on our return journey. When our vessel was finished, we floated it on the river but kept it secured to the land. We loaded the horses first. I led Duchess and the cart to ensure that it was balanced then the two officers followed, leading their own horses. The raft did not seem to sink too much. With the men loaded, Bob took Caesar's reins as the captain would operate the steering board.

"Push us off. I will try to compensate for the current with the rudder but I expect that we will end up further downstream. I will try to find a clearing where we can land. You polemen need to push together."

Seamus said, "We shall sing a work song, sir."

Seamus started the song. His repertoire meant he had one that made it easier for the poles to push at the same time. The river was lively and, once again, I spoke quietly to Duchess and it calmed not only her but the other two horses. They had become familiar with my voice and it appeared to reassure them. My attention to Duchess meant I did not observe our passage as closely as the men with the poles but when the movement became less violent and I was able to look up I saw that we were just twenty feet from what looked like a beach. We ground on the sand and the stones. We led the horses and the cart off first and while Bob went back to help the others haul the raft up onto the beach, I held Caesar's and Dublin's reins.

The officers held a council of war while the sergeant and the rest of the section tied the raft to trees ready for our return passage. I was able to overhear their words.

"By my reckoning, Richard, there should be a road just a mile north of here."

The lieutenant looked and pointed, "And that looks to be a small trail that the cart could use."

I knew that if I was alone I would have no chance of survival as I could not work out when we were in the trees, which was east and which was west. The two officers had compasses as well as a map. Comfortingly, they seemed to know what they were doing.

The captain turned to me, "Well Smith, you are our carter, what do you think?"

I saw the opening and it looked just about wide enough. "I might need to use my bayonet to clear some of the undergrowth sir, but, aye, I think so."

"Good, then we make for the road and camp once we reach it." The captain rolled up the map and shouted, "This is the last order in English. From now on we speak French or whisper. We will make camp soon and then we change into blue." He smiled, "Allez, mes amis!"

He began to hum a tune as he put his foot in his stirrup. I whispered, "Sir, what is that tune?"

He turned and leaned in close to me, "It is the Marseillaise, the song of the Republicans."

With the lieutenant and the sergeant at the rear, we headed along the trail. The captain used his sabre to clear any branches that threatened to impede our progress and, being on the back of Caesar, was able to hack in two the serpent that hung down from a branch. After a little over a mile, I saw that the light was brighter ahead and sure enough we found the road. We spent a short time removing the insects, especially the spiders, that had dropped onto our uniforms and into the cart while the two officers consulted their maps and compasses again.

"Allez."

With the captain leading the way we travelled along the road. Not as good as one we might have found in England, it was still much easier than the trail. We did not encounter a village but we found an area that had been cleared of trees. It looked as though someone had attempted to farm it, there was the remains of a crude house, but failed. It suited us.

Captain Tucker pointed and said, "Piquets."

We all understood that word as it had been one of the commands we had practised. We soon had a fire going and water on for both a brew and food. I fitted the horse's nose bags and put a little of the food I had brought for them into each one. The former farm had enough for them to graze but I liked to give them better food when I could.

While the food was cooking the captain held up his blue uniform. We all nodded and changed from the red of the East India Company to French Republican blue. We donned our old tricorns. They were shapeless enough to suggest that they had seen serious wear. Those with the rosettes attached them while others tied the tricolour sashes that had been delivered with the uniforms around our waists. Captain Tucker and the lieutenant went around the camp to inspect us. They seemed satisfied. I saw that Sergeant Grundy's uniform had the three stripes but also what looked like a repaired bullet hole. I wondered if the previous owner had died in battle. The captain had told us that some of the uniforms were from the dead but others were taken from prisoners. It looked like the only one we could positively identify as being from a corpse was the sergeant's and he did not seem put out by it.

We knew that we were close to the part of the land where we might find the French so little was spoken and what we did speak was in French. The two officers seemed happy to converse in French. Ben and I tried a little and found that we could understand one another.

We had sentry duty at night and that meant we were all a little more tired as we headed along the road. That first day north of the Krishna River we made thirty miles for the road was quite well maintained. When we stopped the two officers and the

171

sergeant held a conference, shielded by the three horses. It was in whispered English but I was close enough to hear it.

The captain had decided that as we were forty or so miles from Hyderabad and this was the main road into the city from the south west and south east, we would camp and wait for any messengers travelling along the road. I saw that it was a crossroads but there was no village. The land was relatively open and I spied grazing for the horses. We set up a camp and erected two of the tents. The captain produced, like a conjurer, a tricolour flag which we put on an improvised pole. I knew that we were all about deception. Any French messenger would see what they expected to see; a French detachment camped close to water. They might wonder the purpose of the detachment but they would not be wary. While we had been south of the river the two officers had gone over the plan as often as they could. We were told that there would be sentries hidden in the trees on the road from the south west. When anybody came close to the camp the sentries would ensure that their escape route was covered and Captain Tucker would use his French and his rank to engage them in conversation. For the first time since we had returned to the fort at Calcutta, we had loaded and primed weapons. I was curious to know how the pistol would perform. I feared that when I discovered that, it would be in the heat of battle.

We settled into a routine. We had no idea how long we would be there and so each day either the sergeant or the corporal would lead men into the forest to forage. If we were French soldiers then we would hunt and gather food and so our actions seemed natural enough. We had not seen anyone on the road but we knew we might be observed. This was not a jungle and was more open. There were deer to be hunted and when we heard shots fired from our men we were not unduly worried. The first day two small deer were hunted and we ate well. Aadyot went with the foragers each day for he knew what we could eat and what was poisonous.

I was spared the hunting as I was in charge of the three horses. Either the captain or the lieutenant was always with the sentries on the road. Their French would be invaluable. I was left to keep the fires burning and watch the horses. I also had a routine. When the sentries were set and the foragers left I would add fuel to the fire and boil water. While the water came to temperature I would take the three horses, one by one, to fresh grazing. I gave each of them a walk to loosen their bowels and allow them to do so away from the camp. Our own latrine was also in the forest. When I returned I would scoop the boiled water into the waterskins using the funnel we had brought. That done I made a brew and put on the stew that we would eat. We found that by cooking, as Seamus said, the life out of the meat, the stew was more nutritious and the meat easier to digest. We had grown used to Aadyot's spices and even enjoyed them. In such a manner a week passed and the foraging meant that no one was bored. I found that I could understand more French than when we had started. I could also speak it, after a fashion. There were travellers on the road but it was always Captain Tucker who spoke to them. He asked them their business and made it sound as though we were an official French patrol.

It was the middle of the afternoon when I heard the sound of a horse's hooves coming down the road. There had been no horses on the road in the week we had been there. It was still too hot and a nap would have been welcome but we had learned to be alert. The flag was visible from some distance away but the captain and the sentries were hidden. The lieutenant and corporal were with me in the camp and my hand went to my pistol butt. The lieutenant shook his head and held his hand up palm out. I took the ladle and went back to the pot to stir it. I saw the blue uniforms and an officer on a horse. He was viewing the camp and, behind him, I saw the blue uniforms of a French detachment. Some of the men were mounted behind the officer. I recognised stripes on one of them. The other soldiers wore uniforms so similar to ours that we could have been part of the same unit. Like ours, there were differences between the men's attire. Some had tricorns, some bicorns and a couple wore forage caps. These men had seen service.

Ben sidled up to me and whispered, "Here we go."

Half of the men were foraging and although I could not see all the French detachment, they looked to be at least equal in number to us. I saw the captain and our men move from the trees towards the detachment. There would be just eight of us and nine of them. The French officer dismounted and I heard laughter as the captain led them into the camp. He was a good actor. As we had planned, two men, Dai and Seamus, stayed to watch the road for any others while the rest fanned out behind the nine men of the French detachment. I saw that they had primed and cocked their muskets.

The lieutenant hissed, "You two, keep quiet."

We nodded. Neither of us wore our blue tunics, just our waistcoats. Ben, like me, had a pistol. Our pistols were not in our belts but lay cocked and primed close to hand. He went to the dixie with the tea and began stirring it. We had the pot between us and any danger. Although the French officer, who looked remarkably young, appeared at ease, I saw that the sergeant was looking suspiciously at the camp, especially the horses. I realised that even Duchess was a better horse than the one ridden by the French officer. He would wonder at Caesar and Dublin which were clearly superior mounts. I saw him turn to say something to the grizzled veteran next to him. Both the sergeant and the man to whom he spoke had huge moustaches and looked to be older than the fresh-faced men that they led. Their uniforms also showed that they had seen action. They were patched.

Captain Tucker said, loudly, in French, "Food for the lieutenant and his men. They have travelled far and are tired."

I had no idea what French soldiers serving in India either ate or drank but it was clearly not tea. Even as Ben took a ladle of tea the sergeant was raising his primed musket. I noticed they had not attached their bayonets. It was aimed at the lieutenant. I picked up my pistol as Ben dropped his ladle and reached for his. The lieutenant's pistol was not primed and he drew his sword. I raised the pistol and aimed it at the sergeant. I pulled the trigger and a heartbeat later there was a huge puff of smoke. The ball was larger than the ones in my musket and it hit him in the face. The ball ended his life quickly and as he fell back he discharged his musket into the air as he died. The lieutenant took advantage of the smoke to leap at the other veteran and lunge, expertly, at his throat. I drew my bayonet as Ben fired his pistol at one of the other Frenchmen. Four muskets barked and more Frenchmen fell.

Captain Tucker shouted, his sabre held to the officer's throat, "Cease fire."

Smoke billowed around us. The young officer and the three survivors looked shocked. Five of their number had been slain in a heartbeat. The lieutenant shouted, "Drop your muskets, you are now our prisoners."

The men complied while the young officer was frozen in shock. The captain said, quietly, "Your sword, Lieutenant."

"But you are French!"

The captain gave a sad smile, "A ruse de guerre, we are English."

Sergeant Grundy and the rest of our men raced into the camp having heard the musketry and knew what it meant.

The lieutenant said, "Corporal, take charge of the sentries and well done. You too, Smith, that was smartly done."

The captain said to the French officer, "Would you like help to bury your dead?"

The young man stood proudly and said, "No, we shall do it if you have the tools."

"Smith."

"Sir."

"Shovels."

"Sir." We had two and I went to get them.

"Sergeant Grundy, watch these men as they dig. Private Byers, collect the weapons."

"Sir!"

"Sir!"

We took the blankets that the dead Frenchmen wore en banderole and rolled them around the bodies. It was little enough but it showed some respect.

The two officers went to the French officer's saddle and took the leather satchel from it. I saw that the bag had a wax seal which Captain Tucker broke. He read and then smacked the letter, "We have what we need. The resident will find this more than useful." He turned to the lieutenant, "Richard, could you hold out here for another ten days or so?"

Lieutenant Crozier frowned and then said, "I suppose so, why?"

"I need to get these back to Madras and my cousin. According to this letter from General Bonaparte, the French are closing on

Cairo. This," he smacked the letter again, "would persuade the Nizam to back the French."

"You can't go alone, Geoffrey."

The captain turned to me, "Smith seems to be resourceful. He saved your life today, Richard. How about I take him? He can ride the French lieutenant's horse."

"Well, Smith?"

"I am game, sir, if the captain thinks I can manage it."

He smiled, "I think, Smith, that if you put your mind to it, you could do anything you choose."

"Then I am your man, sir."

"Excellent and you might as well put on the red tunic once more. According to this letter the French troops who will be there to aid the Nizam are based in Mysore, to the south. Until they know that their letters have been intercepted, they will not move."

Chapter 16

We left the next morning. We had two waterskins. One filled with boiled water and the other with tea. We had some dried deer meat and that would have to do until we reached Madras. Before I left, I gave Bob instructions about the horses. It was a wrench to leave Duchess.

I had not ridden before and it took some time for me to become less fearful of falling off. The captain gave me advice, telling me to use my knees and to try to relax. It was easier said than done. That said, I found that by talking to the French horse it made the journey less threatening. We rode hard and I knew that my buttocks would be sore. This time I would not have the cook's grease to ease my chafed skin. Camping in the Deccan forest was not as scary as doing so in the jungle but I was still wary of reptiles and spiders. The captain seemed aware of my fears, and he chattered constantly to keep my mind off things. He did not give me all his secrets, but I learned a little as we headed for the Krishna River. This was not the first time he had been a spy. He had spied for the Duke of York in the Netherlands, and it was there that he had met Colonel Wellesley. "I hope that he has returned from Penang with his regiment. Company battalions are all well and good but what we really need is a British battalion. The 33rd will fit the bill nicely."

When we finally reached the Krishna River, we were both surprised to see red coats on the other side. The captain took out his 'bring 'em near' and laughed, "I say, here is a spot of luck. It is my cousin, the resident. We won't be away for as long as I feared." He cupped his hands and shouted, "Cousin, we have the dispatch. We have a raft here but no means of getting it over."

His cousin cupped his hands and shouted his reply, "I have the 33rd with me. We shall see what they can do." He turned to speak to the officers with him.

We dismounted.

"Smith, get a fire going, eh? I don't know how long this will take."

"Sir."

I soon had one going. I heard the sound of axes on the other side of the river. I then went to take the saddles from the horses. I did not want them getting saddle sores. My journey so far had shown me that the French horse was not a good one. She had stumbled more than once and we had been forced to go slower as a result. I gave them both a nosebag as I tied them to a low branch, after first ensuring that there were no reptiles in the trees. We did not want the horses to be spooked.

When I had finished I saw five redcoats walk towards the opposite bank, without tunics and with improvised paddles. Another six men brought a freshly hewn log. The log was placed in the water and one end of a rope was tied to a tree. The five men straddled the log. Four had paddles and the last man had the other end of the rope coiled around his chest. Most of the rope lay in the water. As soon as they began to paddle, I saw that the rope would help to keep them stable. As we had experienced they found themselves drifting downstream. When they reached the bank, they all helped to move the rope up to the raft.

The one at the fore saluted, "Sergeant Patterson, sir, that was interesting. At least we didn't see crocodiles."

"They like slow water, Sergeant. You were safe enough."

"Thank God for that. Brown, tie the rope to that tree and make it head height and tight." As the four men went to obey the sergeant said, "The resident said to leave your horses here, sir. He will speak to you and then you can go with the battalion to Hyderabad."

Captain Tucker pointed to their legs. They were covered in leeches, "However, you might try to remove those."

"Urgh, little bastards! Sorry sir." He went to remove them.

"Don't do that. That will just result in something worse. Smith."

"Sir." We had experienced leeches and knew the best way to get rid of them. I took a small burning brand from the fire and said, "Hold still, Sergeant, this should work." As I touched each leech they fell and I soon had the dreadful little bloodsuckers removed.

"Thanks, Private." He turned to his men, "Right you lot, the doctor has attended to you. Sort out the rope." The sergeant looked at the raft, "This is handy."

"These chaps made it."

The sergeant looked at me and my facings, "Company man, eh?"

"Yes, Sergeant."

The rope secured and with four men on the poles, the sergeant and I pulled on the rope while the captain steered the raft back across the river. It was much easier this way and we soon reached the other side. The resident, wearing a straw hat and a colonel also wearing a straw hat waited for us.

"Well done, Geoffrey. This is Colonel Wellesley. Colonel, my cousin, the Honourable Geoffrey Tucker."

The stern-faced colonel said, "I believe we have met before, sir."

"Yes, sir, the Netherlands."

The resident said, "I have a tent and we need to speak." He looked at me, "And your man?"

The captain smiled, "Go and find a brew, Smith."

"Sir!"

I smelled the fire and headed for it. A corporal was tending to it, "Any chance of a brew, Corporal?"

"You have a mug?" One thing I had learned was that you always had your mug with you as well as your spoon and your knife. I whipped it around from the back of my belt. He grinned, "An old hand and there I thought that you were a new recruit." He didn't know that I was, but I had been a quick learner. He ladled some into my mug and pointed to a table where there was a metal jug of milk and sugar. "Goat's milk."

I nodded, "I have been here long enough to get used to it."

He suddenly looked at the river, "You were on the other side of the river?"

I nodded as I added the milk and the sugar, "My section made that raft. They are waiting up the road with some French prisoners."

He called over a sergeant, "Hey, Sergeant, this bloke has been in contact with the French."

My words drew a small audience of idlers. The sergeant looked at me sceptically, "Froggies? Where?"

"A couple of days march north of here at a crossroads. We shot five and captured another four. That horse I am riding is the officer's mount."

The sergeant nodded, "Well, lads, it looks like we might get some action at last." I noticed as he spoke a whole sentence that he had a northern accent. He was a Yorkshireman. "Here, Hardcastle, give me a brew, too." He held out his mug. "I am right fed up," he pronounced it '*reet*' "with marching and sailing and then doing bugger all. We might as well be with the Duke of York in the Netherlands if we wanted to do nowt."

An officer came along, "If you have nothing better to do than stand around gossiping like a bunch of old ladies, Sergeant Charlton, I am sure I can find work for you."

He drained his mug and said, "Righto, Lieutenant Smythe. Come on, lads, follow me."

The officer looked down his nose at me, "And where is your officer?" He had an arrogant supercilious tone.

I kept my voice level, "Speaking with Colonel Wellesley, sir." Sometimes you find you dislike someone and there is no real reason for it. So it was with me and Lieutenant Smythe. He was young and that didn't help. The two officers I knew both had experience and knew how to talk to ordinary soldiers. This one did not. It was clear to me that the sergeant and the men would simply move away from the officer and continue to do nothing. They were not like our section; I could see that.

The officer sniffed. He wanted to order me to do something but could think of nothing, "Well, carry on then."

When he had gone, I said to the corporal, "Are all your officers like him?"

He laughed, "No, thank the lord, his father is the adjutant. His father is alright. A bit of a stickler for rules and regulations but his son, well, he is wet behind the ears, knows nowt and thinks he knows it all. He had better watch out that when we do go into action he doesn't get a ball in the back from one of his own men." One again I heard Yorkshire in his voice.

We chatted, inconsequentially, about our mutual experiences of India. I learned that they had arrived in Calcutta not long before us only to be sent to Penang which, apparently, lay to the east across the sea. The action the sergeant had sought had not been forthcoming and they embarked once more to sail to Madras. They had spent a great deal of time at sea. We had seen far more action than they had.

"So, you have never fired a musket in anger?"

The corporal shook his head, "No, but you have only had an action with eight men. That doesn't count."

I was going to tell him about the bandits and then stopped myself. It would sound like bragging. Just then Captain Tucker came over having emerged from the command tent.

"We will spend the night here, Smith, and tomorrow lead a company of the 33rd to the rest of the army. The colonel will be with us, and we shall ride into Hyderabad."

"Sir, what about the horses? We can't leave them over there on their own."

He smiled, "You are an enigma, Smith, by your own admission a confirmed self-serving thief and yet you worry about animals." He rubbed his chin. "Get yourself some food and then I will have you taken across the river on the raft to attend to them."

As much as I didn't want to be on my own I couldn't abandon the horses. Despite the fact that neither of the horses was Duchess I had grown used to the French horse which I had named, in the absence of knowing her real name, as Froggy.

The corporal said, "Food will be ready in an hour, sir."

"Right then. Have food and then I will have you taken across the river."

The food, when it was ready, was adequate, but it was nowhere near as tasty as our food. What they did have was bread and it was child's play to secrete a loaf in my tunic. I also took some root vegetables for the horses. I even managed to fill my pockets with some oats that the 33rd had for their porridge.

I presented myself at the command tent. The captain, his cousin, the colonel, and a captain were seated outside enjoying a smoke.

"Ready for duty, sir."

The colonel turned to the captain, "Captain Smythe, this chap needs to be ferried across the river."

"Right, sir. I will get the men for you."

He strode off and Colonel Wellesley said, "Mr. Tucker here has been telling me of your adventures. You sound like you are a young man with spirit."

"I just do my duty, sir."

I learned that the colonel rarely smiled but I saw a twinkle in his eye as he said, "Volunteering to sleep on the other side of the river sounds like above and beyond, Smith. I look forward to seeing the rest of your motley crew. They sound like a wild bunch of men."

I grinned, "Oh that we are, sir."

The captain returned, "Lieutenant Smythe has the men at the raft."

I saluted and turning smartly, headed for the river. Sergeant Charlton and eight men were there and the lieutenant was at the steering board. Two men held the rope. I stepped aboard and the lieutenant said, "Push off together." His tone sounded pompous.

He tried to steer us directly across the river, but the current was too much and the men on the ropes were in danger of being pulled overboard. I went to the rope to help them and said, "Sir, you must steer at an angle. The current is strong here."

"When I need your impudent advice, I shall ask for it."

The sergeant sighed and said, "He is right, sir. Push the rudder to your right and we should be able to steer straighter."

He frowned and then did as was suggested. The raft straightened and the three of us were able to pull us across the river. He said nothing as I jumped ashore. I pointedly said, "Thank you, Sergeant Charlton. Have a safe voyage back." I winked at him.

Laughing he said, "Aye, and thank you for your advice."

I stood and watched as the lieutenant tried to fit the steering board at the stern of the raft. He could not do it. I wondered if his reddening face was embarrassment that I was watching him studiously. I was enjoying his discomfort. Eventually, one of the privates helped him and they pushed off to cross the river once more. He had heeded my advice, and the passage was smooth enough.

I turned and went to the horses. I had brought nosebags. There was little enough grazing, but they could drink at the river and I had enough food to satiate their hunger. After they had

eaten, I led them, one at a time, to drink at the river. That done I
tethered them to the reptile-free tree and made myself a bed on
the ground. I chose a sandy patch of beach. Then I collected
kindling and built up a fire. I would smoke my pipe, but I wanted
insects and the other creatures of the night kept as far away from
me as I could. The fire would make sure that the horses were
safer too. By the time darkness fell I had a cheery fire blazing
and sitting smoking my pipe, I felt at peace. I knew that this was
a moment when I could simply slip away. I had enough of the
geography of the land in my head and I had two horses. I
persuaded myself that a hue and cry would follow and I would
be caught. I would choose a better time. Even as I snuggled
down to sleep I wondered if I was just seeking an excuse to stay
with the captain and the rest of the section. Was I changing?

I slept surprisingly well and was woken by the bugle, across
the river, calling reveille. The horses appeared to be no worse for
their night alone and after I had made water, I took out my loaf
and cut a hunk from it with my bayonet. I had some dried
venison with me and after I fed the fire, I toasted the bread and
the venison on my bayonet. The toasting made the venison less
dry as it released a little fat, and I enjoyed a reasonable breakfast
with the last of the cold tea. I gave the horses the root vegetables
and the oats. They both seemed to enjoy the unexpected food. I
saddled both horses for I knew that the captain would wish to
leave as soon as he had crossed.

The first soldiers across were accompanied by Captain
Tucker, He had with him a skin of fresh tea and some fried ham
between two slices of bread. "Couldn't have you starving,
Smith."

"Thank you, sir." I ate my second breakfast knowing I still
had half a loaf.

Colonel Wellesley came on the second crossing. He had with
him a young lieutenant, not Lieutenant Smythe. They both had
horses. He turned to the captain, "How far to the road, Captain
Tucker?"

"Not far. No more than a couple of miles." He pointed,
"Down that trail, sir."

"Then let us head down it, Lieutenant, bring Captain White
and the rest of the company when they land."

"Sir."

The captain pointed, "Lead on, Smith."

"Sir."

I dug my heels and Froggy trotted off quite happily. A good breakfast does that.

We reached the road and while we waited the colonel said, "From what I have been told your section is not attached, as yet, to a Company battalion."

"No, sir."

"And they have lived off the land for, what is it, ten days?"

"Longer, sir."

"I think I may well have a use for you. I need men who can think for themselves. And you Mr. Tucker, or is Captain Tucker? What are your plans?"

He took out a cheroot and using a flint, adeptly lit it, "I have the rank of captain, sir, but the regiment in which I served no longer exists." I was intrigued.

"I have a mind to use officers such as you, Captain," he emphasised the word, "to act as scouts and messengers to find out what our enemies are up to."

"You mean spy, sir."

"That is such an ugly word but I suppose you are right. If you agreed to this then you would be attached to my staff."

"And paid, sir?"

The colonel sounded surprised, "Oh, I thought that you had money?"

"My cousin's family are the ones with money. I am like my father, penniless, although without his addiction to gambling."

"Then you shall be paid. I will leave the details to the adjutant. He is good at that sort of thing."

We heard noises from the forest as the company marched along the trail.

The colonel did not wait for them all to emerge. He simply said, "Lead on, Captain Tucker. I am anxious to get to Hyderabad as soon as possible."

We reached our camp in two days. The colonel, it turned out, was a hard taskmaster and thought nothing of riding forty miles in one day. I rode just behind the colonel and the captain so that I was privy to much of their conversation. None of it seemed private and was more to do with the campaign. I learned much as I studied the rumps of their horses. The commander, I discovered, was General George Harris. I had heard the name in Madras. He had fought in the American War of Independence. However the colonel made it quite clear to Captain Tucker that as his brother was the Governor and he, Colonel Wellesley, commanded the best regiment in India (they were his words) that he would command. I found myself smiling that a colonel would tell a general what to do. He had, it seems, brought over twenty eight books with him and had studied the Marathas and other enemies on the Indian sub-continent. He knew their strengths, they were, he said, their rockets and artillery, and he knew their weakness, their leadership. He would try to avoid the one and use the other to his advantage.

I smelled the smoke before we reached the camp and said, "The camp is just ahead, sir."

Captain Tucker turned in his saddle, "You remembered?"

"No sir, I can smell the camp and…Sergeant Grundy's feet."

He laughed, "You are a card and no mistake, Smith. I shall miss you when we part."

It was Edmund and Bob who were on guard duty on the road and they greeted me cheerily, "Hey lads, look who is back! You have lost your sixpence Dai, he isn't dead."

The colonel shook his head, "Clearly not regular soldiers, Tucker. Not even a salute."

The captain smiled and shook his head, "Sorry Colonel. Come on boys, how about a salute for the colonel."

They both snapped, "Sorry, sir," and brought their muskets to attention.

Sergeant Grundy shouted, "Stand to."

The colonel sniffed, "I have seen better-organised beggar's camps."

I did not dislike the colonel as much as Lieutenant Smythe but Colonel Wellesley was not a pleasant man. He was arrogant and had a superior attitude. I would be glad to get back to my comrades in arms.

He turned in his saddle and shouted, "Captain Smythe, pitch our tents. We will spend one night here and then push on to Hyderabad."

"Sir, Sergeant Major, see to it."

"Right, you shower, let us show these company men how to make a decent camp."

The colonel's attitude, it seemed, had rubbed off on the rest of the battalion. I dismounted and waited for the captain to do the same. He handed me Caesar's reins and said, quietly, "There is nothing wrong with the camp, Smith. The colonel is wrong."

"Sir."

I led the two horses to Dublin and Duchess who both gave me such a welcome that the colonel's words were forgotten. I tied up the two horses and then took the saddles and placed them on the conveniently horizontal branch of the tree. I saw that we had almost used the food I had purloined in Madras. Out of the corner of my eye, I saw the officer's servants lead the horses of the 33rd to their own lines. They were far away from our horses. It was almost as though they feared to be contaminated. It did not worry me. The place they had chosen, whilst closer to water, was also a place plagued by flies. The servants would spend as little time as possible there. I groomed the two horses but, in reality, I was working out where they kept the food for the horses. They had wagons and when the carters brought the draught animals, I saw soldiers taking a sack of food from the back of one of them. I marked it. When I was satisfied that I knew which one it was I headed for our camp.

"Well, Smudger, let us know what we are about, eh?"

I shrugged, "I don't know much, Dai, just that we are going to Hyderabad with a letter from the captain's cousin. I think we will be based there for a while."

"And what about these pretty boys you have brought? What of them?"

I smiled, "They have seen no action and none of them have even fired their muskets in anger."

Sergeant Grundy came over, "Corporal, take a couple of men and escort our prisoners to the 33rd. Get their weapons from the cart. Find a Lieutenant Smythe. He is to take charge of them and, Smith, take the French officer's horse to their horse lines."

"Right, Sergeant. Byers, Williams, with me."

I stood and went back to the horses. John Williams picked up the four French muskets and the officer's sword. He smiled and pointed to the other four muskets, "He said nothing about those, did he?" We did not know what we would do with the weapons but they had to have a value.

I put the saddle and saddle cloth loosely on Froggy's back and led her through our camp to the horse lines on the other side of the road, closer to the river. Even as I approached, I was plagued by flies. There was a sentry lounging against a tree. I saw, above his head, a huge spider, the size of my hand, "Private, you might want to move from there."

"Why?"

I shrugged, "Oh, I don't know, maybe to stop that spider dropping down your tunic." He looked up and started.

"Jesus!" He brushed it from him and then stamped down on it.

I tied the French horse's reins to the rope line and placed her as close to the colonel's as I could. I stroked her mane, "Bon chance, Froggy." I could not see where they had put the saddles and I asked, "Where do your lot keep the saddles?"

Without turning for he was studying the tree and trying to find another spider, he said, "In the last wagon." I saw that he was fitting his bayonet. He would go hunting for the spider's companions.

There was no guard at the wagons, the company who had accompanied us were erecting tents. I saw that the saddles were on one side of the wagon and sacks of food on the other. One of the sacks was open and it was too good a chance to miss. I hefted it on my back and as I passed the sentry, who was still searching the tree for more insects, I said, "See you later."

"Aye, and thanks for the warning." He did not take his eyes off the tree.

I hurried back to the cart and placed the food in the bottom. I arranged the French uniforms on the top and went back to our camp. It was petty but I felt better about the theft.

Once more we had no duty. The 33rd took that on. We had our own food although the captain had managed to obtain some fresher salted meat from the 33rd. He was not seen as part of our band and the colonel had consulted him about the roads close to the camp.

That night the lieutenant and the captain came back from the 33rd's camp with our orders. The captain seemed quite happy about them, "Colonel Wellesley, it seems, is keen for us to continue to be the advanced guard. We are to lead the way to Hyderabad."

In contrast, the lieutenant had returned from the meeting with an angry-looking face, and he said, "We are to be the ones to trigger any traps that may await us. He will not risk his precious battalion."

Captain Tucker sighed, "Richard, it makes sense. You are company soldiers, and the people of Hyderabad will not be surprised to see you. You have Aadyot and the sight of a sepoy will make them less fearful. The colonel does not want to fight a war if he can avoid it. The Nizam is not our enemy; Tipu Sultan is. We will fight but not in Hyderabad. This way we have first choice of camping ground, eh?"

The captain was certainly a half-full sort of officer. I agreed with him. I for one did not want to ride in anyone's dust.

Chapter 17

Colonel Wellesley rode with us. He was not a likeable man but he was not a coward and if there was to be an attack then he would be at the fore to deal with it. Captain Smythe and his son, the unpleasant lieutenant, led the 33rd. I was at the rear of our detachment and each time Duchess dropped her dung I took perverse pleasure in knowing that it would be the two of them who would pass over it first. We had one camp before Hyderabad, and we had the choice of the best site for our camp. I waited until I was unobserved before I filled the nosebags of our three horses and they enjoyed the 33rd's rations I had pilfered. Sergeant Grundy had also persuaded the lieutenant to ask the Colonel for some of the grog ration that the 33rd enjoyed. Surprisingly enough the colonel agreed, and a small barrel of the rum ration was given to us. We would not abuse it. We should have had the ration from the first in Calcutta, but we had spent so little time there that we had not been given any. The same was true in Madras. That night we all enjoyed the luxury of no duty, a tot of rum and a pipe of tobacco. For us, it was as good as it would get.

Hyderabad had a French garrison although we saw no tricolours. We were stopped at the gate by a French lieutenant. I was close enough to hear the exchange. Both the colonel and the captain spoke French well and quickly, but I was able to pick up enough to know that the colonel had demanded entry to the town. As the rest of the 33rd appeared behind us the lieutenant took off his hat and grandly gestured with it for us to enter. We rode directly to the palace of the Nizam where we saw a mixture of French and palace guards.

The colonel dismounted as did the captain. "Lieutenant, be so good as to remain here until my senior officers arrive then you may find somewhere to camp. I will speak to the Nizam with Captain Tucker." He gave a rare smile, "I would like to thank the East India Company soldiers for their service to me. You will be needed again but until we have this part of India back under British influence, you can rest on your well-won laurels."

When the 33rd arrived it was Captain White who spoke to us. Captain Smythe simply ignored us. "Let us know where you camp," he smiled, "you seem to find the best places to do so. We will be here until the colonel has established our position."

Lieutenant Crozier nodded, affably, "We will do so." He waved over Aadyot, "Private Aadyot, find out from the locals where would be the best place to camp, eh?" He flipped him a silver coin, "Use that."

"Of course, sahib, I would be honoured."

When he had gone the lieutenant said, "This looks a little more promising. There is a market here and if the colonel is successful then this might be a pleasant little billet."

When Aadyot came back it was with the news that there was a lake and trees close by to afford shade. He had been given good directions and we left the city to head to the north where we did, indeed, find a lake. We pitched our tents fifty yards from the water and close enough to the trees for shade without being plagued by insects. I took the horses to drink. I checked first for any creatures that might harm either them or me. Bob now acted as my assistant and while I led two horses he led the third. We anticipated a longer stay than usual and so the sergeant ordered the digging of a latrine. While half of the section erected all the tents, the rest of us foraged for wood and anything else that we could find.

"Corporal, send Aadyot back to tell the 33rd about this billet."

"Righto. Aadyot."

"Yes, Sahib."

"Tell the 33rd where we are and try to get us some milk for our brew." He tossed him a couple of coppers.

By the time the advance elements of the regulars arrived, we had a fire going and food was being cooked. Aadyot had procured some milk for us and to our great delight it was cow's milk. Our sepoy was indispensable.

The 33rd chose the flatter ground closer to the water. It meant that they had beautifully straight lines for their immaculately pitched tents but we knew that they would be plagued by flies and flying insects. We were happy enough where we were.

The next morning Captain Tucker was summoned to the side of Colonel Wellesley. It was then I realised that our gentleman was something of a diplomat. We spent the day doing our washing and cleaning our weapons. The 33rd drilled. The lieutenant realised that drilling was not as important out here as keeping our weapons clean and in good working order. He went into Hyderabad with Aadyot to find fresh flints and other essentials we might need.

That evening the captain did not return until we had eaten and were sitting around our fire smoking. He had with him a bottle of whisky. That was a special treat. He was a good man and he gave us all a tot. It would help us to sleep. He also gave us information.

"We now have an ally. The Nizam of Hyderabad was given the letter from my cousin. He now knows of Napoleon's defeat in Egypt. The French General has fled back to France and his fleet has been destroyed by Admiral Nelson. The Nizam has had a miraculous change of allegiance."

Lieutenant Crozier asked, "And the French?"

"Aah, it seems that the French who remain, one hundred and forty-five officers and fourteen thousand men are to remain in the pay of the Nizam." That was a much larger number than we had expected. The resident, it seemed, had forestalled what could have been a disaster. If those Frenchmen had joined with the soldiers in Mysore then the 33rd would not have been able to deal with them.

Sergeant Grundy shook his head, "Doesn't seem right fighting alongside Froggies."

"Colonel Wellesley needs every man he can get his hands on. The Tipu Sultan has a huge army. Some say there are fifty thousand of them. We have just four thousand European troops in India and while we have many sepoy battalions, without the men led by the Nizam we would have no hope of success. No, Richard, we need the Nizam and that means we need the French too." He smiled, "The Governor General is on his way here with more British troops and when he arrives then we will head to Mysore. The Governor General sent a letter to the Tipu Sultan demanding that he submit to British authority. We shall see what his response is likely to be."

"That means we will be here for a while."

"At least a month. The colonel has sent for men to be on his staff. He likes to be in control. This section will be his eyes and ears and I will be one of his…what is the word…" he beamed, "spies!"

As we were likely to be here for some time, the next day I took the opportunity, when the tent I shared with Bob and Edmund was empty, to bury my treasure beneath my bed. The belt was chafing my skin and in this climate that could result in an infection. I took to going shirtless whenever I could. Most of the section were the same and our skins were now becoming tanned. The scowls we received from the NCOs of the 33rd when we did this made us smile.

The colonel returned from the palace three days after our arrival and a day later a group of new officers arrived at his command tent. The captain wandered over to greet them and he chatted with the colonel. We were drying kindling for the fire and preparing food. We were intrigued by the conference as we knew it meant action. When the captain came back, he said, "Things will move a little more quickly now. Those three officers are the colonel's staff. Captain William Barclay is the Adjutant General. Captain Colin Campbell the ADC. He hates the Tipu as he was his prisoner for forty-four months. He knows the tactics the Tiger of Mysore will employ. He is a good man. The last is Captain John Blakiston who will be the Engineering officer. If we have any siege work, he will be most useful."

While we worked at our camp the 33rd drilled and had musket practice. I suppose it made sense for them to do so as they had never been under fire or been asked to discharge their weapons at an enemy. We did not need to as we were confident in the use of our muskets. I had managed to get some grease in the town and I used that on my chafed skin.

I do not know if it was the arrival of the three officers which upset the equilibrium of the camp of the 33rd but two days later we heard the drums and bugles sound as the battalion was summoned to witness company punishment. We had no idea what was going on until Sergeant Grundy explained, "Some poor sod is going to have their back laid bare. He will be spread across a gun wheel and lashed."

Bob asked, "What for, Sergeant?"

He shrugged, "Could be anything. Sometimes it is justified, for theft and the like, but often it is just some officer exercising his control."

We were all thieves and the thought of being whipped for doing what, to us, came naturally, seemed terrifying. The ranks of the battalion hid the spectacle from us but after the silence that followed the charges being read out, we heard the sound of a whip as it struck the unfortunate soldier's body. Not seeing it made it seem worse, somehow. We counted and there were one hundred strokes. I could not imagine what the soldier's back would look like after such a flogging. As the battalion was dismissed, we caught a glimpse of the soldier when he was taken to the lake to have his bare and naked back washed. He looked as though he still wore his red tunic.

That evening as Bob and I took the three horses to be watered and to wash their coats, I met Corporal Harris and a private who were collecting water.

He recognised me, "I wish we had an officer like you have. You seem to have the life of Riley at your camp."

Bob nodded, "Aye, the captain and the lieutenant are both good blokes."

I nodded towards the patch of sand which was still a little bloody, "What happened this morning?"

"It was that bastard, Smythe."

"The captain?"

"No, the waste of skin that is his son. He reckoned that Private Cope did not obey a direct order." He shook his head, "We had been firing all morning and the muskets made him a little deaf. He is not the sharpest knife in the drawer at the best of times but he didn't deserve to be whipped. His back is a mess."

His companion said, darkly, "It was wrong and the whole battalion knows it. There will be retribution."

Corporal Harris snapped, "None of that, Harry. It is over and done. Sergeant Charlton has had a word with Captain White. Let us see if that makes a difference."

When we told the others Sergeant Grundy nodded, "Aye, I have heard of such things before. A sensible officer lets men's ears adjust after musket practice. Sergeants give the orders and we know how to shout so that even the dead can hear us!"

Two weeks later the Governor General arrived with General Harris, and it was clear that something was going to happen. We used the time well and bought what we might need from the market in Hyderabad. It was while we were there that we heard of the French mutiny. It was Aadyot who was told of the incident. The French officers had refused to serve alongside the British. The French officers had all been sent out of Hyderabad. They would be sent to France but Aadyot's informant thought that some would head for Mysore. The bulk of the men who remained were retained in the army of the Nizam but with British officers. When we told the lieutenant he nodded, "This will be the opportunity for some East India Company officers to be promoted and paid for by the Nizam. They will be older men who seek to increase their pensions."

"You aren't tempted, sir?"

"No Corporal Neville. You are stuck with me I am afraid."

For my part, I knew that the day we lost Lieutenant Crozier would be the day I ran. With our ally now secure, orders were given and we prepared to move south to Vellore. Being so close to the main camp and with Captain Tucker constantly speaking to the colonel we learned of the make up of the army.

The cavalry would be the 19th and 25th Regiments of Light Dragoons. We had more infantry than cavalry: the 12th, 33rd, 73rd, 74th, 75th, 77th and the Scotch Brigade would be the infantry. Bob was delighted that five of the battalions would be Scottish. We also had some Swiss mercenaries: the Regiment de Meuron. They would meet us at Vellore. There would be ten battalions of Company Sepoys and all of our artillery would be native. The Nizam was bringing his whole army and that included sixteen thousand cavalrymen. The captain also told us that another column would move into Mysore from the west. The Bombay column would be led by General Stuart. The French element would be left in Hyderabad and that pleased us all.

Colonel Wellesley did not wait for the Nizam to muster his army and the order was given to break camp. We left the Deccan plateau to head south. We were at the fore. Until the cavalry arrived, we would be the ones called upon to scout. I dug up my treasure and the belt was wrapped around my waist once more.

The days without it, allied to the grease I had applied, had helped my skin to lose its redness.

We had almost four hundred miles to travel and, by the time we reached Mysore, we would all need new boots. The 33rd would be in the same position as we were. When we stopped to camp I often spoke to the men sent to find water. They seemed confident that their colonel would find them boots. Now that he had an adjutant general, he was able to manage such matters. We had been resupplied with powder and ball. I had implored the lieutenant to issue them directly to the men as poor Duchess was already, in my view, pulling too much. He agreed to my request. The extra food I had stolen was paying dividends but she still seemed too thin for my liking.

When we finally reached Vellore it was already an armed camp. The colours of the uniforms and the sheer numbers of soldiers and horses took my breath away. As had been predicted there were new boots for us and even some new uniforms. Colonel Wellesley was exercising his brother's power well. He made sure that his men had all that they needed.

Our two officers were summoned to a meeting and that allowed us to choose the food we would eat. Aadyot had proved to be a good forager. We would give him a handful of coins and he would come back with fresh food that enlivened our diet. By the time the two officers returned the food was ready and we were all in a good mood. The mood changed after the meal.

It was the lieutenant who addressed us. "Well, boys, the holiday is over. Colonel Wellesley and General Harris have met and they have a strategy." He smiled, "We, it seems, are a key part of it. Captain Tucker will be what Colonel Wellesley calls an exploring officer. He will be accompanied by Smith. The cart will be left here and Duchess will become a saddle horse."

Captain Tucker took a draw on his cheroot and said to me, "We have a saddle arriving this evening."

I tried to take it in. Poor Duchess would have to carry my weight. I felt guilty that I had eaten so well.

The lieutenant continued, "We will be ditching the cart although I suspect that the 33rd will use it, hand drawn of course. We will be the scouts and our tents will be taken with those of the 33rd as will our cooking pots. I fear that our days of independence are over. We will be the first to leave the camp and the last to return. Our food will be cooked for us and our tents erected by others."

I glanced around at the faces of the others. No one liked it but we knew we had been lucky thus far. It was Ben who asked the question that was on my mind, "Sir, what is an exploring officer?"

The captain tossed the stub of his cigar in the fire, "In simple terms, a spy. Smith and I will wear the French tunics once more. The Tipu Sultan has many Frenchmen in his ranks. Redcoats would attract musket balls. I hope that we will not be seen but, if we are, then the blue coats buy us time. Smith will wear a straw hat and I a bicorn. Smith will leave his musket here and one of you will let him have your pistol as a second weapon." He smiled, "Private Smith has shown that he can learn languages well and, as he has demonstrated on more than one occasion, he is more than capable of thinking on his feet."

I felt the sympathetic eyes of the others on me. Our success had been when we had stood together. We were brothers in arms and I felt the same fear as I had when I had feared that Ralph Every was close to catching me. Even as the thought passed through my mind the positive side of my brain came up with the cheery thought that this would be a perfect time for me to run. South of us was Mysorean land. If I could pass through, then I would be able to reinvent myself somewhere else. My gold was intact and I would be mounted. Most importantly, no one would look for me. They would assume that I had been killed.

The lieutenant smiled, "Let us enjoy this bottle of rum, a gift from the colonel. If nothing else we shall sleep well tonight."

Everyone, it seemed, was concerned that I would be in danger. They all knew that even if the section found the enemy there would be others to stand shoulder to shoulder and they could fight and perhaps die, together. My death would likely be a lonely one. Men like Seamus and Dai trusted their comrades before officers. We liked Lieutenant Crozier and thus far he had done well but we relied on each other more.

Sergeant Grundy said, "I will watch your musket for you."

Ben handed over his pistol, "Here, Bill, have this. You will need it more than me" He also gave me his bag of balls.

"Thanks."

Edmund reached into his pack, "Here, Smudger, these are French. I took them from one of the dead Froggies before we buried them. They don't fit me and I was going to sell them. If they fit you then you are more than welcome to use them." He handed over a pair of French boots. "Course, when you get back, I want them returned. They are worth a couple of bob."

"Of course."

I unlaced my boots and tried on the French ones. They were well made and they fitted. I guessed that one of the two veterans who had been killed knew the value of boots and had invested in them. I handed my boots to Ben. Unbeknownst to my comrades they were already helping in my escape.

With the 33rd as sentries, we were able to enjoy the rum, a pipe or two and a few songs and stories. It felt like the last meal of a condemned man but the thought that I could run made it easier for me to bear.

When the saddle was brought by the light dragoon trooper then the reverie ended. He had, in his hands, a saddle, saddle bags and a saddle cloth. I took them to Duchess and tried them on for size. I spoke to her as I did so. "I am sorry, old girl, but you won't be pulling from now on you will be carrying. I hope I am not too heavy." She whinnied and Dublin nuzzled me with his head. "Don't you worry, Dublin, you will be looked after by one of the others but not me. I will keep an eye on the little lady." The saddle fitted and I hung it over the horizontal branch next to Caesar's.

By the time I returned to the camp there were just the two officers and Sergeant Grundy talking. The rest of the men had retired to their tents. Their faces as I approached told me that they had been talking about me. The lieutenant said, "Take this as a compliment, Smith. Everyone thinks highly of you. You speak French reasonably well and you can talk to the Indians too. You are perfect for the role."

Captain Tucker said, "And, with luck, you shall return with a little profit from the experience."

I just wanted to return alive or, if things worked out the way I planned, to start a new life.

Chapter 18

We rose before dawn. The section would begin their work while the rest of the column breakfasted. The light dragoons had only arrived the previous day and the horses needed time to recover. Until they were fighting fit then it would be the East India Company who were the eyes and ears of the army.

I would not be needing my knapsack and red tunic, nor my shako. They were given to Ben to carry for me. The others would take it in turn to carry my pack. The boots I left with Aadyot. We ate our last breakfast with the others and then I saddled Duchess. She was unused to the saddle and the saddle cloth. I saddled her more carefully than I had done with either Caesar or Dublin. She seemed happy enough. Then I prepared myself. The newly acquired French boots were a good fit and came halfway up my calf.

When the captain saw them he approved, "They are better for riding than your army boots, Smith."

I nodded. They would also give me a disguise when I ran. Army boots would simply mark me as a deserter. I had new clothes in my saddlebags and I could shed the uniform. I donned the blue tunic and straw hat and then put my feet in the stirrups. They needed adjusting and Captain Tucker came over to shorten them for me. There were no holsters for the pistols and so I had them stuffed in my belt. I felt like a highwayman.

"Time is wasting, Smith." The captain mounted and dug his heels into the flanks of Caesar and sped off down the road. I had no time for a farewell and I just waved my hat as I urged the game Duchess to follow. I caught up with the captain who had realised that I was a novice rider and my horse was not the equal of his. He had wisely slowed down. As we rode he said, "If we meet anyone then we speak French. You are my servant so just 'oui monsieur' will probably suffice."

I nodded for I was feeling guilty that I would be running and not be able to say goodbye properly to my comrades. I had never intended to but I had become attached to all of them. They felt like family.

"Where are we heading, sir?"

"The Tipu Sultan has his fortress in the heart of Mysore at Seringapatam. It is about two hundred miles away. Our job is to find them before they see the redcoats of your chaps or the horses of the Light Dragoons. Both would give away our intentions."

Two hundred miles would be a five-day ride, although I was experienced enough to realise that we would come across some of the Tipu's men before that. We rode through a land that was likely to be hostile. The first thirty miles were the easiest as it was so close to the Madras Presidency that they were more neutral than hostile. As darkness approached, we spied a village. We dared not use English in case it was reported, and the captain tried to mime asking for shelter and food using a mixture of hand actions and French. The blank looks on their faces told him he was not understood. I tried some Bengali. I had, like Aadyot, been trying to learn the words of the people who lived in this part of the world but I knew too few. As soon as I spoke the first words the headman smiled. They corrected my pronunciation and then told me, it took three attempts before I understood them, that there was an empty hut we could use and that we could share their food. I repeated what I could of their words in French and the captain beamed. He took out some French coins and handed them to the headman whose face lit up.

We ate a simple spicy stew that tasted a little of goat. We had our own blankets and after I had fed the two horses, using the nosebags we had brought, we settled down in the hut. I think that the captain was desperate to speak to me but he did not trust my French enough. For my part it was more evidence that I was in a good position to run. I could speak to the locals and when I had used Indian words, they had smiled. I was glad that I had met Aadyot.

When we were on the road and there was no one in sight the captain thanked me, "Well done, Bill. That was smartly done last night. I am not much of an exploring officer if I can't speak the language. I would appreciate some lessons from you when this is all over. Now let us push on. I would like to make more miles today."

"Sir, Duchess is not as strong a horse as Caesar. I would not have her injured."

"And you will not. I grew up with horses and I can tell you that while Duchess does not look it she is more than capable of carrying you and making better time than you hope. Trust me, Bill, I dare not risk your horse for without you and your mount I am unlikely to be of much use to the Governor General. I promise you that she will not be harmed by carrying you on her back."

Sir Arthur's brother had been at Vellore with General Harris, and it told us just how important this campaign was. It had elevated the desire for every officer to do well. For those of us who were the rank and file it mattered not who led the army. We were still at the bottom of the pile.

That second night we found an outpost on the road manned by some of the Tipu Sultan's men as well as a French ensign and two soldiers. This time it was the captain who took charge and his smooth tongue, I understood more than I had expected, bought us a billet and food for the night as well as a stable for our horses. I understood enough French to know that the main army was still sixty or so miles to the west. They believed the story that the captain had a message for the Tipu Sultan from Paris. The story would not have worked with an experienced officer but the ensign was about my age and still wet behind the ears.

Once again the captain waited until we had a clear road before he spoke in English. "That was a bit of good fortune. We shall push on today and, with luck, we shall soon find their army and return to the main column with no one the wiser." Knowing that we were now in a territory where French was the spoken foreign language helped. We did not find their army by dark but we did find shelter. There was a French plantation and the owner welcomed the captain like a long-lost friend. That would have been my chance to run for I was taken to the servant's quarters. Their French was as bad as mine and so I used a mixture of poor French and bad Bengali. They were nice enough people, and I was fed well. I went to see to the two horses just before I retired and, as I gave them both a fresh nosebag, I contemplated running. There was no logical reason not to but I liked the captain. I persuaded myself that it would be easier to disappear on the way back. He had told me of his plan not to use the main road when we neared the outpost, but to take to the forest. That would be my opportunity.

The French plantation owner gave us food and a skin of wine when we left. It seemed he had enjoyed the captain's company. We rode hard knowing that we would find the enemy soon and then we could return to the main column. We saw the flags and the camp when we neared the place that the captain identified as Mallavelli. He had managed to see a map when he had enjoyed brandy at the plantation and he knew it was an important place. We left the road and made our way through the forest, the better to view their dispositions. The captain took out his 'bring 'em near' and while I held Caesar's reins he stood on the saddle and leaned against a tree.

"They have occupied a piece of higher ground. Their camp is below it and I can see cannons and revetments." He lowered himself into the saddle and put the 'bring 'em near' back in its case. "I think they outnumber us but I did not see many French soldiers. The men manning the guns are from Mysore and I did not see their dreaded rockets."

As we turned to ride back to the road I asked, "Rockets, sir?"

"Yes, Bill, they are a frightening weapon fired from a metal tube. Even Colonel Wellesley fears them. They can fire faster than normal artillery and unlike a cannonball, they travel so fast that they cannot be seen clearly as they approach."

Sergeant Grundy had told me that artillery fired cannon balls and they could be seen in the air. They were still deadly but if you had your wits about you and were far enough away from the guns you could move out of the way.

"What now, sir? Back the way we came?"

He shook his head. "We have to avoid the plantation and the outpost. Those are two sections of the road we need to avoid."

"What if we get lost, sir?"

He grinned, "We won't. I have my compass but from now on, I lead. You stay four lengths behind me. Just in case I get in trouble."

When we camped ten miles east of the plantation, we found somewhere with grazing and water. Thanks to the generosity of the plantation owner we had food and with a fire going to keep away flies, we slept well.

Knowing we had passed one danger we pushed on and used the road. We passed through the village where we had stayed. No one appeared to give us a second glance. At this camp we had a poorer night of sleep as there were more flies and we had less food. We both rose early and left as the sun was rising ahead of us. I knew that we were getting closer to the main column and if I was going to run it had to be that day. We were riding through a forest which had been partly cleared of timber. It was undulating and as the captain was keenly watching the ground ahead, I gradually slipped back. I reasoned that he would be close enough to our lines that he would not be in trouble. When he disappeared from sight, dropping into a dell, I reined in. This was my chance for a new life. We were getting close to our lines and the captain would be safe. I wheeled Duchess and prepared to head south. The sound of the pistol shot arrested my movement. The smell of gunpowder drifted over. I heard voices and shouts from ahead. They were indistinct but sounded French. I should have gone. I could have gone but I liked the captain. More, I knew that if he did not report back then my comrades in arms might suffer. I could not bear the thought of them dying because I was looking out for myself. There would be other opportunities to run. I took out my pistols and loaded and primed them both. I rammed them in my belt and then stroked Duchess' mane, "It is time for you to become a war horse, Duchess."

I did not follow the trail taken by the captain but went further south. I was aided by the fact that the ground fell away naturally. The sound of voices grew. I used the trees for cover and reasoned that their attention, whoever they were, would be on the captain and the trail leading west, the direction from which the captain had come. I reined in and, peering through the undergrowth and low branches of the trees, saw that there were men gathered around the captain and they were fifty paces from me. It was too great a range for the pistols but I was able to identify the numbers. There was a French officer and four Mysorean warriors. At least I took them for Mysorean. They rode small horses, little bigger than Duchess and they had swords and pistols. The French officer had a sword and he held a pistol that was pointing at the captain. I reasoned he must have another pistol for I had heard a pistol shot. I saw that they had not taken

Captain Tucker's sword which hung from his saddle. The five men had completely surrounded Captain Tucker preventing his escape. I realised that if I moved slowly enough I could approach much closer. I inched Duchess slowly up the slope using the trees for cover but avoiding brushing into branches which might make a noise.

When I was about thirty paces away the French officer backhanded the captain across the face. His movement and the sound of the slap made all six horses move and I knew that this would be my best chance. I drew a pistol and rode at them. The French officer had his back to me. I knew he was the more dangerous of the five and I did not hesitate. I aimed at his back. I knew I could not fire whilst moving and I reined in. It was when I stopped and raised my pistol that one of the Mysorean warriors saw me and pointed. I fired at the Frenchman as the officer turned to look at the danger. I hoped the ball would hit him but as he was turning I was not sure. The smoke obscured them and I rammed it in my belt and drew my second. The warrior who had shouted the warning came at me. He had a sword in his hand and was just five paces from me when I saw him. I fired and this time I saw the ball hit his face. His head disappeared and he fell from the back of the horse.

I was weaponless but the captain had three opponents. I shouted, "Charge!" as though I was leading a regiment of cavalry. It was madness, of course, for I had no loaded weapons nor a sword but the three survivors did not know that I was alone and unarmed.

Through the thinning smoke, I saw the captain draw his sword and slash it across one man's throat. The remaining two warriors, hearing my cry and seeing me charging, chose discretion over valour. They turned and fled. I rode up to the captain. He had a bloody nose and I saw that he had a wound to his leg. There was a blackened hole where the ball had hit him and blood dripped down.

"Reload your pistols and keep an eye on those two although I don't think that they will return." He dismounted as, with shaking hands, I reloaded my pistols. I rammed them in my belt. The French officer was dead. My ball had hit higher than I had aimed. The hole in his throat was enormous. His horse was still there for his foot was still in the stirrup. The other two animals had run off to follow the two warriors. Despite his wound the captain was all business. After taking the Frenchman's foot from the stirrup he checked the tunic and took a pistol as well as the sword. He hung them on Caesar's saddle. He found a purse and tossed it to me, "To the victor go the spoils. If you are not too squeamish you may have whatever the other two men have. I shall just tie something about this wound."

I dismounted and tied Duchess' reins to a branch. The warrior with the slashed throat had a pistol and a sword. I took them as well as his purse. The one I had killed had a sword and a purse. I fastened the two swords to my saddle and put the pistol in my saddle bags.

The captain had tied a tourniquet to his leg and nodded toward the French officer's saddle, "Take the saddle holsters and then lead the horse. We have to get away quickly. I do not think that those five were alone. The enemy have their own spies out and we have used up all our luck."

"Can you ride, sir?"

He laughed, "Well I cannot walk, can I? Yes, Bill, I can ride."

I tied the reins of the captured horse to my saddle bags. We rode directly for the road. We needed to make up lost time. I recognised where we were and knew that we had to pass the outpost. The captain seemed to anticipate my question, "Have a pistol ready and we shall gallop through as though the devil is behind us."

I drew and cocked a pistol. The young ensign would not be harmed when I fired. If we fired the smoke and the noise would scare him. When we had passed through earlier, the two men with him did not even have powder in the pan.

We rode slowly until we neared the outpost. The ensign turned and said something to the two men with him. When they reached for their powder flasks the captain shouted, "Now, Bill!"

I dug my heels in. We were slow to move for the French horse was attached but once Duchess moved then the French horse started to open his legs. The captain had no such anchor to slow him and he reached the three men well before me. He fired his pistol, and the three men took cover. As I neared them I fired too. The ball went nowhere near them as Duchess' head dipped just as I fired. It mattered not for we were through and by the time they recovered we would be beyond the range of their muskets. We rode hard for a mile or so and then slowed. A few minutes later we heard hooves ahead.

The Sergeant of the 19th Regiment of Light Dragoons and his patrol had their carbines out for they must have heard the shooting. He recognised the captain for he said, "Stand easy lads." We reined in. "We heard firing, sir, was that you?"

"It was indeed. There is a French ensign and a couple of native soldiers a mile or so ahead."

"Right lads. Put your carbines away. The column is just three miles up the road, sir."

We rode slowly along the road for poor Duchess had gone above and beyond. To my great delight, we soon came upon our section. Seamus and Dai were between the shafts of our cart. Seamus shouted, "Heaven be praised! Smudger is back and Duchess!" The cheer I was given made me feel warm.

The captain chose that moment to turn and ask, "Back there, Bill, why were you not behind me?"

The old thief and liar in me helped me to adopt the mask, "You know Duchess, sir. The slope was too much and I was resting her. Good job I did, eh? We both might have been taken."

Although he nodded and said, "Yes, damned fortunate," the look in his eyes told me that he did not completely believe me.

Chapter 19

The captain rode to report directly to the colonel, Governor General and General Harris. He would also see the doctors to have his leg tended to. He smiled as he left, "Thank you again, Smith." We were back with the column and the familiarity of the road was forgotten. When we reached the section I saw that they had the cart again and I smiled at the expressions on the faces of Seamus and Dai who were pulling it. I put my blue tunic back in the cart and retrieved my red one.

It turned out that no one wanted the cart as the regiments all had wagons. Once the dragoons had taken over the scouting duties the section had retrieved it. We took the saddle from Duchess and put her between the shafts again. She seemed happy enough. Seamus and Dai were just pleased to be relieved of their role as draught animals. I fastened the captured French mount to the rear. I had plans for the beast. I had not escaped when I had the chance but I now saw that it was possible to do so. The French horse was a better one than Duchess and would enable me to disappear. But for my misguided sense of duty I would have been far away already.

We camped at the outpost. The ensign and the rest of the guards had been taken prisoner. Having passed through it twice, I was able to direct the lieutenant to the best campsite. The three purses jingled too much and, as soon as I could I made the excuse that I needed to empty my bowels and I headed to the forest where I put my new found coins with my burgeoning treasure trove. I was truly a rich man and when I ran I would be able to be a landowner.

I had little to do once I had seen to the three horses, and I sat to enjoy a pipe of tobacco while the others erected tents and cooked food. We only needed three tents. The lieutenant, sergeant and corporal all shared one and the rest of us did not mind the cosiness of two. While they cooked the food, I told them what we had discovered.

Sergeant Grundy nodded, "About time we had some proper action. Those lads in the 33rd will get a shock when they have to charge into artillery fire."

The lieutenant had been listening. "No matter what happens when we do meet them at, where did you say it was, Smith, Mallavelli?" I nodded, "Seringapatam is another matter. It is a fortress with a river around it. I spoke with the engineering officer, Captain Blakiston. It will be a bit bloodier there than some hillside in the back of beyond."

His sobering words ended the conversation.

We did not see the captain that night, nor the next day. We moved on and our muskets were all kept to hand. I pointed to the place where we had been ambushed. Even though we had light cavalry as skirmishers, I knew that they would only watch the road. The captain and I had moved easily enough through the trees and so could our enemy. We kept a wary eye out for an ambush.

Captain Tucker finally returned to our camp when we had the food already cooking. I had attended to the three horses and I was pleased with their condition and they were settled. I had named this captured mount, Froggy, as I had the previous one. I made a fuss of him, he was a gelding, as I planned to use him to escape. I needed him as my friend. Duchess might not be a fast horse but the French officer's mount looked as though it was.

The captain was limping when he returned but other than that he looked well. He had new breeches on and a huge smile on his face.

"You and I, young Private Smith, are the apple of the Governor's eye. He seems to think you are some sort of lucky charm and wishes to promote you. I told him, of course, that was unnecessary but a guinea or two would not go amiss." He flipped me two guineas.

He was right. Gold was better than a stripe any day of the week. "Thank you, sir."

"And once we have rousted the Tiger of Mysore from his lair at Mallavelli, we shall be called upon again." He nodded towards Duchess, "And now you have a decent mount. I impressed upon his lordship the need for you to be well mounted. Duchess can resume her duties and Hogan and Evans need no longer perform an impression of a pair of draught animals."

Everyone laughed.

As we ate, Aadyot said, quietly to me, for we often ate together, "You have won much honour and gold. You are indeed a lucky man."

"And it is thanks to you." I took a florin from my waistcoat pocket, "This is for you."

"But I did nothing."

"You taught me some of your words and for that I am grateful. I would learn more." My little trip had shown me the need to speak the language of the land.

The next two days saw us draw closer to Mallavelli. I learned at least ten words a day. The French had been handy but my lessons from Aadyot would be my ticket out of the company.

The road was familiar to me. When we passed the plantation I saw that it was deserted. The French owner had fled. He might return, such men were opportunists, but the captain thought that he would err on the side of discretion. We reached Mallavelli towards the evening and this time two Madras battalions were placed before us as sentries. Our enemy had been forewarned and there were more men present than when we had scouted it out. I suspect the two men who had fled from us had reported back.

There was an officers' call and Sergeant Grundy was left in command of the camp. Normally a lowly officer like the lieutenant would not be invited but our work thus far could not be ignored. I made sure that the three horses were not only tethered but hobbled too. I wanted no opportunist from the enemy to steal one away.

When the officers returned we were informed that we were to be used along with the 33rd and the Highland battalions to bolster the centre of the line when we attacked the enemy. The British cavalry would be on one flank and the native cavalry on the other. The East India Company battalions would support our attack and the Nizam of Hyderabad's army would be our reserve. Nothing was said outright but I suspected that our leaders did not trust to the troops of our ally. When we won then the Nizam's troops would have more confidence.

It was the lieutenant who explained our orders. "The colonel intends to spearhead the attack with the 33rd. Accordingly we and the light company will be the skirmishers and we will be spread out before the other companies."

Edmund said, "Skirmishers, sir?"

The lieutenant nodded, "A thin screen of men who snipe and harass the enemy."

I saw Sergeant Grundy open and close his mouth. I knew him well now. He did not like the order, but he would support his officer. John Williams, however, had no such qualms, "Sir, let me understand this. We walk in front of the army to close with the enemy." The lieutenant nodded, "That is madness. They will open fire and we will all be killed."

The captain threw the butt of his cheroot into the fire, "It is the standard formation, Williams. The Tipu's men will adopt the same formation. Their light infantry will also advance."

John was in a belligerent mood. I had shared a tent with him and knew that he could be argumentative just for the sake of an argument. "With due respect, sir, that is an easy thing for you to say. You will be sat on your horse with the general."

"Williams!" Sergeant Grundy brooked no ill discipline.

"No, Sergeant, it is better that this is explained here. We do not want any man to break on the morrow for that could be disastrous. I will be with you and advancing. The difference is that you will have muskets and I will have a pistol and sabre." He nodded to Lieutenant Crozier, "Lieutenant."

"It is simple, Williams, we have better muskets and we are better trained than the enemy. We will not advance in line but in pairs. Sergeant Grundy served in a light infantry regiment, and he knows how this works. We use the ground for cover and one man kneels to load. One man fires while the other reloads. Our job is to precipitate the enemy into attacking. When they do the bugler from the 33rd will sound the retreat and we run back to our lines, turn and kneel before the front rank."

Sergeant Grundy said, "You aim for the officers and their gunners if you can."

Seamus laughed, "Sir, when we practised at sea we could barely hit anything."

Lieutenant Crozier nodded, "True, but you were firing at a single piece of wood. Here you will fire at a solid line of men. The officers and both rank and non-commission will likely be

together, with the bugler and standard bearer. Hit any of them
and it is a victory." He turned to me, "Smith, you have hit more
men with musket and pistol ball than any. Can you give Hogan
some tips?"

I saw in their faces trust. I was one of them. They were not
convinced by either officer or the sergeant. They knew I would
not lie. The old Bill, the thief from the docks would have happily
told a lie but Private William Smith of the East India Company
would not be untruthful to his comrades in arms. I sighed, "It is
true, I have taken lives. Before I joined I am not sure I could
have killed a total stranger, but at the fort and on the patrols I
have endured I have come to realise that if I do not try to kill my
enemy then they will kill me." I saw Ben and Bob nod. "I kept
still when I fired and I aimed at the biggest target I could, their
middles. Two of those I killed, the ones where I used a pistol,
were struck in the neck and the head but I aimed for the middle. I
watched them fall and I saw them die. In the fort I could not be
sure what I hit but as I am here, and they are not, then I must
have hit them. My advice is to aim low." A sudden thought came
to me as I remembered the men at the brazier in the fort, "Sir,
will we be using muskets with bayonets?"

The two officers both looked at the sergeant who said, "No,
son, but when we run back you pull your bayonet out and as you
kneel, you fit it. When the enemy attack, the bayonet will be
your best defence."

There was silence except for the crackling of the fire.

Sergeant Grundy must have realised that there was little point
in arguing against the orders for he shook his head and just said,
"We will leave our knapsacks here and take ball and powder with
us. Have a good drink before you leave for the day will be hot
and dry."

Dai asked, "What if we need to pee, Sergeant?"

The old soldier laughed, "Ah, that is the secret weapon of the
British soldier. If we fire long enough, then the barrel of your
musket will clog. Pee down the barrel and it will clean it." He
chuckled, "Keep your wedding tackle away from the barrel
though. It will be hot."

For some reason that made us laugh and bawdy comments about men's manhood took our minds away from the prospect of dying.

"Get a good night's sleep and we rise before dawn."

"Sir, what about the horses and our knapsacks, Lieutenant Crozier?"

"Good question, Smith. Aadyot, you will be the guard for our camp."

The sepoy said, "Sir, I am a member of this section. I should fight alongside my comrades."

"And you will, Aadyot, but not tomorrow. The general and the colonel, not to mention the Governor General, are all confident that we can defeat the Tipu. This war will not be won tomorrow but when we take Seringapatam. You will fight alongside your friends."

The depth of feeling for our comrade was shown when the others all gave him their treasures to hold. They trusted him and knew that he would hold them until the battle was fought and won. I headed for the horses. They were my friends and while I trusted Aadyot, I knew that they would miss me and, if I was to die on this foreign field, I would say goodbye to them.

I filled their nosebags and then spoke to each one, "Froggy, I hope that I get to know you better when I return. Caesar, you are well named, farewell." I kissed his muzzle. "Dublin, you need to watch over Duchess. She is a lady and needs your care." He nodded his head and slobbered me with his tongue. People say that animals are dumb but they are the ones who do not know them. Finally, I went to Duchess and touched my forehead against her as I spoke, "I hope that I shall return on the morrow Duchess but know that," I put my mouth to her ear, "you are my favourite and I worry more about you than any other. Take care. You are a loyal horse and deserve your name." I put my forehead against hers again and we stood in silence. I could almost feel her thoughts.

"You are a strange one, Bill."

I turned as Captain Tucker came along. I was embarrassed, "Just feeding the horses, sir."

He smiled, "You were saying goodbye," I said nothing, and he came closer to me and his voice became serious, "I confess,

Bill, I came here because I thought you might do as you did on the road and run. I can see now that is not what you were doing."

The old Bill came to the fore and I said, defensively, "Me? Run, sir? The thought never entered my head."

He smiled in the dark, "You and I have had totally different upbringings, Bill, but we are similar in nature. You and I know the truth. I should warn you that if you do run, I shall not hinder you, but Colonel Wellesley is a stickler for discipline. You would be hunted down and punished. Few men survive a thousand lashes."

I lied, "I will not run, sir."

That night, as I lay in my tent I could not sleep. It was not the fear of battle but the realisation that I had missed my chance to run. I should have done so the moment we landed at Calcutta. I had become known and the captain was right. I would no longer enjoy the anonymity I had before I stepped down the gangplank and landed in India.

My troubled sleep meant I woke before dawn and I went to make water. The sentries, from the 21st Carnatic battalion, were between our camp and the enemy, on the heights. Behind me lay the tents of the 33rd and the generals. I was trapped and could not run. I had to accept my fate and fight this day if I was to survive. I still wanted to run but the well-meant words of Captain Tucker rang in my ears. I needed a better plan. I fed the fire and filled the pots with water. We needed a good breakfast and a mug of tea.

Sergeant Grundy rose not long after I had put the tea in the dixie. He nodded and smiled, "Good lad. I will give you a hand."

Even before he had returned Aadyot had risen and smiled at me, "Is there anything you wish me to watch for you, Smudger?"

"Keep your eye on the horses, especially Duchess."

"Of course."

The sound of our voices soon woke the rest and we were all dressed before the bugle blew to rouse the rest of the camp. Fried salted beef wrapped in the bread we had been issued the day before was a good breakfast. Aadyot ate his own concoction. With a mug of tea, we were as content as any man who was facing his last day on earth. Those who had never been soldiers would not understand the apparent calm. The old Bill would have laughed at the fatalistic view, but I was satisfied.

A sergeant came from the 33rd, he had a jug. He smiled and handed the jug to Sergeant Grundy, "I am Sergeant Oldcastle of the Light Company 33rd Foot. Captain Kincaid's compliments and he has sent over this rum, for your lads."

"Thank you, and most welcome it is."

He nodded, "Today we shall see who are soldiers and who are not."

Sergeant Grundy poured the same amount into all our mugs, even the two officers. It was an equitable distribution. We would be fighting and the musket balls would not discriminate between officer and rank and file. I drank the rum infused tea and, not being used to it coughed.

Seamus laughed, "Sure, and I will drink yours for you if you wish, Smudger."

"That is all right, you big Mick, I will endure the discomfort stoically like a man!" He laughed and clapped a huge ham-like arm around my shoulder.

That done we prepared for the day. I would take my two pistols with me and I loaded them both. We had cleaned our muskets the night before and we loaded them. The sharpened bayonet was in its sheath and when we fastened our tunics and donned our shakoes, we were ready.

The bugle call sounded for us to take our positions. We nodded to Aadyot as we left the camp. Any words that were necessary had already been spoken. We marched behind the two officers with the sergeant and corporal bringing up the rear. I saw Sergeant Oldcastle and the officer I took to be Captain Kincaid leading the one hundred men of the Light Company from their camp. We would be under their command. The sun rose and showed the enemy moving into their positions on the higher ground.

Captain Kincaid came over and offered cheroots to our officers. They took one each and lit them from his. We were all close enough to hear their words, "Your fellows have, according to the colonel, seen more action than we have. I would have your men on the right." He smiled, "It is the place of honour."

I was not sure about the honour. If that meant it was the most dangerous place then I would have another enjoy that dubious privilege.

"Right, lads, to the right." Sergeant Grundy led us to the right as the Light Company took up their positions. Behind us we heard the drums as the 33rd and the Highlanders were marched into their lines. We had been told that they would be three ranks deep. When we retreated to the shelter of their muskets, in places it would be four men deep. It was a reassuring thought. We had discussed our pairings the night before and I was to be with Ben while Bob would be with the sergeant.

As we waited, my mouth felt dry. I wondered if that was due to the rum. I glanced to my left and saw the Light Company in pairs. Looking to my right, there was nothing. Our cavalry was echeloned behind and formed a solid line with the centre companies. I looked back and saw that the grenadier company, the tallest and, according to some, the best men in the battalion, were also on the right. I took comfort that when we ran, if I was still alive, I would have the protection of the grenadier company and the cavalry.

We had barely found our place when the enemy sounded drums and horns. We would not have to attack. They were attacking us!

I learned later that it was two thousand men who charged down the slope towards us. At the time it seemed as though their whole army had descended.

Sergeant Grundy was calmness itself, "East India, present."

So much for skirmishing. We would be firing as a line company.

The Mysorean warriors with swords as well as bayonet-tipped muskets and even spears charged down the slope so quickly towards us that it was like a huge roller at sea. They were like wild men. The pirates who seemed to be so reckless were similar in the way that they attacked. Perhaps their lives were so poor that they did not care if they lived or died. I wanted to live. I smiled when some of them discharged their muskets as they charged. They were balls that were wasted. It was Sergeant Oldcastle who shouted, "Fire!"

Sergeant Grundy repeated the command but Ben and I were already squeezing our triggers. The flash and bang along with the smoke effectively hid the men who were charging us. We both began to reload.

Normally we would have been ordered to fire a second and third volley but the speed of the charge negated the second volley. The enemy were bounding down the slope like hares. "Independent fire at will."

This was not the leisurely reloading of a practice fire. I raised and fired as soon as I was reloaded. It was a heartbeat faster than Ben. I had been someone who could pick a lock quickly. I had fast fingers. The nearest warrior was just forty paces from me and I aimed at his middle. Even as I reloaded I saw him tumble and roll down the slope. I was reloading and firing now without any thought. When the bugle sounded and the order came to fall back the nearest warriors were just ten paces from us. I had no time to reload but, holding my musket in my right hand I drew and fired a pistol into the face of the warrior who was raising his sword exultantly to split open my head.

"Run!" I turned and obeyed Ben's command. I had long legs and I opened them as I ran the one hundred paces to the grenadiers whose muskets were being raised. I saw the sergeants with their halberds ensuring that the ranks were straight. I slid the last five paces and turned. I jammed my pistol in my waistband and began to reload.

Behind me, I heard the commands as the 33rd Regiment of Foot prepared to fire their first shots in anger.

I had reloaded and, remembering Sergeant Grundy's words, fixed my bayonet. I knelt and aimed my musket at the mob of wild charging warriors. I heard the command to present. I was not sure if I was to fire when the front rank did but it seemed prudent to do so. I aimed at the forest of brightly coloured warriors who hurtled down the slope towards us. They were just forty paces from us when I heard the command, "Fire!"

I had never heard so many muskets fire at once. The Madras artillery had also opened fire and my hearing went. Smoke filled the ground before me. It was like a fog on the River Thames in November. I could see nothing. I fired and reloaded. Hearing no commands meant I was, effectively, on my own. I reloaded and fired as fast as I could. The barrel of the musket became hot and burned my hands. I would wrap a cloth around it the next time I fought in a line, if I survived this encounter. A body crashed to the ground, through the fog, before me. As I reloaded for the umpteenth time I noticed that he had no face and had been struck in the chest by more than one ball. I fired again and again.

Suddenly a grenadier's hand tapped me on the shoulder. I looked up and he mouthed something but I could not hear his words. He made a slashing gesture with his arm and I guessed he meant to cease fire. I reloaded and stood.

The first sounds I heard were the cheers that rolled down the battalion. I glanced down the line and saw Ben and Bob, along with the sergeant were still alive. I could not see the others but smoke still drifted along our front.

Ben grinned, "We are alive."

His voice sounded distant but I heard it.

The Yorkshire grenadier behind me said, "By but you are a game cock and no mistake. I thought you a cockerel ready for the plucking but you fired and reloaded like a veteran."

I grinned and looked through the smoke which was gradually thinning. My mouth was dry and my fingers were blackened from the powder and scorched from the barrel. We had killed many of the enemy, but they still held the field. They had withdrawn just a hundred paces up the slope. I wondered about peeing down my barrel. I felt sure that my gun would be clogged but this did not seem the time. The next command guaranteed that I would not have time to do so.

"Fix bayonets."

My bayonet was already fixed. I wondered if I should have done so. It was too late to change now. The muskets became heavier. The ones who had never fired a musket with a bayonet would have to adjust their aim when next we opened fire.

Sergeant Grundy then shouted, "East India, take a position to the right of the grenadiers." He sounded as though he was out of breath already.

Ben and I were almost at the end of our line and we were the first to stand just forty paces in front of the light dragoons commanded by General Stuart. They were even more reassuring than the grenadiers.

It was as the others joined us, this time not in skirmish order but in a small line that I saw one was missing, Edmund Byers. As his friend John Williams passed me, I said, "Edmund?"

He shook his head, "He was speared."

There would be time for mourning if we survived but the death was the first one in the section since the pirates had attacked. It made me fearful. So long as none of the company died then I might survive. It was just one death but that was portentous.

It was clear, as we stood and waited, that the enemy were preparing for another attack. I saw men, possibly their holy men, exhorting the ones who stood before us, presumably to die well. Fresh men were being fed into the line.

The next command took me by surprise. It was the voice of Colonel Wellesley, "The 33rd will advance. Sergeant Major."

"Battalion, march!"

There were fifes and drums with the battalion and they sounded giving the battalion a rhythm. Lieutenant Crozier shouted, "East India, march."

I was between Ben and Bob. We kept time.

The Mysorean warriors opened fire when we were one hundred paces from them. Balls flew over our heads but none of our section was hurt. I saw just two of the 33rd fall. There might have been others but only two were close to us. The Mysorean warriors had to have fired more than a thousand muskets but if the handful of men who had fallen was a measure of their success, then they had failed. I saw them hurriedly reloading. They were not as quick as we had been and when, at a range of sixty paces, we were ordered to halt, I braced myself for the next fusillade. Surely they could not miss again so badly.

"Present!"

The sergeant major's command was repeated by Sergeant Grundy. As we raised our muskets I saw the enemy raising theirs. This was a race and the losers would, in all probability, die.

"Fire!"

Our muskets belched a heartbeat before I heard a foreign voice give a command to the Mysorean warriors. It meant our musket balls struck their line even as they were squeezing their triggers. For us the range was almost perfect and, as we reloaded and through the smoke, I saw that we had hurt them. I reloaded by jolting the ball down the barrel.

"Charge!"

The command took me by surprise. We were going to make a bayonet charge uphill against a superior enemy. We all ran and I heard the wild Celtic screams of Seamus and Dai as they lowered their bayonet tipped muskets and charged the shaken Mysorean warriors. My slight delay meant I was not in the fore and I followed Ben and Bob.

I saw that some of those on the ground were not dead and were slashing swords at legs as they passed. I watched a grenadier skewer a man. This was kill or be killed. Even though they were demoralised, men will not simply roll over and die. They were fighting and they had the advantage that they were above us. I saw Bob and Ben parry two spears that came at them and a third man appeared. I raised my musket and snap fired. He was just ten yards from me and I could not miss, even with a bayonet at the end. He fell to the ground writhing and clutching the hole in his stomach. It would be a slow death.

I had discharged my weapon and now I would have to use the bayonet. I had used a bayonet at the fort and so, when I ducked beneath the swinging scimitar and lunged, I was more confident than I might have otherwise been. He had misjudged his strike because of the slope, and I tore my bayonet into his stomach and, twisting, ripped it to the side. It was as though I had released a basket of red snakes. I stepped over his dying body. We were amongst the enemy now and I stood between Bob and Ben as Mysorean warriors tried to get at us. Unlike the 33rd we were a thin rank and as such, an easier target. Bob and Ben discharged their weapons and men fell. It was then I heard the cavalry bugles as they sounded the charge.

It was Captain Tucker who realised the danger that we were in. We stood between the cavalry and the enemy. He yelled, "East India, quick march, thirty paces to the left!"

The three of us turned and ran. Perhaps we had more idea of what was about to happen than the Mysoreans for they did not run but saw our flight as weakness. I had to fend off a musket with my own as we ran. The warrior was level with me but was a shorter man. I parried his bayonet away and lunged. I caught his hip and I knew that I had hurt him but he was a brave man and his lunge caught me in the middle. It was like being punched but I felt no pain. I feared he might succeed a second time and I swept my bayonet up and across his head. It tore through the cheekbone, and he dropped his musket and ran.

I glanced down and saw the slash from the bayonet but there was no blood. My luck was holding.

I heard Lieutenant Crozier shout, "East India! To me! East India! To me!"

I saw that some warriors, recognising the two officers had surrounded them. We did not hesitate but ran into the fray. Seamus was in his element and he wielded his musket like a war axe. He slashed and stabbed screaming Gaelic curses. I plunged my bayonet into the back of one man. I was learning all the time, and I knew that a sideways rip could open a wound and end a man's life more quickly. I did so.

"Watch your back, Smudger!"

I whipped around, whirling my musket as I did so. I barely deflected the long spear and I saw the warrior pull it back. I remembered my loaded and primed second pistol and I pulled, cocked and fired it in one motion. There was the inevitable delay which enabled the warrior to thrust his spear towards my head. When the ball hit his head, just three paces from me, I was spattered with his blood and bits of his bone. My tunic and breeches looked as though I was working in an abattoir. The ball knocked him and his spear backwards. I stuck the pistol in my belt.

It was at that moment that General Stuart's horsemen hit the flank of the Mysorean army. There was a crack like thunder followed by screams and shouts that were as loud as the musketry at the start of the battle. The warriors had discharged their weapons. Their spears and muskets were not presented in a solid line and the horsemen simply tore through them. The ones facing us turned and ran.

I heard Colonel Wellesley shout, "Keep your bayonets in their backs. If we do not kill them today then we must fight them again tomorrow."

We were tired and sweaty. Our faces and hands were grimed with powder and blood but we obeyed the order.

Sergeant Grundy was the oldest of us and I saw him on his knees, "Are you hurt, Sergeant?"

"No, son, just bloody tired. Get after them while I catch my breath. Go on, son, I will be right behind you."

I ran and soon caught up with men whose backs were to me and were trying to avoid the horses that were looming up from their right. Three of them died without even knowing I was there. We reached the top of the hill and their encampment. We had caught up with all those that could be caught by men on foot. The Madras horsemen had joined in the chase and the two brigades of horsemen could do more damage than we could. We stopped to catch our breath.

The Lieutenant said, "East India, stand fast."

I looked at my comrades. Only Edmund and the sergeant were missing. Everyone looked as I imagined I looked. Dirty, dishevelled and bloody. It was not our blood but that of our foes. I saw the lieutenant and captain congratulating each other and then spied the rest of the section as they entered the tents.

The old Bill resurfaced. There would be loot in the tents. It might not be gold or silver but there would be objects that could be sold. I chose a tent that no one had yet entered. The reason was clear. It had been struck by an artillery round and although the fire had gone out there was the smell of roasting flesh. I steeled myself and entered. There were three bodies and they still smoked. I was not an expert but it looked to me as though the explosion had killed them and the wall of flame had begun to char their bodies. I was about to turn and leave when I spied a small box. Although it was hot to the touch I opened it. Having smoked a pipe for some time I could bear heat a little easier now. In it were some gold coins and jewels. I did not know what the jewels were but I guessed that, as they were red and green, they were rubies and emeralds. There was a dead Mysorean soldier with a knapsack on his back nearby. I took the knapsack and emptied it. There was nothing of value within and I put the small chest inside and slung the knapsack on my back.

The other two corpses had rings on their fingers. It was a grisly task but I removed them. They both had decent swords and I took those too. I put the rings in my tunic pockets and left the tent. I slung my musket. What I needed was some way to carry the swords and keep my hands free for any more treasure. There was a dead Mysorean soldier lying on the ground. He had been bayonetted and had bled out. He had a thick belt and fastenings for a sword. Someone else had taken the sword but I took the belt and attached the two swords to it.

The captain and lieutenant shouted, "East India, to me."

We all reluctantly left our looting and joined the two of them. I looked to have the least treasure for all that was visible were the two swords. George Mainsgill had a large chest and was grinning from ear to ear.

The captain said, "If the colonel sees you with the chest, Mainsgill, he will have you whipped for looting."

"But sir, everyone is doing it."

"Yes, Mainsgill but captured swords and weapons are considered spoils of war. A chest looted from the dead is not."

The lieutenant shook his head, "Mainsgill, I can see that you were never a thief. Empty the chest and put the contents in your tunic and your pockets. The captain and I will pretend we saw nothing." As the rest obeyed, he said, "Anyone seen the sergeant?"

I looked around and said, "I saw him just before the last charge. He said he needed a rest and would follow." I looked down the slope and saw that he had not moved, "There he is, sir." I ran down the slope. Sergeant Grundy was lying flat on his back and looked a little grey. When I reached him I saw that his breathing was irregular, "You need a doctor, Sergeant. You look like death."

He smiled, "Just a bit tired, lad. I had a bit of indigestion and a pain in my arm from holding my gun too long but that has gone."

The two officers arrived. They took one look at him and Captain Tucker said, "Smith, get to the camp and bring one of the horses. He is in no condition to walk."

"Sir," I ran.

I heard the others as they came to the aid of our sergeant. I made the camp in as short a time as possible but I still feared that I might be too late. It was one thing to die in battle but the sergeant just looked deathly ill. Surely he could not die of indigestion. I would disobey the order. The sergeant needed the cart. It was big enough to hold him and it would be easier to load him than put him on the back of a horse.

Chapter 20

Aadyot looked up as I ran into the camp. I simply shouted to him, "Empty the cart and I will get Duchess."

"What is wrong, Smudger?"

"The sergeant has been taken ill."

Between us we had the cart and Duchess ready quicker than we had ever managed it before and we both headed up the slope, urging our horse to move quickly. The sergeant was clearly unhappy with the fuss and when he saw the cart he became angry.

"I don't need a cart, Sir. I am fine now."

Captain Tucker said, "As you know, Sergeant Grundy, I am not one to use my authority recklessly, but I am ordering you to allow us to put you in the cart and take you to see a doctor."

He sighed. He was an old soldier and obeying orders was second nature to him, "Sir."

Seamus and Dai lifted him in the cart and were as gentle with him as though he was a newborn baby.

I led Duchess back through the battlefield. The ones who had been dying were now dead. Medical orderlies were carting our wounded men back to the doctors. As we walked Lieutenant Crozier said, "He won't be seen quickly, you know that."

Captain Tucker asked, "Why not?"

"No wound and it is musket balls and sabre cuts that are the stock in trade of the army doctor. We need a civilian doctor."

The two of them looked towards Mallavelli, the small town that nestled close to the battlefield. We reached the camp and as Sergeant Grundy was taken to his tent Captain Tucker said, "Smith, saddle Froggy. You and I will find a doctor."

"Me, sir?"

"You can speak to the locals easier than I can. We need a European doctor. His nationality does not matter."

If I could help Sergeant Grundy, I would. "Sir." I went outside to saddle the horse.

I said to Aadyot, "What is the local word for doctor?" He told me and I nodded, "Fetch Froggy and my saddle. I need to drop something in my tent, first." I had realised that I still had the pack on my back and it was laden with treasure. I went to my tent and stuffed the pack inside my empty knapsack. I saddled Froggy while the captain saddled Caesar. I had wondered why the captain had not asked Aadyot but as he dug his heels into Caesar's flanks and galloped off, the reason manifested itself. He could rely on me to ride hard and not fall off. We could not afford for two of the company to require medical help.

The small town was in uproar. Some of the Mysorean refugees had fled there and the locals had cowered in their homes when the musketry and sound of battle filled the air. Now all came outside. The battle survivors were fleeing and the sight of two red uniforms hastened the last of them. We reined in and the captain tried, first English and then French as he asked for a doctor. There were blank looks from the locals. He turned to me, "Over, to you Smith."

I dismounted. One thing I had learned was that it was the gestures and body language that made the locals more amenable. I handed my reins to the captain and gave a little bow with my hands together. The man did the same and smiled. I just said the word Aadyot had given me. It sounded unlike any word I had used before but I trusted my friend. The man nodded and pointed to a large house with a gate and a wall running around it. I bowed again and after thanking him, I remounted. The captain had seen the gesture and we rode to the house. The gates were closed. We banged on them but to no avail.

"Smith, climb the wall and open the gate. They must be sheltering inside."

I climbed onto the saddle and reached the top of the wall. My skills as a thief came back to me and I easily scaled the wall and dropped inside. The gate was just barred and, after lifting the bar, I opened the gates and the captain led my horse inside. He dismounted and I saw that the only way in or out of the house was through the gate. There was a small stable. The captain went to the door and banged on it. "I need a doctor. Please open the door." There was no reply. He turned to me, "Go to the stable and see if there are horses within. If the stable is empty, then the doctor and his family may well have fled."

I tied Froggy to the hitching post that was close to the front door as the captain banged on it and, first in English and then in

French, demanded entry. I ran to the stable. Inside there were three horses. Two were the kind of horses we called hackneys in England. Good enough riding horses but not for the battlefield. One of them, however, looked to be a good horse. I stroked its mane and spoke to it as I examined it. It was as good a horse as Caesar. This was a soldier's horse or an animal belonging to a fine gentleman and did not belong to a doctor. Armed with that information I left the stable. When I emerged I walked to the back of the house. There was no gate in the wall and the door at the back of the house looked like a servant entrance. I ran back to the captain.

"There are three horses, sir, and one looks to be a soldier's."

"Load your pistols." He did the same and when that was done he banged on the door and shouted, "I am Captain Geoffrey Tucker and I represent the British Government. I demand that you open this door or we will be forced to break it down." He repeated it in French and we waited.

We heard noises from within and then I heard the bolts being pulled back. Our hands were close to our pistols. If we had to then we could draw and fire them quickly enough. It was a European and a turbaned warrior who opened the door. He was not a well-dressed warrior and the sword that hung from his belt was nothing special. He was not the owner of the horse.

The man spoke accented English. He sounded French, "I am Doctor Armand Lavalle." He looked at us both, "you do not seem as though you need medical help."

"We do not but we have a man who collapsed on the battlefield."

He tried to close the door on us as he said, "You have army doctors."

The captain pushed the door open and stepped inside, I pushed the warrior aside, "Get your bag, Doctor, and come with us."

He shook his head, "I have a patient here and I cannot leave him."

There was something suspicious about this. I could see that the doctor was being shifty and so could the captain. He nodded, "Very well. Smith, bring the patient here." He winked, "And Hogan and Evans."

"Sir." The two biggest men in the section would be intimidating enough.

I went outside and threw myself onto Froggy's back. I galloped through the open gates and was back at the camp in a few minutes.

The lieutenant looked up, "Did you find a doctor?"

"Yes, sir, but he wants the sergeant there. The captain wants Seamus and Dai to pull the wagon."

"Hogan and Evans, fetch the sergeant and put him in the cart. Bring your muskets too." He looked at me, "Is something amiss, Smith?"

"Just a feeling, Sir. Could I take Aadyot too? His language skills might help."

"Of course, Private Ganguly, get your gear and go with Private Smith."

"Yes, sir."

I led Froggy as the sergeant was hauled towards the small town. He complained, "I don't know what this fuss is about. I feel fine."

Seamus laughed, "And your face looks like the grate at home when we cleaned out the fire. Sure, and it is a fine day for a stroll, Sergeant."

Dai said, quietly, "What is this all about, Smudger? You asked for us by name."

"The captain thought we might need a couple of big lads. There is something queer going on at the house. Keep your wits about you."

"Righto."

Seamus and the sergeant had heard my words too and they nodded. Once we reached the house I said, "Take him inside, lads. I will bar this gate. It is the only way in or out."

The two of them carried the sergeant inside as I barred the gate and then took Froggy to the stables. I walked to the wall on the far side of the house. I looked at the house a little more closely this time. I saw what I had missed before. There were two more outbuildings. One was open-sided and had an oven. The other had a door and was clearly a latrine of some sort. I drew my pistol and approached the door quietly. Usually, such places were left with their door open to alleviate the stink. This one was closed but I could not see that the captain would have allowed anyone to go outside. I walked up, silently, and listened. I could hear breathing from within. With the cocked pistol in my right hand, I jerked open the door with my left. Cowering within was a well-dressed Mysorean. His clothes were of the finest quality and the many rings on his fingers glistened gold, red and green. This was the owner of the horse and he was not using the latrine, he was hiding.

"Move," I repeated the word in French and then Bengali, I used the pistol to gesture to the house and I kept it in his back. When we reached the door, I did not move the pistol but I tried the door with my left hand. It was locked. I knocked on it. "It's me, Smith."

Aadyot opened the door and his eyes widened when he saw the prisoner.

"Lock the door behind us." As I passed through the kitchen, I saw the servants seated around the table. I said, over my shoulder, "Aadyot, stay here and keep your eyes and ears open. They may say something that we find useful."

"Yes, Smudger."

I passed the bedroom where I saw the doctor examining the sergeant. Dai and the captain were with him. I pushed my prisoner forward into the room where Seamus and the other Mysorean waited. As soon as the warrior saw my prisoner his hand went into the folds of his robes and he brought out a knife. Seamus was waiting for just such a move and he felled the man with a mighty swing from his ham-like right hand. The man fell to the ground.

The captain heard the noise of the fall and came racing in, his pistol levelled. "I think, Captain Tucker, that we have the owner of the fine horse. He was hiding in the latrine."

The captain nodded, "And he is the reason the good doctor did not want us to enter. He was lying about having another patient. What is so important about this man that he must be hidden?" He turned to the man and said, in French, "Who are you?"

The man said nothing, but his eyes betrayed the fact that he had understood the words. "Hogan, secure this man." He pointed to the unconscious warrior.

"Sir." The big Irishman flipped the unconscious warrior over and, taking off the man's turban, used it to secure his hands.

"Smith, ride to headquarters and find the Governor General. Tell him what we have found. Tell him that Captain Tucker suggests he comes here, incognito."

"Me, sir?"

"You are known, Private Smith, and you can be persistent."

"Sir."

"Hogan, go and bar the gate when Smith has gone."

"Sir."

I galloped through the camp to the company flag that marked headquarters. I recognised Sergeant Charlton. "Sergeant, I have an important message for the Governor General."

"Give it to me and I will see it is delivered."

"It is not written down, Sergeant, and Captain Tucker insisted that I deliver it personally."

I saw a frown on his face. He seemed to be debating with himself. Eventually, he nodded and said, "Barlow, take charge. Private Smith, come with me."

We entered the tent which was awash with officers. Colonel Wellesley, his brother, the Governor General, General Harris and the three staff officers were standing around a table. Colonel Wellesley turned at our approach. He saw me and frowned, "Yes, Sergeant Charlton?"

"Private Smith here has a message from Captain Tucker for the Governor General."

The colonel shook his head, "Well give me the message and begone, Smith."

I stiffened, "Sir, with due respect, I was commanded to give the order to Lord Mornington and no one else."

General Harris looked as though his face was going to explode, "You are a company soldier. Tell me the message."

"Sorry, Sir, orders are orders."

I saw Lord Mornington smile, "You were one of the chaps who rescued the Hardcastle family were you not?"

"Yes, My Lord."

"Then I believe we can allow you some latitude. Gentlemen, allow me to speak to this bold soldier alone, eh?"

Colonel Wellesley nodded and headed towards the table with the tea urn. General Harris, however, glowered and glared at me.

Alone in a corner of the tent, his lordship said, "Now then, Private, what is so important that you risk the wrath of the general, eh?"

"Sir, we found a doctor to tend to our sergeant who was taken sick. Whilst there we took a prisoner. Captain Tucker believes that the man is important and asks you to come incognito to see for yourself."

"Important?"

"Yes, my lord. He is dressed in fine robes, he has many rings on his fingers and he rides the finest horse I have yet seen." I paused, "He was hiding in the latrine of a French doctor's house."

He nodded, "Captain Tucker is a good man, and your report indicates that you concur with the captain."

"I do, my lord."

"Very well." He raised his voice, "Gentlemen, continue with your plans. I will go with Private...?"

"Smith, sir."

"With Private Smith."

His brother, Colonel Wellesley, said, "Do you need an escort, my lord?"

"No, I think I will be safe enough, Arthur." He took his cloak and with a straw hat upon his head, he strode from the tent. Once outside he said, "Sergeant, find me a horse."

One was soon found and he mounted. Like his brother, he was an accomplished rider and it seemed but moments before we reached the house. The gate was barred so I stood on Froggy's back and entered the way I had the first time. I unbarred the gate and brought in Froggy.

His lordship dismounted, "I can see, Smith, that you are a most resourceful sort of chap." He handed me the reins of his horse. He pointed to the door, "In here?"

"Yes sir. I will take these to the stables."

I fastened them both up and had just entered the house when I heard Lord Mornington exclaim, "Mir Sadiq! Captain Tucker, you have made a most interesting discovery. This is the 1st Minister of Tipu Sultan."

I peered through the door. The captain and Lord Mornington were towering over the man they had called Mir Sadiq. Seamus was grinning and the bound prisoner, dried blood on his face, was looking most unhappy.

Captain Tucker said, "Get a brew on, Smith, and see how the sergeant fares."

I went into the other room and saw that a bare-chested sergeant was asleep. Dai was watching the doctor suspiciously. The doctor wiped his hands, "I was telling your friend here that the sergeant has suffered a mild heart attack. I have given him a sedative. When he wakes you can move him but tell him that his days as a soldier are over."

I looked at Sergeant Grundy and knew that it would break the old soldier's heart. The army had been his life and the East India Company had offered him a second chance.

The doctor smiled and it annoyed not just me but also Dai. "If you don't mind, I would like to see that my…, my other guest is well."

Dai's fingers tightened into fists, "You stay with the sergeant, Dai, Seamus can handle the doctor."

"Aye, alright."

I went into the kitchen where Aadyot was chattering away to the servants. "Aadyot, ask them to make a brew, for everyone, eh?" His words were fired like bullets and when he turned, I asked, "Well, what did you learn?"

"That the man you found is an important man. Only Tipu Sultan ranks higher. He was at the battle and took shelter here. The doctor is an agent of the Tipu and the French."

It all made sense now. I wondered what the Governor General would do. We made the tea and took it to the others. Lord Mornington beamed, "A cup of tea, just what we need. Captain Tucker, you and I need to speak alone to Mir Sadiq…Doctor you have tended to your patient here, enjoy a cup of tea with our men."

Captain Tucker nodded, "Hogan and Smith, escort the doctor out and then Smith, you return to guard this door."

The doctor looked as though he was going to complain but Seamus put one of his huge hams in the middle of his back, "Do as his lordship says, Doctor Darlin', otherwise you will have to tend to your own bloody nose."

I grabbed the prisoner and said, "Up."

We took them into the other room. That way Seamus and Dai would have Aadyot to help them although I did not think they would need any help.

I returned to the door and heard the buzz of conversation from within. After what seemed an age Captain Tucker emerged, "Saddle and then fetch Mir Sadiq's horse around to the front." A question formed in my throat but Captain Tucker just said, "Do what I say, Smith. You are a bright lad so trust his lordship and me. This is all for the good."

"Yes, Sir."

I saddled the fine horse and led it to the front of the house. Captain Tucker emerged, "Smith open the gate and when the street outside is clear give me the nod."

"Sir."

I unbarred the door and peered around. The street had largely cleared. The battle was over and it was getting on for the time people would be cooking food. As soon as the last woman entered her home with a pot of water from the well, I turned and waved. Mir Sadiq, a cloak around his shoulders galloped out, almost knocking me to the ground.

"Close the gates, Smith."

By the time I had entered the house again, Lord Mornington had finished his business. He turned to me, "You and I, Private Smith will return to headquarters. Captain Tucker, once again we are indebted to you." He waved a hand at the rest of us, "And this fine body of men. Your service will not be forgotten. Fetch our horses."

I felt I had to volunteer the information Aadyot had discovered. "Sir, you ought to know that the doctor is an agent of the French as well as being a supporter of this Tipu Sultan."

He smiled, "I had worked that out already but it is good to hear it confirmed. You are a bright lad. Well done!"

Not a word more was said as we rode back to the camp. When we reached the tented village food was cooking and I felt hungry. It had been hours since we had eaten breakfast. "Wait here, Smith."

I dismounted and stood with Sergeant Charlton. "So what have you been up to?"

"Can't say, Sergeant."

He was about to say something when Captain Colin Campbell emerged, "Sergeant Charlton, ask Captain White to bring a platoon of soldiers. We need them to guard some prisoners."

"Sir."

The Scottish officer looked at me, "His lordship is most impressed by you and your fellows, Smith. Perhaps General Harris has misjudged you."

"A lot of people do that, Sir. We are used to it."

He laughed, "The colonel said you were an impertinent sort of soldier. I see what he means."

By the time I had taken our relief to the house, it was dark and Sergeant Grundy had awoken. We walked back to our camp where, the moment we arrived, we were inundated with questions. Before he had left the house Lord Mornington had sworn us all to secrecy, although I doubted that we would have told anyone about the information we all held. Lord Mornington was playing some sort of game but I could not see how it affected us. Our main concern was Sergeant Grundy.

Back at the camp the questions were all about the doctor's prognosis and no one gave a jot about the mysterious prisoner. Lord Mornington would be pleased.

It was Dai who broke the news of his condition to the sergeant when he woke. He looked desperately at the lieutenant, "Sir, I do not want to retire. What would I do?"

Dai said, "Sergeant, I heard the doctor. He said that the next heart attack would kill you."

I saw the determination on the sergeant's face, "Evans, I am an old man. Not old like lords and such but for a soldier I have lived longer than anyone I know. All my old comrades are dead. I am the last." He smiled, "I didn't think I would be. I have served with some good men but I reckon you lot are as good a bunch of soldiers as I have ever led. If I am to shuffle off to that last mess in the sky, then let me choose how and when." He looked at Lieutenant Crozier, "I swear that I will not be a burden, sir. You let me get on with my job, eh?"

We all looked at him knowing that he had just sentenced himself to death. The words, when I spoke them, seemed to come from another, "Sergeant, I have been fortunate and collected a few guineas. If the thought of a life of poverty is all that is stopping you then take my money. I can always make more."

The smile he gave me was almost tearful, "Smudger, Bill, that is the kindest thing anyone has ever said but it is not about being poor. It is about being needed and doing something useful. Neville here will make a good sergeant but he is not ready, not yet anyway. I promise that if I feel a little like I did when Smith found me I will stop. Keep your money, Son, I just need my brothers in arms."

Everyone looked at Lieutenant Crozier. It was his decision. Captain Tucker said, quietly, "Richard, for what it is worth I think the sergeant is right. He might die of a heart attack but then again he could die of a bullet or a sword. I would be dead now if it hadn't been for Smith's quick thinking. We are all soldiers and any soldier who thinks that he is guaranteed a peaceful old age is deceiving himself."

The lieutenant nodded, "From now on, Sergeant Grundy, you ride Smith's horse. Smith, teach the sergeant to ride." The sergeant looked as though he was going to object. The lieutenant pointed his forefinger at him. "The back of a horse or retirement."

Sergeant Grundy sighed, "I hope you are a good teacher, Smudger!"

Epilogue

I had to teach the sergeant on the job, as it were. We began our march to Seringapatam the next morning. Getting on the horse was bad enough but getting him to sit straight was a nightmare. He didn't seem to want to use his knees and he had little control over the reins. He was keen to learn but he sat on the French horse as though he was a sack of potatoes. No one laughed and no one commented. We all liked our sergeant and if this bought him more time so much the better. When we were in camp no one allowed him to do anything physical. We told him he was there to give orders. Aadyot proved how invaluable he was. He told the lieutenant of some of the foods his people used which seemed to help the old, the ones, he said, with weak hearts. We began to use more of those spices, like turmeric and ginger. The sergeant objected but he had a whole section and two officers who put him in his place. In that fashion, we made our way to Seringapatam, the Tipu Sultan's fortress in the bend of a river.

We learned that the Tipu was procrastinating. He was trying to delay a confrontation. Lieutenant Crozier thought that he was holding out for more help from the French. He sent letters to Lord Mornington asking for peace talks. We learned this from Captain Tucker who was constantly in use as a sort of consultant. He was not asked to be an exploration officer again for the simple reason that we knew where the Tipu was but his skills were used by the colonel and his brother.

When we reached Seringapatam we made a camp and the fortress was surrounded. The only one of us who had been on a siege before was Sergeant Grundy. He took great delight in showing off his knowledge. It seemed to vindicate his decision to remain a soldier. For my part, I now had the means to start not just any life but a prosperous one. I knew that I could run, and I was constantly making plans to do so but, while we all pitched in to make the sergeant's life as comfortable as possible, I was content to remain a company soldier. I consoled myself with the fact that I was now richer than I had ever been and my new profession seemed to afford more chances of becoming richer than my former life as a thief. Ralph Every had done me a favour by seeking my life for he had, inadvertently, given me a new one. I did not know how I would be able to run but I knew that if the chance came again then I would take it, and in a siege who knew what opportunities might present themselves?

Glossary

Bombay - Mumbai
Bring 'em near - telescope
Calcutta - Kolkata
Havildar - a sergeant
HCS - Honourable Company ship
Jangheas - short jodhpurs worn by native infantry
Squits - diarrhoea.
Tiddly oggy - sailor slang for the sea

Historical References

The East India Company ruled large parts of India and had three Presidencies: Madras, Bombay and Calcutta. The British Government, however, had imposed their own Governor General on the company, which meant that while most of the soldiers who fought in the battles I describe were company soldiers, the British Government sent British troops. The Duke of York's campaign in the Low Countries had not gone well and India was a place where Britain could not only defend British controlled land but enjoy victories over the French. There were European soldiers and native soldiers, generally referred to as sepoys. They had cavalry and artillery arms but the bulk of the troops were infantry. The Europeans were not, in the main, considered to be good soldiers. The fictitious section I describe, a sort of nineteenth century Dirty Dozen, are better than most of those who were in the company ranks.

I made up the missionary incident but I am a storyteller and I wanted to give my hero the chance to redeem himself after a life of crime.

The main events in the book: the Battle of Malavelli, and the letters to the Nizam are historical facts. The Resident in Madras did intercept letters that indicated the French were trying to add Hyderabad as an ally. Despite his junior rank, Sir Arthur Wellesley was the de facto commander of the army led by General Hunter when Mysore was invaded. His brother, the Governor General, was with the army and that may have contributed. The 33rd made an uphill bayonet charge against many times their number. They were led in the charge, by Colonel Wellesley.

The next book will begin with the siege of Seringapatam. Mir Sadiq was a real person and he was instrumental in the siege. I have made up the connection with Lord Mornington but, as will be revealed in the next book, the link was there.

Books used in the research
The Military History Book

Armies of the East India Company 1750-1850, Reid and Embleton
The first Anglo-Sikh War 1845-46, Smith and Noon
Wellington's Infantry (1), Fosten
Wellington's Regiments - Ian Fletcher
Wellington's Military Machine - Haythornwaite
The Napoleonic Source Book - Haythornwaite
Nelson's Navy - Brian Lavery
Assaye 1803 - Millar and Dennis

East Indiaman

Other books by Griff Hosker

If you enjoyed reading this book, then why not read another one by the author?

Ancient History

Roman Rebellion
(The Roman Republic 100 BC-60 BC)
Legionary

The Sword of Cartimandua Series
(Germania and Britannia 50 A.D. – 128 A.D.)
Ulpius Felix- Roman Warrior (prequel)
The Sword of Cartimandua
The Horse Warriors
Invasion Caledonia
Roman Retreat
Revolt of the Red Witch
Druid's Gold
Trajan's Hunters
The Last Frontier
Hero of Rome
Roman Hawk
Roman Treachery
Roman Wall
Roman Courage

The Wolf Brethren series
*(*Britain in the late 6th Century)
Saxon Dawn
Saxon Revenge
Saxon England
Saxon Blood
Saxon Slayer
Saxon Slaughter
Saxon Bane

East Indiaman

Saxon Fall: Rise of the Warlord
Saxon Throne
Saxon Sword

Medieval History

The Dragon Heart Series
Viking Slave *
Viking Warrior *
Viking Jarl *
Viking Kingdom *
Viking Wolf *
Viking War*
Viking Sword
Viking Wrath
Viking Raid
Viking Legend
Viking Vengeance
Viking Dragon
Viking Treasure
Viking Enemy
Viking Witch
Viking Blood
Viking Weregeld
Viking Storm
Viking Warband
Viking Shadow
Viking Legacy
Viking Clan
Viking Bravery

Norseman
Norse Warrior

The Norman Genesis Series
Hrolf the Viking *
Horseman *
The Battle for a Home *
Revenge of the Franks *

East Indiaman

The Land of the Northmen
Ragnvald Hrolfsson
Brothers in Blood
Lord of Rouen
Drekar in the Seine
Duke of Normandy
The Duke and the King

Danelaw
(England and Denmark in the 11th Century)
Dragon Sword *
Oathsword *
Bloodsword *
Danish Sword*
The Sword of Cnut*

New World Series
Blood on the Blade *
Across the Seas *
The Savage Wilderness *
The Bear and the Wolf *
Erik The Navigator *
Erik's Clan *
The Last Viking*
The Vengeance Trail *

The Conquest Series
(Normandy and England 1050-1100)
Hastings*
Conquest*
Rebellion

The Aelfraed Series
(Britain and Byzantium 1050 A.D. - 1085 A.D.)
Housecarl *
Outlaw *
Varangian *

The Reconquista Chronicles

(Spain in the 11ᵗʰ Century)
Castilian Knight *
El Campeador *
The Lord of Valencia *

The Anarchy Series
(England 1120-1180)
English Knight *
Knight of the Empress *
Northern Knight *
Baron of the North *
Earl *
King Henry's Champion *
The King is Dead *
Warlord of the North*
Enemy at the Gate*
The Fallen Crown*
Warlord's War*
Kingmaker*
Henry II
Crusader
The Welsh Marches
Irish War
Poisonous Plots
The Princes' Revolt
Earl Marshal
The Perfect Knight

Border Knight
(1182-1300)
Sword for Hire *
Return of the Knight *
Baron's War *
Magna Carta *
Welsh Wars *
Henry III *
The Bloody Border *
Baron's Crusade*
Sentinel of the North*

War in the West*
Debt of Honour*
The Blood of the Warlord
The Fettered King
de Montfort's Crown
The Ripples of Rebellion

Sir John Hawkwood Series
(France and Italy 1339- 1387)
Crécy: The Age of the Archer *
Man At Arms *
The White Company *
Leader of Men *
Tuscan Warlord *
Condottiere*
Legacy*

Lord Edward's Archer
Lord Edward's Archer *
King in Waiting *
An Archer's Crusade *
Targets of Treachery *
The Great Cause *
Wallace's War *
The Hunt*
The Prince and the Archer*

Struggle for a Crown
(1360- 1485)
Blood on the Crown *
To Murder a King *
The Throne *
King Henry IV *
The Road to Agincourt *
St Crispin's Day *
The Battle for France *
The Last Knight *
Queen's Knight *
The Knight's Tale *

Tales from the Sword I
(Short stories from the Medieval period)

Tudor Warrior series
(England and Scotland in the late 15th and early 16th century)
Tudor Warrior *
Tudor Spy *
Flodden*

Conquistador
(England and America in the 16th Century)
Conquistador *
The English Adventurer *

English Mercenary
(The 30 Years War and the English Civil War)
Horse and Pistol*
Captain of Horse

Modern History

East Indiaman Saga
East Indiaman*
The Tiger and the Thief

The Napoleonic Horseman Series
Chasseur à Cheval
Napoleon's Guard
British Light Dragoon
Soldier Spy
1808: The Road to Coruña
Talavera
The Lines of Torres Vedras
Bloody Badajoz
The Road to France
Waterloo

The Lucky Jack American Civil War series

East Indiaman

Rebel Raiders
Confederate Rangers
The Road to Gettysburg

Soldier of the Queen series
Soldier of the Queen*
Redcoat's Rifle*
Omdurman*
Desert War
An Officer and a Gentleman

The British Ace Series
(World War 1)
1914
1915 Fokker Scourge
1916 Angels over the Somme
1917 Eagles Fall
1918 We will remember them
From Arctic Snow to Desert Sand
Wings over Persia

Combined Operations series
(1940-1951)
Commando *
Raider *
Behind Enemy Lines*
Dieppe
Toehold in Europe
Sword Beach
Breakout
The Battle for Antwerp
King Tiger
Beyond the Rhine
Korea
Korean Winter

Tales from the Sword II
(Short stories from the Modern period)

Books marked thus *, are also available in the audio format. For more information on all of the books then please visit the author's website at www.griffhosker.com where there is a link to contact him or visit his Facebook page: Griff Hosker at Sword Books or follow him on Twitter: @HoskerGriff or Sword Books @swordbooksltd
If you wish to be on the mailing list then contact the author through his website.

Printed in Great Britain
by Amazon